Anchor Point

Newman Fire Dept Series

Rae Fields

HEA Books LLC

Copyright © 2024 by Rae Fields

All rights reserved.

This is a work of fiction, created without use of AI technology. Names, characters, places, and incidents are products of the author's imagination and are used in a fictitious manner. Any resemblance to actual persons, living or dead, events or locales are entirely coincidental.

Without in any way limiting the author's exclusive rights under copyright, any use of this publication to "train" generative artificial intelligence (AI) technologies to generate text is expressly prohibited. The author reserves all rights to license uses of this work for generative AI training and development of machine learning language models.

No part of this book may be reproduced in any form or by any electronic or mechanical means, including information storage and retrieval systems, without written permission from the author, except for the use of brief quotations in a book review.

Developmental and Line Editing: Jessica Snyder, HEA Author Services

Copyediting and Proofreading: Brooklyn Marie with Brazen Hearts Author Services

Cover design: Kari March

www.raefields.com

ISBN-13: 978-1-961803-06-0 (ebook)

ISBN-13: 978-1-961803-11-4 (print)

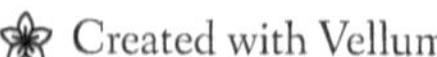 Created with Vellum

For Mom, I love you

Chapter One

Olivia

"As mayor, let me be the first to welcome you aboard, Chief Hawkins." Paul Smith, a plump older man behind a gleaming large desk, rose from his luxury executive chair. Surrounded by his lush office, he reigned as a small-town mayor. Pompous. Arrogant. Condescending. That was probably why he felt comfortable letting his gaze skim suggestively down my legs as I took the seat across from his desk.

"Mr. Bloom assures me that you come highly recommended and will be an asset to our department and community." His perusal traveled somewhere south of my chin with the words.

Irritation prickled down my back at the derisive tone as he said the word "chief," even as he objectified me as a woman.

Maybe being as old as Methuselah compelled him to treat women as his own personal plaything.

Maybe it was his true, good-old-boy colors showing, and he really didn't hold me in high regard.

Whatever the case, he didn't take me seriously, and I didn't trust his toothy grin for a second.

"If you need *anything*," he continued in that slightly annoying, slightly suggestive manner, "anything at all, please don't hesitate to reach out."

He might as well have winked as he said it.

I bit my tongue against the cutting remark that threatened and stood, smoothing my jacket as I accepted the offered handshake. My movements drew the old bird's eyes directly to my breasts.

Great. My new job as fire chief was off to an inauspicious start.

"Thank you, Mr. Mayor. I appreciate the opportunity," I replied, letting the ice princess seep into my tone.

Plenty of men had looked my way, always seeing the curvy package and not the powerhouse leader. Those men learned quickly that I was a professional, and I didn't suffer fools. But I was new here and needed this job. So I forced down the part of me that wanted to bite the man's head off.

Cornelius Bloom, the city manager, stood from the other guest chair and cleared his throat. "Yes, Chief Hawkins. Welcome to the City of Newman. I'll take you down to Human Resources. Once you've had time to get your paperwork processed, we'll take a tour of the city, maybe stop by the stations to introduce you to your crews."

I looked over to find his gaze fixed on my face, another plus in his favor. "If it's all the same to you, I'd prefer to meet with the captains first before meeting with the entire department, if possible."

"Certainly," the mayor bubbled, speaking over Mr.

Bloom. "Of course you want to meet the men working under you." Then he winked.

I steeled my spine, suppressing the eye roll that threatened. This egotistical asshole was going to be my boss. I'd dealt with his kind of misogynistic attitude my entire career, and I knew how to handle myself to get what I wanted. He'd get used to seeing a woman in uniform, and then he'd begin to see me as the woman in charge, and the respect would grow. That was my plan, anyway. But it sucked to have to set these boundaries and lay the groundwork first.

"Excuse me, sir," I replied, letting the steely tone I'd developed seep into my words. "They are officers. I am an officer and a professional. With all due respect, please extinguish the innuendo. I've been in the fire service for nearly fifteen years. I can guarantee you I've heard every joke, every wisecrack. And none of them are remotely funny. I'm here to do a job. I'm here because you needed a fire chief."

Mayor Smith huffed in response, his face turning red as he bumbled a response. I tuned him out, spinning on a spiky heel toward the city manager.

Red-faced, Mr. Bloom blurted, "Thank you, Mr. Mayor," before ushering me to the door and leading me down a long hallway.

City hall was housed in a modern red-brick building. One side of the hall was lined with doors, with the names of city offices labeled in matching font. On the other side, light filtered through tall windows that ran the length of the hall, showcasing a well-landscaped courtyard. Tile floors gleamed underfoot, our footfalls echoing off the high ceiling. A nice, top-of-the-line building for a small town. I was hopeful that the fire stations would be equally as nice.

The quaintness of the town and the classiness of this

building alone had been an enticing part of the move from South Carolina.

"Please excuse the mayor," Mr. Bloom said in a hushed voice. "He's of a different generation."

"Mr. Bloom, age should not be validation for bad behavior."

"No, it shouldn't." He had the grace to look chagrined. "But as an elected official, and our boss, he tends to get away with doing things that others wouldn't."

Not for the first time, I wondered if I'd made a mistake accepting this position and uprooting my daughter Rosie. My interview process had been… interesting. I suppose my resume listed my qualifications well enough. But oddly, when I'd had my interview, traveling from Charleston on the city's dime, my resume hadn't been explored much. Rather, the topics had ranged anywhere from what my worst call had been to the types of equipment Charleston preferred. It was the oddest interview I'd ever had.

I'd still taken the job when they offered it because I couldn't stay in Charleston any longer. My ex-husband had made sure of that.

Mr. Bloom offering the chief's position had been the new start I'd needed. I'd accepted on the condition that they pay moving expenses, and then Rosie and I were on our way to our new town and leaving all the hurt of Charleston behind us.

"Here we are." Mr. Bloom stopped in front of the door labeled Human and Community Resources, as if they couldn't be bothered to have two departments for two such important roles.

"I need to make some calls while you complete your paperwork, but I'll be back in an hour or so, and then we can get started on that tour."

Three hours later, we'd driven the city, and he'd shown me all the "most important" sights, including the three smaller firehouses that would fall under my direction and which roads they closed for parades. He pointed out the city park still undergoing reconstruction after a tornado destroyed the southern portion of town and then other important landmarks.

Bloom ended our tour at the Newman Fire Department headquarters, a two-story block building, with an exterior glass wall showcasing the stairwell and giant red slide.

"We finished remodeling and making upgrades just before the tornado hit. We refurbished the day room, offices, and bunk room, and installed the slide." Pride curled around Bloom's words. "And Station Four was completed the year before that. Our first new facility in over a decade, which also added another new engine company."

He was a likable guy, radiating positivity and smiles, probably in his late forties, with thinning hair and a wiry build. He loved his city and seemed to embrace his role as head cheerleader.

I eyeballed the large headquarters from the parking lot. "And how many personnel are at this station?"

"This firehouse runs the most calls, so naturally, it has the most personnel on duty at one time. We have Rescue One and Engine One stationed here. Rescue One is staffed by two—a driver and a medic. Engine One is staffed by four. There are two apparatus drivers on shift here, one at the smaller stations. Plus a captain at each one."

"And what's the average call volume?"

"Oh, um... I'm not sure right offhand ..."

Up until now, he'd spouted information like he was reading a brochure. I wanted to tell him he couldn't scare me away with his answer. I'd asked the same question in my follow-up interview, so I knew the answer. Throughout the day, I'd gathered that the administrator wasn't so much connected with the department's issues as he was just showing off the pretty, positive things.

But I needed to know if I had an ally when it came time to approach a city council governed by a misogynistic mayor.

I gave him a thin smile to set him at ease. "Never mind, I'll pull the information I need from reports. Let's see the rest."

His relief was palpable. "I'll show you to your office, and then we can discuss meeting with the captains." We started through the open bay doors. "Fair warning, there may be some resentment there. We passed over a few of our own to hire you."

It made sense. I'd felt like there'd been more to this story from the get-go. I followed him into the stairwell, our footfalls echoing in the cavernous space. Keeping my voice soft, I asked, "Was there a reason to go outside of the department?"

"We had a former chief who made some... poor decisions. Naturally, it affected the department. We hired an interim chief, a retiree, but then the tornado happened, and with already having staffing issues... our search for a new chief was delayed while we put the city back together again."

A second fumble. But this time, I wasn't letting him off the hook. Something had gone down in this department, and knowing the details would help me navigate this onboarding with my new crews.

"So, the personnel are burned out and don't trust leadership is what I'm hearing."

"I wouldn't call it burned out, but they are tired of change and are ready to move forward."

"And the 'poor decisions of the former chief'? What does that mean?"

From this vantage point at the top of the stairwell, the glass wall lent a good view of the rest of the block. Cars buzzed by on the one-way, double-laned street. To the left, the center of town boasted a historic courthouse. Across from the station, residential homes had been converted to businesses. Beyond that lay quaint neighborhoods, with well-manicured lawns and large front porches, most with rocking chairs or porch swings.

Inside headquarters, the bay was filled with natural light. Clean, with a fresh coat of paint. The equipment, although in good condition, showed signs of age.

At the other end of the bay was a large empty office. The station was eerily quiet. No personnel milling about, though all the trucks were in the bay.

"I'm sorry, Chief Hawkins, his personnel record is confidential." He turned to the doors, effectively ending the conversation. That was fine. I'd pave my own way and make this department my own. "This side of the stairwell used to be a municipal building. The other side is the living quarters. We moved the fire administration to this new wing as part of the renovation."

A clerk at the front desk gave me a warm, welcoming smile, but Mr. Bloom walked right past her without introducing us. Then, once again, I followed him down a hallway.

He opened a door and swept his arm with a flourish into the room. "Welcome to your new office."

It was small—industrial carpet, a simple desk and file cabinet, and a row of little windows high along the back wall. Possibly a converted storage room. Definitely a far cry from the fancy offices of city hall.

"I'll leave you to get settled in now." He checked his phone, swiping through messages. "I have another meeting that I need to get to, but I'll check in with you tomorrow morning."

And with that, my new boss left me hanging. *Thanks for tossing me into the deep end of the pool, buddy.*

I sat in the chair and took a moment to breathe, finally allowing myself to relax.

I thought about texting Rosie to see how her day had been, but a knock sounded at my door.

The clerk stood in the doorway, smiling at me. She had on a business casual outfit paired with sensible shoes. The tips of her blond shoulder-length hair curled slightly outward, and she wore minimal makeup.

"Hi, Chief. I'm sorry to interrupt. I thought we might go over a few things." She indicated the notepad she held.

I straightened and motioned to the guest chair.

"Certainly. We can start with your name." I tried for a polite smile. My face was going to crack from all the pleasantries.

Chuckling, she entered the room and took the seat across from me, leaning forward to offer her hand. "My name is Cathy. It's a pleasure to meet you. It's going to be nice having another woman in the department."

She sounded positively thrilled, but her comment struck me as odd.

"There are no other women in the department?"

Cathy shook her head. "There are some female medics, but they work for the county. We're it for the fire department."

A whole department of men only? It was unusual but

not unheard of. And I had a sneaking suspicion I'd just uncovered why my interview process had felt so peculiar.

"You seem surprised, Chief."

"I am. I want to know why and how."

Cathy shrugged. "There are some in other departments nearby, but in all of my years working here, there's only been one female firefighter. Of course"—she cocked her head conspiratorially—"she had to work doubly hard to prove herself."

"Do they actively discriminate?" With the mayor's attitude, it wouldn't surprise me. They needed me for their numbers.

"No. I think it's more that we rarely have turnover, so we don't have open positions very often. It's a small department in a small city—when people get hired, they usually stay. So no other women besides you and me."

This situation added another layer to the trepidation building in me. Suddenly, taking the position felt like a mistake.

I frowned at the thought, then refocused on my clerk.

Cathy was open, friendly, and I had no doubt she was the glue that held this department together. In my experience, there was a line between bosses and subordinates. Being friends usually didn't work.

But I could be pleasant. Cordial.

I didn't want to make enemies on my very first day, aside from the mayor. I could use an ally in the department, but years of needing to remain guarded had taken its toll and become my default.

"Anyway"—she shifted under my direct gaze—"I didn't know your sizes." She'd slipped into a professional get-shit-done voice that I immediately respected. "However, I've coordinated with the uniform shop, and they have the departmental patches ready. If you'll jot down your sizes, I'll make a quick call, and they should be ready this evening. I can run by on my way in tomorrow morning and pick them up."

She checked her notes, ticking off boxes as she changed topics.

"I also ordered you a laptop, and IT should be by any minute with it. I got you all set up with account codes, so you'll just need to change your password. And then I thought I could give you a rundown of the software we use."

Another box was ticked off. "Oh, and I ordered you new badges and collar bars."

And now I felt like a total bitch.

She'd really taken care of me. I hadn't even thought to ask about my uniform. I softened the ice princess and let genuine appreciation seep into my tone. "Thank you, Cathy. I appreciate all that you've done. You've certainly set me up to get started on the right foot."

A smile spread across her face, brightening her features. "It's my pleasure, Chief. How about I give you a tour of our office area?"

She walked us through the administrative offices, noting a large conference room, a small unisex restroom, and a nice kitchen with a break area.

"How long have you worked here?" I asked as we made it back to my office.

"Ten years, ma'am." Her words had a weight to them.

"It sounds like those might have been ten hard years."

Cathy held my gaze confidently, having nothing to hide, and oddly, her no-nonsense attitude helped dispel some of my apprehension.

"But the next ten will be amazing, I'm sure." Her warm

tone held a note of supportive assurance, and just like that, she won me over.

This time, I didn't hide my smile. "You're damn right they will."

I had a lot to live up to, following in my father's footsteps and moving through the ranks of the fire service. Now was my time to prove my worth.

The IT guys showed up after that and set up my computer. Cathy gave me a rundown of the programs and then left me alone. Near five o'clock, I gathered my things and walked through the office, pausing at the kitchen to note we had a nice Keurig and an electric tea kettle, beside which a dainty teacup sat. Another thing Cathy and I had in common.

"Chief," Cathy's voice echoed down the hall, "your uniforms are all set. I'll swing by and pick them up on my way in. Remember it's black pants, not navy like the crew."

"Thanks, Cathy."

"And I scheduled a meeting with all the captains, on and off duty. They'll be here at eight thirty, so the shift coming off can get out of here, and the shift coming on can get pass down completed. Plus, you'll have time to get into your badass power suit." She shot me a sly grin. "It's going to be awesome to see their faces when they walk in and find out a woman is now leading this motley crew."

I said goodbye to Cathy at the lot, after she assured me that my new SUV would be coming in the next few weeks, and finally headed home to Rosie, still halfway wondering what I'd gotten myself into.

Chapter Two

Mac

"**W**ell, shit."

I propped a boot on the engine's metal bumper and plucked the toothpick from my lips, clicking open the email from Cathy.

Mandatory captains meeting.

I appreciated that she never minced words and was straight to the point. Her email had no other information in the body of the text other than the date, time, and location.

"What's wrong, Captain?" LT Nate Williams flicked his empty Sprite bottle into the recycle bin at the corner of the bay and joined the rest of the guys relaxing in front of the commercial fans, enjoying the shade from the late-afternoon August sun.

Station Four was the newest firehouse in the city. We had the newest engine, a beautiful Sutphen, equipped to my specs since they'd put me at lead on the build-out team. She was gorgeous. Black top, gleaming red carriage, could hold my crew of four, and was one of my favorite things about being at the new station.

I'd done my time for the department and earned my place as supervisor of Station Four. Over the course of the past twenty-five years, I'd taken nearly every assignment given to me, been on the planning committee for every special event, organized and coordinated funerals, and driven the vintage open-cab truck in so many parades I'd lost track. I think everyone had just assumed I'd always do it.

But my work ethic and ability to make things happen had paid off when they'd asked if I wanted to help lead in getting the new station completed. I'd fought tooth and nail for it, but we had a gorgeous, tricked-out new engine, even if I'd given up on fighting for other updates.

I had five years to retirement, and I was going to enjoy the hell out of them at my station and let some other grunt take command over the brass's special pet projects. It was time to pass the torch.

Four pairs of eyes waited for me to answer Nate's question.

"Mandatory meeting tomorrow morning. So much for getting down to the lake house. I barely have time to make it to the meeting after pass down. Who knows how long they'll keep us. Last time it was half the day."

"What's the meeting about? Can you skip it?" Burgess, the newest addition to our shift and a giant pain in my ass, was doing push-ups in the corner. The guy never stopped. Always working out or doing stupid shit. We were all fucked because he'd had a late-afternoon cup of coffee, and his ADHD had kicked into high gear. He'd be pestering the shit out of us to go do something soon enough.

Mo Jackson, my lead firefighter, looked at Burgess and

clenched one of his big fists as if he wanted to use it. "Shut up, man. Captain doesn't flake out. Maybe you should learn to be more like him."

Burgess puffed up like he was offended but thought better when he caught the look on Mo's face. Nate flopped into a rolling chair and kicked his feet up on the folding table we'd set up in the middle of the bay.

Thoren Watkins, the other firefighter on shift, picked up a deck of cards and started shuffling.

Nate clapped a hand down on the cards Thoren dealt as his phone dinged with a notification. No doubt his girlfriend. Again. The guy couldn't go a single shift without constant check-in, a leftover effect of a time when he'd scared the shit out of her after a particularly bad call.

"Damien just sent a text," Nate announced. "New fire chief is in the house. Went straight to the office and never came out."

Mo picked up his drink and shuffled his ice, watching his own cards fall. "That doesn't mean much. Probably got a bunch of administrative work to do before he can meet with the crew. I can respect that." He glared at Thoren. "Don't fucking deal from the bottom of the deck, you cheater."

I grunted at Mo. He was probably right. This meeting was most likely introducing the new chief.

"I still think they should've given it to you, Captain," Burgess called from the corner.

"Quit sucking up, Rookie." Nate pitched a wadded-up ball toward him. Then immediately jumped from his chair and tossed the trash into the large bin between the bay doors.

I grunted my appreciation for his following my number one rule: Keep My Station Clean.

It was times like these that I enjoyed the most. All of the

crew just hanging out at the station in between calls, when we were all kicked back, the hard work was done, and we were able to relax a bit. Time when we could forge the bonds that made it so we trusted each other when our lives depended on it.

Twenty-four hours spent in each other's space meant we had to make things work and get along. We didn't have to be friends for the forty-eight we were off, but most of this crew was tight even outside of the department.

Hopefully, if the call-gods were kind to us, it would be a quiet night, and we'd get some dinner and rest.

I ran my station in a way that allowed the guys to relax when we could. We worked hard early so we didn't have to work hard all day. We never knew when shit would hit the fan and we'd be up all night.

Luckily, our call volume had declined after a record number of structure fires in the last year. We were due a break. Except for the fact that the son of a bitch who'd started them all had gotten past his security detail while he'd been laid up in the hospital and had fled.

It was just a matter of time before the bastard showed up again. I felt it in my bones, as sure as I could tell that it'd be raining within the next twenty-four hours.

"Hey, Captain? You ever hear any more about that TikTok?" Thoren asked mid-shuffle. He was nonchalant, but I wasn't buying it.

"I don't do social media. You know this."

To his credit, Thoren flushed the tiniest bit. "Yeah, but Kylie is on me to try to find out if you've made contact. You gotta give me something."

The guys under my command were exceptional men with exceptional women in their lives. Over the summer, they'd taken to having cookouts and bonfires and inviting me to join them. At one of those cookouts, Thoren's girl-friend, Kylie, had stumbled on a TikTok post that had sent me into a tailspin of warring emotions.

Floating around on social media was a fifteen-year-old photo from a perfect week in paradise.

I'd gone to the island on my should've-been-honey-moon, intent on nursing my broken heart. Instead, I'd met the most beautiful, most complex, most responsive woman. The funniest, kindest woman I'd ever known. Our chemistry sparked the moment we laid eyes on each other, and by the end of that first night, we'd fucked twice. By the end of that week, we'd explored every fantasy either of us had ever had. I knew her body better than my own.

The caveat of our week-long fling had been not sharing any personal information, only first names. It was one wild, anonymous, nothing-but-fun fling.

By far the best week of my life.

I'd thought about Livvie over the years, wondering where she was—*how* she was. If she still remembered that week as fondly as I did. If she missed me like I sometimes missed her.

It didn't pay to think too hard about what might've been if we'd shared anything other than first names. Hell, she might not have even given me her real name.

I'd been such a wreck before arriving on that island. My whole goal had been to forget. To drink my way through a blissful week, driving away the heartache and disappoint-ment, along with that memory of standing solo at the wedding altar while my world fell apart.

But by the end of that week, I'd been half in love with Liv. I'd been in no shape for a relationship, determined to end the fling on a high note rather than allow it space and time to grow into something real before it crashed and burned.

My mistake.

Because over the years, Livvie had become the one who got away. Though I'd gotten over her, Liv had always been in the back of my mind. She was the standard I held other women to.

And the social media post confused the fuck out of me because it was made by a teenage girl looking for her father.

And that thought turned my insides to jelly, no matter how hard I tried to pretend otherwise.

I pushed aside the turmoil and focused on the facts. This was an old photo of me with Livvie. That's all. The kid could belong to anyone else.

I pushed off the engine and straightened. "No."

He squinted at me, unsure. "Is that 'No, I didn't make contact' or 'No, I don't gotta give you anything'?"

I stuck my toothpick back in my mouth, chomping down, the mint flavor doing little to curb the nicotine I suddenly craved, and let my glare be my answer. Then, to escape further bullshit, I stalked out of the bay.

Thoren yelled after me, "Oh, come on, Capt. Kylie's gonna keep hounding till she gets an answer. You know that."

Nate and Thoren had found new love and settled down, and our crew had grown closer in the process. I didn't envy their new relationships, though I appreciated the way we'd stuck together as a family with the addition of Jordan and Kylie. When the town had needed us to help with tornado recovery, when Nate had been in the hospital, and then when Thoren had, everyone had come together as a unit.

Hell, even that stupid shirtless calendar they kept roping us into... all of it strengthened the brotherhood bond.

But I'd never told anyone of my explosive fling, and they didn't need to know anything about it now either. And I had to quit thinking of families and bullshit. That shit never did me any good anyway.

With a grunt of frustration, I shoved open the door to the living quarters and pushed my disturbing thoughts away. The past was best left in the past. Today was what mattered.

And right now, I was going to pack my bags to attend this fucking meeting first thing in the morning, instead of heading to work on my boat.

I walked into the conference room at headquarters with five minutes to spare. Nodding at the other captains, I grabbed the closest seat facing the door. This fucking meeting was infringing on my personal time, and I had a ton of shit to do.

My crew had taken one look at me this morning and hightailed it to safer parts of the station. I couldn't seem to keep the scowl off my face, despite knowing I needed to play nice with the city administrator and mayor.

It was just an extra hour. It shouldn't be such a big deal. But I was over the administration's underhanded politics and HR's fluffy, feel-good bullshit.

And, fuck, but I was exhausted.

I loved my crew and the good we did. But I was tired of the three a.m. bullshit headache calls, like last night's run on a guy who'd been sick for three days, hadn't taken any meds, and suddenly needed to be transported in the middle of the fucking night.

I'd find something else, a new job that didn't require nightly adrenaline rushes, but I'd worked too damn hard for too damn long to give up on the one thing that'd kept me going—the promise of an early retirement.

From the hallway, I heard Bloom's annoyingly jovial voice chatting it up, and the equally annoying voice of the mayor as he openly flirted with Cathy, the department's administrative assistant.

Being at the new station meant I didn't come to HQ as often, but Cathy was one of ours.

If that old man offended her and ran her off like he'd done his assistant... I bristled, halfway out of my seat when they entered the room. The mayor was first through the door, greeting the four of us with handshakes and back claps.

I took a sip of coffee to hide the sneer that threatened every time that asshole was around. Fucking politician.

Bloom followed in his wake, equally as fake with his too-big smile and jokes. The city manager was a nice enough guy outside the office, but when he was in city-manager mode, he had a kiss-ass way about him. The dichotomy between his two faces made me not trust him. And it was too fucking early to deal with politics and bull-shit agendas today. I was supposed to be at the lake and would've been if they hadn't fucked up my plans with this meeting that could've been an email.

I hid behind my coffee again, avoiding direct eye contact with either of them by shifting my attention to the door as the next person entered.

She was tall, decked out in the formal fire department uniform. Her stark white coat a striking contrast to the fitted black skirt. Her dark hair was coiled into a tight bun at the nape of her slender neck. She looked professional and smart, and the vaguely familiar expression on her face indicated she'd take no shit. I let my gaze roam down her body, no doubt like the rest of these assholes were doing. Across the table, Roberts was checking out her legs as she passed him. She filed in and stood next to Bloom, clasping her hands in front of her.

A glance down at her hands showed the only indication that she might be feeling something other than the calm coolness she projected. The pointer finger of one hand rubbed against the knuckle of her thumb. It had been her tell way back when we'd met at the cocktail bar. Then, the simple movement had been entrancing. Now, she twirled a shiny thumb ring, equally hypnotizing.

In an instant, I was transported back in time. The last time I'd seen her, that hair had been a glorious mass of long dark curls blowing in the wind as we'd kissed goodbye on the dock of the private resort. Before that, those curls had been splayed out over a pillow beneath me. I'd buried my face in her graceful neck, and my body in hers.

I shifted in my seat, adjusting the uncomfortable, immediate hard-on pressing against the zipper of my uniform pants.

What in the hell?

This was Livvie, my Livvie.

Except she wasn't. She was polished, with a cold air about her.

The Livvie I remembered was flowy and bright. Soft and romantic.

This woman was professional and sharp. Not a bad thing, just a difference I couldn't reconcile in the moment.

The mayor's introduction was a buzz of words that didn't penetrate. Then the city manager smiled his bright white smile and added to the noise.

All I paid attention to was the brass shield on her uniform coat, indicating that my perfect fling partner was now my new boss.

She made eye contact with each of the captains as they were introduced. From the fog, I heard my name called, and then her eyes were on mine.

A bolt of lightning ripped through me, shredding my insides. Threatening to blast me from the inside out. Every sound in the room was magnified—the scraping of chairs as they sat, the voices I'd known for so many years—all rumbling together in a massive cacophony in the too-small room. All my nerve endings lived outside of my skin, exposed, sensitive, raw. The scratch of my shirt across my back, the too-tight cuff on my arms, the press of the shears in my leg pocket. All of it was too much.

But if seeing me affected her, I couldn't tell. She moved past me, on to the next guy, like nothing had happened, and then launched into a speech.

Hearing her speak solidified any doubts I had, as the voice I'd heard gasp in ecstasy now covered bullshit department business.

Two things hit me at once.

This was not the same woman I'd spent my perfect week with. And I was fucked because my body remembered every minute of our time together.

Chapter Three

Staring down the barrel of a loaded gun might've been easier than keeping my composure while coming face-to-face with my daughter's father.

As it was, a bead of sweat rolled down the center of my back under his direct stare. I barely managed to contain the squirm that my body so desperately wanted.

Thankfully, I'd opted for the full power of the formal dress suit of fire chief. A stark white jacket that proudly bore my badge and deftly concealed my overactive sweat glands.

I'd worked my way through the ranks, and I knew the level of respect the uniform alone granted me. The rest I'd have to earn on my own.

Except, now, I faced off with the one man I thought I'd never see again. A man who'd haunted me every single day for nearly sixteen years.

And I couldn't let on. Couldn't let them see the shock

that threatened to drop me to my knees, the fear that he would hate me once he knew the truth, the regret that things had turned out the way they had. I had to be professional and composed.

Focusing on the city manager while he spoke, I inhaled slowly through my nose and exhaled just as slowly, rubbing my finger over the warm metal of my thumb ring. As always, the movement calmed me.

This first meeting with my new command would set the tone. I needed to exude confidence and control, despite what was quickly becoming the worst moment of my life.

Cathy had thoughtfully prepared some homework for me. A file containing the headshots and names of the commanding officers that I hadn't had time to fully review prior to the meeting. At that moment, I regretted not taking a moment to at least look it over. Maybe then the surprise of seeing him wouldn't have rattled me so much.

And these men seeing me as anything other than in charge was unacceptable.

Mr. Bloom finished with his long-winded introduction, and it was time to face the men around the conference table.

"Thank you, Mayor Smith, Mr. Bloom. I appreciate the opportunity to serve the city of Newman." It rankled to have to basically kiss ass, but it was smart to play nice on the first week of the job. I turned and addressed the men who would be working for me, my mask of HBIC—Head Bitch in Charge—firmly in place.

"Good morning. First, let me say thank you for coming and being on time. I'll keep this short and sweet. I'm sure you have a full day ahead of you, and this last-minute meeting probably challenged your plans."

I glanced around the room, noting the body language of the four captains. Three sat at the table, one stood along the wall in front of an old-school dry-erase board. All had assumed some form of defensive pose. Arms crossed over chests, closed off.

I'd been correct in my assumption that they wouldn't appreciate the inevitable disruption of their schedules. And some of these men no doubt had thought they'd be in this role, giving orders rather than taking them from someone else, much less a woman.

A girl could choke on the amount of testosterone in the room.

"Second, to answer the question I'm sure you have. Yes, I'm qualified for this role. I've got fifteen years of fire service. I'm a certified paramedic. I graduated at the top of my class with a fire science degree and completed my master's in emergency management."

The looks on their faces told me what I needed to know. Book smarts wouldn't cut it, and they weren't down with political games either.

"But my real mettle comes from a long family history in the fire service. My father was a fire chief and my grandfather before him. I grew up learning fire strategy and hearing about issues that departments face. In every department I've been a part of, I've completed the mandatory training that all personnel are required to have, including mandatory PT hours, and have been as much a part of change—improvement—as possible. I worked my way through the ranks to assistant chief at my former department by being a damn hard worker and being invested in the department. I have five life-saver commendations and twelve for bravery." Even if they didn't believe my words, maybe they'd realize my work ethic.

"I've been on the front lines. I'm not here to make your lives miserable. I'm here to support this department and make us the best we can be."

From there, I dropped into a prepared speech about what my expectations were, ensuring them that I would not change their current operating procedures unless I knew of a better way to handle certain aspects, and I wouldn't change things just to change them. By the time I got done speaking, most of the men had dropped their defensive posture.

"Now, if you'll please do me the honor of introducing yourselves."

One by one, they stated their name, where they were stationed, and their years of service.

Until that moment, I'd avoided meeting his gaze. He sat forward, forearms on the table, hands clasped loosely as he studied me. "I'm Mac Collins, captain at Station Four. Twenty-five years of service."

I was impressed that he hadn't once let that steely gray gaze drift down my body like it had the night I'd met him in that tropical beachside bar. Now, instead of heat in his gaze, there was accusation, disbelief, and a touch of hostility.

I nodded in greeting as if we hadn't known each other intimately. As if I didn't have a massive secret that I needed to share with him. Instead, I addressed the room at large. "I'll stop by each of the stations over the next few days to meet the men and women on shift. I'm open to hearing what you feel our issues are and look forward to working with you to resolve them."

The mayor took a step forward, placing himself a step in front of me. I stifled a groan of frustration. It was going to be a challenge working for this weasel.

"Well, gentlemen, that'll be all for today. You heard the little lady."

I bristled, and it took all of my willpower not to shred him on site. But eviscerating him publicly would gain me no favors. I'd have to bide my time and be strategic with the mayor.

"She's willing to listen to ways we can improve, and the mayor's office wants to support you. Within the bounds of the budget, of course, so don't think this is an open invitation for a Christmas wish list."

Masculine chuckles filled the room, though Mac didn't even smirk. The captain propped at the back of the room, Thompson, pushed off the wall and stalked away. Captain Roberts, seated across from Mac, stared at my legs suggestively as he stood. He offered a handshake that lingered a touch too long to be professional and said his goodbyes. Another battle I had expected and had won before.

The mayor and administrator had already turned and engaged in conversation about a tax referendum meeting. I'd been effectively dismissed, and the whole thing stunk of good-old-boy politics, misogyny, and sexual harassment.

Mac, Captain Collins—I couldn't think of him as Mac— pushed to his feet and met my gaze. Once again, the heat of it ran the length of my body, and I turned toward him against my better judgment.

No doubt about it. There was still some kind of powerful magnetism between us.

"Chief Hawkins," he acknowledged before striding out of the room, the bite of my name lingering in the air.

He wore the standard navy-blue tactical pants that everyone else wore, but somehow, his cupped his butt in exactly the right way and molded to his thighs, leaving the impression that they were just as thick as I remembered.

And I was a terrible person for objectifying him, especially when I had just endured the same. I would not be the creep hitting on her subordinates.

Finally, the room emptied, and I pressed the back of my hand to my brow and sank to a chair to gather my composure for a moment.

"That went well." Cathy's voice broke my moment of silence.

I glanced up to find her leaning against the doorway.

She smirked. "Except for Thompson being his regular ray of sunshine and stomping off in hunt of puppies to kick."

My jaw dropped. "He doesn't..."

Her laugh was a twinkle that brightened the otherwise gloomy room. "No, Chief. I was joking." She tilted her head as if pondering. "But you know, I don't know what he does on his off days, so it still could be a possibility."

I straightened and walked toward her. "What can you tell me about the others?"

I wanted—needed—information, especially about one man in particular, but I didn't want it to seem like I was fishing.

"Not much to tell. You've got the best of the best for captains. They are all good men and have moved through the ranks."

"What you aren't saying is that I haven't, and in their eyes, that might be a problem."

Her head waggled in a nonresponse.

"Well, Cathy, just because I haven't risen through the ranks here, doesn't mean that I haven't done my time. I have plenty of boots-on-the-ground service in Charleston."

"I don't doubt it, ma'am. But then again, I'm not the one you have to prove it to."

By the end of the day, Cathy and I had been through the budget, had a list of equipment—most of it needing to be upgraded five years ago, save the new equipment at Station Four—and a to-do list a mile long.

But first, I wanted to talk to Rosie.

Seeing my daughter's eyes in the man across the room had been unnerving. The sudden need to take her and run home was strong. It was too coincidental that we'd landed here, of all places, where her biological father lived and worked. Yes, I definitely needed to have a conversation with my daughter.

I dialed her number on my cell, and of course it went straight to voicemail. A glance at the clock showed three thirty. She wouldn't be off the bus for another half hour at least.

Somehow, between now and when I got home, I had to piece together how this stroke of bad luck had happened and how I was going to handle it. It was just a matter of time until she found out the truth.

And I prayed that she could handle it.

I also prayed that he would accept meeting her once he found out the truth. But this was fine, just a small complication.

* * *

"Rosie, sweetheart? I'm home," I called as I let myself into our new townhouse. The rental was nice enough. Good neighborhood, close to work, good school district.

Everything had moved so swiftly since Rosie tipped me off to the job opening and I had applied on a whim.

At the time, I'd been so relieved that everything had fallen into place. The job interview had gone well, and we'd found a nice place to live, just in time for Rosie to start her freshman year of high school.

Looking back, her overzealous attitude and total acceptance of uprooting our lives was... unusual. I'd expected some pushback over her having to start a new school, and high school at that. But my precocious daughter had been elated.

Now, as she be-bopped into the small kitchen and greeted me with a hug, I realized how completely she'd played me.

"How'd it go today, Chief?" She'd started calling me Chief instead of Mom the moment I got the job offer like she was proud of me. What I'd once considered a sweet sentiment suddenly seemed all wrong.

"It was a good day," I replied, dropping my work bag to return her hug. Despite everything, she was the love of my life, and no matter the circumstance, we were in this together. I pulled back, cupping her face. "How about you? Did you have a good day at school?"

Her steel-gray eyes flitted away, and she pulled away from me, heading to the fridge, where she searched the contents for something to magically appear.

"Meh. It's high school, I guess. Did they get you a car today?"

Rosie had started dreaming of driving over the summer, yearning for freedom while stretching every boundary I set. While I'd agreed to loosen the reins on her in safe situations, I wasn't used to dropping her at the movies or letting her hang out unsupervised.

She was still my little girl, and I wasn't ready for her to grow up. "Not yet. Cathy, my new assistant, tells me it should be here soon."

A small squeal pealed through the kitchen, echoing off

the bare walls. My daughter, so fiercely independent and ready to tackle the world on her own. Apparently, it was a given that if I had a department-issued car, she would get mine.

I kicked off my shoes at the table and plopped onto the couch. We didn't have much in the way of furniture. Aside from her bedroom furniture, a couch, an oversized chair that Rosie had labeled her reading chair, and a small coffee table were all that we had managed to move with us. We didn't even have a television.

I'd wanted a fresh start for Rosie and me after the divorce, but establishing a new home was expensive, and it was taking some time.

I propped my feet on the coffee table and relaxed.

"Don't get so excited, sweetheart. You still have nearly two years until you turn sixteen. And we still need to check the state requirements on learner's permit requirements and how long you have to wait after that to get your license."

The refrigerator door slammed shut, the few bottles in the door rattling. "I know, Mom." She plopped next to me, resting her head on my shoulder.

"So did you have to go all badass on anyone today?" She pulled my hand into hers, absently tracing the lines of my palm with the tip of her finger. Memories of another set of hands identical to hers, except more masculine, doing the exact same thing the night we met roared to life. Was it possible that they had the same soul? Now that I'd been face-to-face with him, I recognized so many similarities in their mannerisms. What I remembered of his, anyway.

"No, sweetheart. And I don't think I'll have to."

Quietly, she traced my fingers, turning over my hands, fiddling with my rings, especially the new turquoise-and-silver band I'd bought to replace my wedding set. She had a matching one on her finger.

"Did you get to meet the rest of the department?" Prior to today, I wouldn't have thought anything of her innocent question. But now... I had my doubts as to how innocent my daughter actually was. My heart broke a little.

"I met my captains." Rosie tensed up beside me. A definite tell if I'd ever seen one. I continued as if I hadn't noticed. "I'll meet the rest of the crews starting tomorrow and spend the next three days meeting everyone."

I pulled my hand from hers and wrapped my arm around her shoulder, snuggling her into my side. It wasn't often that I got to snuggle my baby girl anymore. Resting my temple against her silky hair, I breathed in her scent, cherishing the moment. The floral shampoo she'd always used a familiar balm in a sea of unexpected events. "What about you? Did you meet some new friends today?"

"I met a girl named Shae. She seems really nice and had the prettiest braids. She sat next to me in art class."

She plopped her feet next to mine on the table, playing footsie as she told me all about her new friend and her awesome art teacher. I wanted so badly to interrogate her, find out if my suspicions were accurate. If she knew about her biological father.

The week with Mac had been so much more than anything I'd ever experienced. The deepest connection, the most fulfilling experience of my life, aside from the angel I'd been gifted to raise.

"So this move has been a good one?" I asked. If I could just keep her talking, maybe she'd give me the opening I needed.

"So far, so good." She tucked her head further into me, scooting down into the couch to lay her head on my chest. If

I didn't know any better, I'd think she was trying to be extra sweet. But I knew my rebellious child. These snuggle sessions were rare, and she'd never extended them to get closer.

My Spidey senses were tingling. There was more to her story than she was letting on.

"What about you? Is this move everything you wanted it to be?"

"So far, so good." I echoed her words on a grin. She'd tensed up when I mentioned my crew. I needed to explore that more. "My visit to the stations starts tomorrow, and I'll have a chance to meet the rest of the department. But the captains were all nice. I felt very welcomed."

"Were any of them cute?"

"Honey." I leveled my gaze on her. "They are my subordinates. It doesn't matter if they are the most handsome men in town, they aren't for me."

"Shae said they do this firefighter calendar, and all the guys in it are hawt."

"You mean attractive."

"No, I mean haaaawt." She giggled, fanning her face as she drew out the word. "At least that's what Shae sounds like when she says it." We shared a chuckle. "So, are any of them in it? Maybe we should get a calendar just to make sure."

I choked on air.

"Rosa Nell Hawkins," I started when I could find my voice. "Young lady, you will not pursue this line of thought. These men work for me. We will not be ogling them."

She sat up, whipping around to face me. "It's for charity, Mom."

If eyes could roll any harder, I'd be surprised.

"Anyway." She settled back into the curve of my arm.

"Shae showed me a bunch of pictures from when the tornado came through. I checked them out."

I let the silence ring, hoping she would continue.

"There was this one old guy. He was decent looking. He'd done some real hero shi—stuff during the storm. I was just wondering if he works for you. If, you know..." She picked at the frayed hem of her jean shorts. "Maybe you met him? You know, to find out if the stories were true."

"Don't think I missed that slip. Good catch on not cussing, by the way." Honestly, this child tested my nerves sometimes, and aside from her tendency to cuss, she was a good kid. But good kid or no, we weren't ready for the discussion she seemed to be headed for. So, like a big chicken, I hedged and made a mental note to do some research about the tornado.

"I haven't had a chance to talk to anyone about it, but I'll let you know after my station visits. How's that?"

She didn't like my answer but didn't push.

"Tell me about the rest of your day, sweetie. You made a new friend named Shae. Anything else good happen?"

She pushed off the couch, gathering her backpack. "It wasn't terrible. But I'm not sure about that bus."

"What do you mean?"

Dragging her bag across the room and rifling around in it, she produced a handful of paperwork for me to sign. "There's a crew of kids on there who make me feel sort of weird."

"What'd they do?"

"They're just... not nice. Made fun of some kids. Normal bullsh—stuff."

"Good catch, again."

She dug out a notebook and opened it to her agenda. My girl was organized and shared my love of planners and journals. I admired her profile while she shuffled some papers. She really was the best part of my life. She paused on a page, a frown marring her features.

"Okay, Mom, don't yell." She flipped a page up so I could see it. On it was a list of mandatory supplies.

I sighed because the absolute last thing I wanted to do was run to the store for school supplies. "Tell you what, I'll drive you to the store, and you start filling out forms on the way. We'll also stop and grab a bite to eat, because I'm starving and don't feel like cooking."

An hour later, we were headed home, takeout in hand, and Rosie was making her sales pitch. "Well, hear me out. I have to wait two whole years to get my license, and that's going to suck. I don't want to ride the bus with those jerks. I need some wheels. Besides, I could be finished with my homework way before you get home, and I could cook and have dinner ready when you get home if..."

I rolled my eyes. This was classic Rosie. No telling how long she'd been planning to make this pitch. Might as well let her finish before I shot her down. She tended to have off-the-wall ideas that she didn't think all the way through.

"If you get me a bike." She tossed the words out like she hadn't been leading up to them over the last hour of our conversation.

"That's actually not a bad idea." At a red light, I gave her the side-eye. "When did you come up with this plan?"

"Today, on the bus," she offered with the nonchalance of a teenager.

"And what made you, she-who-is-allergic-to-exercise, decide that riding a bike appealed to you?" I flipped on a blinker and turned into our complex. There was enough lighting that it felt safe. We had a two-story townhouse, and though there was no garage, there was plenty of space to store a bike for her.

"Shae rides hers every day. They have a great place to lock them up, and it's out of the weather so they don't get ruined. It's less than a mile to the high school, and I can take neighborhood routes so I don't get on the main road. And it'll have me home, like, an hour sooner. And it's faster than walking."

She really made a good argument, and I didn't blame her. I hated riding the bus when I was a kid. Plus, if we got two bikes, it would be something we could do together.

"Bonus, if you get a bike too, there's a cool bike path on the other side of town, and it'd be something we can do together."

My kid was a damn mind reader.

But she made some valid points, and I was willing to consider it. "Okay, you little psychic, we'll check into it this weekend."

She bolted out of the car, plastic bags rattling. "I can't wait to tell Shae."

I locked up the car, swallowing my emotions. My little girl was growing up, spreading her wings. Pretty soon, she would fly from the nest. And I wasn't ready for that part of my life to change.

And on the heels of that thought, an overwhelming sense of guilt clouded in. How much disservice was I doing by keeping the truth from them? I really owed it to Mac, and to Rosie, to introduce them.

I had tried to find him. But with not even knowing his full name, nor where he was from, even social media was a bust. And Tim had been such a good father in the beginning, I'd been selfish and taken the easy option out. Tim had known about Rosie and had chosen us anyway, so there was no need to dig deeper—to make things harder. Even if I felt crushing guilt that Mac may have wanted to know his daughter. What if he'd been alone in the world all this time, and I'd cheated him out of her love?

Now it seemed my choice to stop looking for him was rearing its ugly head. I just prayed the consequences wouldn't destroy us all.

Chapter Four

Mac

Two days passed between shifts. Forty-eight hours that would've been glorious if I hadn't spent the whole time thinking about a certain new fire chief.

Where had she been all these years? And how fucking ironic that she was now my boss, much less in the same line of work as me. And how the fuck was I supposed to react? And who was the kid from the TikTok video?

I pulled up to the station, fully aware that she'd be making her visit today.

"Morning, Capt," Big Mo called, too fucking cheerful for my mood. I grunted a hello, stalking down the hall to my bunk.

I tossed my bag into my locker, yanking my sheets and blankets out. She'd probably show up in that damn tight-ass uniform and send all these yo-yos into heat. Again.

I snapped the sheets tight. Why did she have to show up here? Why now? And why couldn't she wear normal, loose-fitting, tent-shaped uniform pants? I flapped the blanket over the sheets and tucked the end before smoothing the corners.

"What?" I barked to the presence in my doorway.

"You okay there, Capt?" Nate stood with a shoulder propped on the doorframe. "Everything go okay at the lake?"

"Everything's fine."

His eyebrows shot to his forehead. "Really? It's just that, I've never seen anyone make a bed up with that kind of vengeance."

I needed to get my shit together. These guys depended on me to keep my cool. It was all they'd ever known, and they deserved better from me.

"The guys said the new chief is making her rounds," he continued, oblivious that I absolutely did not want to talk about the chief. I didn't even want to think about her. I'd spent the last two days thinking about her, to the point that I was ready to confront her, then maybe kiss her, and then maybe yell at her some more.

"Anyway, Torres said she's really smart. He's impressed. They cleaned the bay for us last night and gave us the heads-up that we might be getting a visit. We don't know when she'll show. So we need to be ready." Nate paused, then asked, "You sure you're okay, Capt? You got some heartburn or something? Your face is all red."

I pulled a toothpick out of my pocket and chomped down, speaking around it. "Nicotine fits still get me from time to time," I lied. "And traffic was a bitch coming from the lake this morning." It wasn't a full-on lie. Other than getting behind school buses, the ride had been fine. No, it was the days, weeks, and months that loomed ahead that had me on edge. "I'd pay twenty bucks to smell a freshly lit cigarette right now."

His brows shot high. I didn't often admit to needing a smoke. "Okay then, I'm gonna leave you alone," he said and cautiously backed out into the hallway.

I resumed my morning routine. This was fucking stupid. I was better than this childish temper tantrum. I could handle her being here. I hadn't let a woman affect me this much in over fifteen years. Hadn't had one get under my skin or consume my thoughts.

Matter of fact, she was the last woman to affect me this quickly, this thoroughly. I shoved the thought back into the box it belonged in and left my bunk in search of my crew.

Inside the bay, between the engine and the rescue truck, was where we spent most of our time hanging out at a cheap plastic table with mismatched chairs.

Except this morning, the table and chairs had been put away, and everyone was busy cleaning the already spotless bay. An old vintage Ford Crown Victoria pulled into the drive and parked in front of the station.

"Who's in that piece of shit?" Burgess called.

"I haven't seen one of those for years," Big Mo replied, propped on his broom. "I thought they retired all the former cruisers after PD got done dogging them." He shook his head in disbelief. "What unlucky SOB got shackled with that?"

Knowing the way the city did things, I could imagine who was about to walk around that corner. I plucked the toothpick from my lips as the quick clip of high heels echoed from the sidewalk.

And then, there she was. Dress jacket crisp and white. And another fucking skirt and heels.

Well, shit.

"Good morning, gentlemen," her sexy-as-fuck voice rang through the bay. A flash of irritation crawled up my spine. I didn't want to see her. Not here. Not like this.

But I was the captain on duty. It was my role to make the introductions and be professional. So I schooled my features and went to greet her.

"Chief Hawkins, meet the crew of Station Four. This is Morgan Jackson, or Big Mo. Nate Williams, Thoren Watkins, and our rookie, Burgess."

The whites of Thoren's eyes blazed as he gawked at her, probably recognizing her from Kylie's photo. She'd aged gracefully, but there was no doubt that she was the woman in the picture. I prayed he'd keep his shit together and narrowed my eyes in warning. Thankfully, she didn't linger on Thoren or notice his stupid gaping mouth.

"Burgess doesn't have a first name?" Swear to God, her eyes twinkled, just like they had in that island bar.

"Rookie," Big Mo teased with a huge grin.

She returned his smile, and my stomach nearly regurgitated the coffee I'd pounded on the long drive to work. This was a fucking nightmare. Add in the fact that she didn't act like she recognized me, and all of it just piled on to the shit I didn't want to deal with. I hadn't changed that much either, so there was no way she didn't know. What game was she playing?

"It's a pleasure to meet you, gentlemen." She took in the bay, eyes lingering on the corner where the table and chairs were neatly stacked. "I appreciate the effort to impress, but I can assure you that I don't expect you to reorganize your lives on my account. I don't mean to interrupt, but I'd appreciate a few moments of your time."

Over by the engine, Thoren and Nate whispered, heads bowed.

I knew exactly what they were whispering about. If I could, I would smack them both in the head for whispering about me. Her. What they thought they knew.

But then again, maybe that was me projecting.

I cleared my throat and snapped our collective attention to the matter at hand. My new boss was in the house, and we needed to find out her agenda and lay down some parameters.

I'd worked too damn long and too damn hard, and I was too damn close to retirement to let some newbie, no matter how gorgeous she was, come in and fuck it up. Regardless of how much my body responded to hers.

Or how hot my dreams had been in the two days since I'd last seen her.

"Conference room is open, Chief," I ground out, ready to get this meeting over with. If being in her space was affecting me this much, I had no idea how I was going to manage the next five years.

The smile died on her face as she took me in. "Let's get started, then." She turned and motioned to my crew of idiots, and like a pack of baby ducklings, they followed her into the station, toddling single file into the conference room where they sat like good little boys.

I scowled. What the fuck? They'd never been so well behaved in their lives.

I wanted to throttle them.

We'd be having a discussion as soon as she left because something was definitely up.

She sat at the head of the table, notepad in front of her, and listened while they addressed everything from uniforms and bunker gear to the state of the equipment.

"Why do we have a four-million-dollar building, and we're using outdated, glitchy equipment?"

"That's a good question, Chief," Thoren piped up. "Maybe ask the city manager or the mayor. We gave them our list of problems before they opened this station, but nothing was done."

I leaned back in my chair, chewing on my toothpick, arms crossed over my chest because it physically hurt to be in her vicinity, but I knew I had to speak up. "I was on the consulting team for the station build-out and equipment specs. More than once, my concerns were overridden in lieu of aesthetics for the building. Thankfully, they listened on the engine requirements."

She turned to face me. "Hence the fancy red sliding doors on the bay?" The full effect of her attention on me nearly stole my breath.

Nate saved me by replying, "The money wasted on those doors alone could've been used to upgrade the equipment. They do look really cool, and the truck is super nice, thanks to Capt. But what does it matter if they leave the little issues unchecked?"

"Having reliable communication is not a little issue." Mo glared at Nate before shifting his attention to the chief. "And that's the administration's mentality too. It's just a radio. What does it matter?"

She made a note on her pad. Efficient, knowledgeable, listening.

From there, more conversation unfolded. She gave each person equal opportunity in the discussion. It really sucked that she seemed good at her job.

I didn't want her to fail, but I also didn't want her here, dredging up old memories. Making me feel things I had no business feeling. Especially when there was no reaction from her at all. She could've at least given me a second glance. I mean, damn. We'd spent a whole week wrapped up in each other. Best sex of my life.

How many times over the years had I wished that I'd gotten my head out of my ass and just asked for her number? How many times had I regretted forsaking the connection we'd had? Had it just been a time-and-place thing? Tropical paradise and a brokenhearted fool looking for a willing someone to make him forget.

And now there was a random kid on social media with a photo of us, looking for her father.

I studied Liv. The avoidance. The stilted interaction. Maybe there was more happening here than her just avoiding me. Maybe I did have a kid, and Liv didn't want me to know.

This was fucking confusing.

"Captain Collins?"

My name from her lips did things to me.

And I'd been so caught up in just staring at her, I'd completely missed a whole-ass discussion. I realized, belatedly, that not only was the entire shift looking at me, but they'd also caught me staring at her mouth.

I met her steady gaze, heart hammering.

"Did you have anything to add?"

The bossy attitude was a total turn-on.

"Has anyone discussed the arson cases with you?"

There. See? I was engaged. And had a contribution that we could work with. Because I was a fucking professional.

Her brow dipped in concern. "No. I'm not aware of any open cases."

I glanced at Thoren and then took the reins, certain he'd rather not have to spill the details about his twin brother. "Recently, we had a situation, a series of arson fires, and an active investigation that culminated in the perpetrator being apprehended after he caught one of our guys in an active structure fire. Both men were sent to the hospital. However, the suspect managed to slip away from his police guard at the hospital."

She sat back in her chair, frowning. "No one has even mentioned it."

"I gave the officer responsible, and his lieutenant, a piece of my mind. Since then, relations with that shift have been... less than ideal. Sometimes hostile, even. I'm surprised you weren't warned about the situation."

Her lips pressed together as she made a series of notes, then met my eyes. "Thank you for telling me."

"There's more to the story," Thoren added flatly. The rest of the crew shifted, bristling in defense of their brother. "The arsonist is my brother."

Had to give her credit. She didn't even flinch. Instead, she grew still, her voice soft and gentle as she suggested, "How about you fill me in on the rest of the story."

"My brother was targeting me because he's a sick fu— person." He cleared his throat, color creeping up from the collar of his uniform shirt. "Anyways, he thought the best way to torment me was to set fire in places he knew I'd respond to. My girlfriend's apartment, her yoga studio, all in my station's zone. We caught him, but not before he'd done irreparable damage."

"Why her place and not yours?"

Thoren shrugged. "Because it would hurt me more if something happened to her."

Chief Hawkins listened patiently as Thoren continued the breakdown of events, making notes on her pad the whole time. I managed to stay involved and fill in missing details, even as I wanted to get my hands on those notes and find out what she kept writing down. Eventually, she wrapped up the meeting.

"Thank you. This has been a very informative meeting, and I appreciate your candor. I've gotten what I needed for now and won't take up any more of your time."

The guys thanked her and left one by one. I waited until they'd all left the room, because if she'd been anyone else, I would've done the same thing. And I respected the way she'd handled the meeting. To the point, direct. No bullshit.

"Thank you, Captain Collins. Your crew has been the most forthcoming of all the shifts. I feel like we've had some good discussion today. I can tell they respect you a great deal." She sat back in her chair, relaxed, in control, her tone conversational.

I mirrored her position, even though I felt anything but relaxed and in control. "I have a good squad."

There was more I wanted to say, things I wanted to ask. About that damn social media post, about the past, about so many things. I shifted and dug around in my pocket for my pack of toothpicks, jamming a new one in my mouth to keep myself quiet.

She picked up a pen, dropping it end over end. Letting it slide down through her fingers, then flipping it over and repeating the process.

She had something on her mind, but I could wait her out.

"Captain," she started, meeting my gaze, "we've met before. Do you remember me?"

Mother. Trucker. We were doing this. I'd been curious, but that didn't mean I was ready.

What was I supposed to say? "Oh, hey, Chief. Yeah, I remember that day we went skinny dipping." Or "Do you still like those fruity drinks?" Or "Yes, I remember every minute of being balls deep in you." Or "I've thought about you all the time over the years and regretted not getting your number." None of those were a suitable reply.

I opted for a safe, affirmative grunt.

Her expression was unreadable, but I didn't miss the slight nod she gave me before she broke the eye contact.

She glanced down at her notepad and spun the ring on her finger. Obviously, I made her nervous. "There are strict no-fraternization rules, I've been told. So I would appreciate your discretion."

After her lack of initial acknowledgment, the words slammed into me and pissed me right off. How dare she assume that I'd be shouting out our business? I pushed away from the table and stood.

"Yes, ma'am. Understood. Did you need me for anything else?" I needed to get the fuck out of here. She'd made herself clear that she didn't want anything to do with me. Held no fond memories, or if she did, they'd meant a lot more to me than to her.

"No." Her reply was soft, relieved. "Thank you, Mac."

Gutted.

I was absolutely gutted.

I'd spent the last forty-eight hours thinking about her, replaying those old memories in my head. Had obsessed over them. Over her. Halfway wondering if we could try again and see if we still had the same chemistry, knowing that would be a colossal mistake for many reasons, at the top of which was because she was my boss.

To make matters worse, it'd also been a long fucking time since I'd had any sort of physical reaction to a woman, and immediately upon seeing her for the first time, my body had responded. A relief and a problem at the same time.

I left her there in the conference room. Stomping down the hall and punching through the doors, needing a cigarette in the worst way, I stalked out to the yard. My momma, God rest her soul, would cuff my ear if she'd seen that.

But I needed to be as far from Chief Hawkins as possible. I didn't need the reminder that I wasn't good enough. Wasn't wanted. Being stuck in a room with her and the vivid memories I'd carried was a slap in the face.

Mo was out back winding the garden hose, water droplets still shimmering on the pickup truck he'd just hosed off.

"You done?" I snapped.

"Yes, sir."

"Good. I'm making a run."

To his credit, he just nodded and stayed out of my way. I caught him watching from the bay as I wheeled out of the parking lot.

I made it to the red light before the tones dropped, and we began an intense day of running calls. By that evening, I'd finally had enough distraction that I'd settled somewhat. I joined the guys, mid-argument, watching golf in the day room.

"I'm just saying that watching YouTube videos of people playing golf is not my idea of watching sports," Nate grouched from his recliner. He was kicked back, an arm behind his head, eyes glued to the golf game in question, despite his denial of enjoying it.

"What would you rather watch, then, Grandpa?" Burgess taunted.

Three voices answered, "The Braves."

Burgess exhaled a beleaguered sigh. "Baseball is so boring."

"And watching golf isn't?" Thoren chimed in.

"Enough." I snapped my fingers, demanding the remote from Burgess. I flipped it to baseball and kicked back in my chair, effectively halting the argument.

Burgess slipped out a few minutes later, mumbling about his iPad.

The back door chimed, and Mike Harrison, the fire marshal, walked in.

Greetings and handshakes were passed around before Mike settled into the recliner next to me.

"What's up, Mikey?" Nate asked.

"Man, fuck off with the nickname."

Thoren chuckled. "But it's so cute when your mom says it."

Mike scowled. "You're pushing it. Just because you overheard my mother say it, does not give you leave to use it."

"How's it going?" I asked.

"Pretty good. Leah's got a late class, so I thought I'd hang out here while I wait on her."

His girlfriend, Leah, and Thoren's girlfriend, Kylie, ran a yoga studio together.

"They got the studio reopened, then?"

"Yeah, man. The new space is working out well. It was a stroke of luck finding a vacant space on the square, but so far, so good. Business is going well for them."

"That's good," I mumbled.

"It's still unsettling that the bastard is still on the run," Mike said. His heavy sigh carried a weight each of us felt.

"No kidding," Thoren agreed. "Like waiting for the other shoe to drop."

On the screen, the Braves hit a homer to take the lead,

and the guys whooped like they were at the park. Just like that, the heavy mood lifted.

When they settled, Mike started again. "I got to meet the new fire chief."

I knew immediately where this fucking conversation was headed.

"She looks an awful lot like that photo Kylie saw on TikTok this summer," he continued, the words loaded with meaning. Meaning I didn't want to think about. Instead, I focused on the game stats scrolling the bottom of the screen.

All fucking day, I'd been dreading this conversation, knowing it was coming because these guys couldn't help but gossip.

"Yeah, she came by this morning." Nate straightened, his attention on me. "So, what's up, Capt? Was that picture legit?"

Thoren dropped the foot of his recliner and leaned an elbow to his knee, fully invested in the topic. "More importantly, do you have a secret love child that we don't know about?"

"Because it seems that maybe you do, and maybe your baby mama is now your boss. That's gotta suck, man. All parts of it." Mo summed up the situation perfectly.

I dropped the foot of my own chair. "Here's the deal."

They all leaned forward, and I wanted to thump each one of them right in the fucking forehead. "She is the woman in the photo. She stated that we'd met before and asked if I remembered her."

There was a collective gasp like they'd just received the juiciest bit of news they'd ever heard. I loathed being the subject.

"But as to the thing Kylie found, she didn't mention it.

We didn't discuss anything beyond acknowledging identities. So I'm not making assumptions, and you nosy little bitches are gonna keep your mouths shut and let me handle it."

Except, I didn't know how.

Maybe that was the underlying frustration that had ridden me all day. I didn't know what the picture meant. I didn't know why Olivia was here. I didn't know who the kid was. Had she come here, knowing she'd find me, to make my life hell? What did she want?

Was this kid mine? And if she was, would that suck? I'd never wanted kids before, but what if I had a grown child? Was I such a bastard that I wasn't worthy of being a dad? Did they want money from me? Why? And why now? Why not years ago?

I looked at the men around me and leveled my meanest, don't-fuck-with-me glare on them one by one.

Normally, it would have them all tucking tail and running to hide, because I could be an intimidating SOB when I wanted to. But these assholes? Nothing I said or did fazed them. They shared a grin between them. One that spread and grew like they were all in on some kind of secret and their whole night had been made.

"Okay, Capt," Thoren cheesed at me. "Whatever you say."

Chapter Five

"**H**ere's how you lock in the rack to the hitch." The young man currently mansplaining how to attach the bike rack to my SUV missed the delicious eye roll I sent to Rosie. But her responding giggle said she got it.

He paused and glanced at us. "What's that?"

"I didn't say anything," my daughter responded. "But, just to let you know, you've threaded that backward."

I loved it when she stood up for herself. The years of taking her camping and hitching the pop-up camper were paying off in her general knowledge.

He glanced back down to the hitch, scratching the back of his neck. "Huh, you're right. I should probably let you do it, then." Teenage attitude laced his tone as he stood and handed her the pin.

Rosie puffed her chest and stepped forward. "Watch and learn."

Pride swelled in my chest as Rosie anchored the rack

and then watched intently while he loaded and secured the bikes. My daughter was growing into a capable young woman. Doing things for herself, proving herself. She ran through the cable lock sequence with him and then looked to me with sparkling eyes.

We took our shiny new mountain bikes for a spin, then stopped for a post-ride ice cream.

It had been a long week, after an equally long summer, so it was time for my girl to enjoy all her favorite things. We flopped onto the couch in our bare townhouse, waiting for the pizza delivery guy, worn-out after a fun day.

"Mom, I need to tell you something."

A thread of discomfort shivered down my spine at her tone. "What's wrong, honey?"

Next to me, my baby girl fidgeted. Like me, she tended to twirl her rings when she was nervous. Whatever was on her mind had her worried. "You know that day I was asking you about the people at the fire department? And I had those pictures from my friend Shae?"

"Yes."

"Don't you think I look a lot like one of them?" She voiced it as a question, but I knew my girl.

My eyes slid closed even as my heart dropped to the pit of my stomach.

I didn't know how she did it. But Rosie had figured out that her biological father was here in this very town.

"Rosie, honey," I started, already dreading the conversation I knew she deserved.

"Mom, just wait. There's something I need to show you."

She rose and went to her book bag, rummaging around inside. I tried to sneak a look, but she held whatever it was behind her as she returned, curling a knee into the couch and sitting facing me.

Then she handed me a picture from a lifetime ago. I took the four by six with a shaky hand, staring at an old image of a younger Mac, his arms around a younger me. The edges of the photo were dinged, one corner slightly bent.

"This was one of the guys in the calendar. I mean, he's old now, but it's still him. With you."

I was unable to respond. All I could do was trace a finger over the younger version of myself. Looking at the picture of the two of us, I was transported back in time to a perfect day on a tropical beach. I was snuggled up to him, my back to his chest, his arms wrapped around me. We were smiling. Happy. And if I was honest, maybe even a little bit in love after a week of spending every minute of every day together.

"Who is this, Mom?"

I finally found my voice. "Where did you get this?"

"I found it in the attic when I was hiding out from Tim and his bad moods one day." Toward the end of our marriage, she'd done that often. "There was an old trunk with letters and journals. When I moved one of the journals, this photo fell out."

I blanched as the underlying meaning of what she was telling me sank in. Rosie had had this all along. And the journals...

She stood and returned to the backpack, bringing a familiar leather-bound notebook back with her. "There are letters in here. But I didn't read any of them."

I met her gaze to check for honesty. I needed to know she wasn't playing games with me. Those letters had been my only outlet as I grieved the loss of what might have been, the mourning heart of a young woman. Not something I wanted my teenage daughter to read.

"Honest, Mom." Her eyes were warm with understanding as she lifted the book to me.

I took it with trembling fingers. Why was it that I could be such a badass, working in a badass field, and yet my hands shook as I faced the reality that my baby-child had managed to find her father, when I had been unable to do so for so many years?

She perched on the edge of the couch, watching me.

"Mom. This is my dad, isn't it." Her voice sounded gentle and wise for a fourteen-year-old girl. And I hated that she had this lot in life, having to find her biological father, especially after the way the man who'd raised her had treated her.

Clearing my throat, I dropped my hand to my lap and forced my eyes to hers. "Sweetheart, I... do you remember when you were eight years old, and you asked me and Tim why you didn't look like either me or him?"

"I mean, yeah. I know Tim isn't my real dad. Plus, after he literally yelled it to the world when I busted him with that cheating hoe—"

"Rosie—"

"—anyway. Yeah. I knew he was my stepdad. That's not what I'm asking. Come on, Mom, you're smarter than this. Stop avoiding me. I'm asking you if the man in this photo is my dad. Because I think it is."

A thought rang loud in my head. I was proud of her for standing up for herself, even if I was the one in the hot seat. Followed quickly by how disappointed in me she must be. But based on when she'd had that fight with Tim and the time that she'd had those journals...

"When did you find this picture?"

She swallowed thickly. "A while ago."

"Before Tim and I split?"

She nodded, and my insides churned. My daughter had been raised in the internet era and had online sleuthing skills I couldn't fathom. I never started a social media account for myself, but I'd let her start her own monitored accounts a few years ago. Now I had to admit to myself that I'd been lax in the monitoring.

"So, you knew, and somehow you found him online. And then you found out about the job, and you told me. All in an elaborate effort to come here and meet some random old boyfriend of mine in hopes he'd be your real dad?"

"Well, when you put it that way, it sounds bad." She slumped back on the couch, crossing her arms over her chest. "I wasn't trying to cause trouble, Mom. I didn't do anything wrong." Her normal teenage petulance made an appearance. This was good, familiar.

Still, she deserved the truth.

I ran a thumb over the book again, unable to find the words to say. Finally, after tense moments of silence, I replied, "I wasn't trying to hide him, sweetheart. I just didn't know where he was or how to find him. And then so much time went by, and I didn't know if I should or if you'd hate me. If he'd hate me." There was so much to unpack, so many half-truths and so much regret.

She perked up. "You met him, didn't you? He works for you?"

I nodded, my gaze drawn to that photo and the memory it represented.

"Did he recognize you?" The hope in her voice almost crushed me. "Does he know about me?"

"No, sweetheart. He doesn't know." For some odd reason, the old shame of being unwed and pregnant by a stranger rose like a knife to my heart. This whole move, the job, now this new obsession of Rosie's to find her dad... it was overwhelming.

I sat forward, the journal blurring as I fought back tears. I placed it on the table in front of us and took my baby girl's hands in both of mine.

"I don't know what you think of me," I started, my voice trembling, "and I don't know if I want to know. I am so ashamed that you found out about him. That you went through this without telling me, because I'm sure you had lots of questions."

I paused, racking my brain as to how to continue. Knowing that I just needed to get it all out and give her the whole, honest truth. She deserved it. Mac deserved it.

"I was scared when I realized I was pregnant. I knew who the father was, but I couldn't find him to tell him. Things were different then. Plus, I was just starting a dangerous career that kept me away from home every third day. I was terrified. When Tim and I started dating and fell in love, I was grateful because he stepped up. He treated you like you were his, he loved you as his own, and once upon a time, he took care of us."

I paused again as the words stuck in my throat. "But no, Mac doesn't know about you. I tried, but I could never find him to tell him about you." A tear leaked from the corner of her eye, leaving a wet trail down her precious cheek, and her hands twisted in mine, gripping them hard.

The simple hold gave me courage. "Sweetheart, I love you more than life itself. I can't help feeling that I've disap-pointed you. That my mistakes are hurting you. I thought Tim would be in our lives forever. But marriages fail, and when he started treating you badly because of resentment he held for me..."

It broke my heart that he'd taken his attitude and anger at me out on her. That I'd brought her into this world not knowing where even to start to find her father. She was innocent in this mess, and I'd carry the guilt for my lifetime. Not just the guilt toward Rosie, but the guilt toward Mac as well. I'd done them both such a grave injustice by taking the easy way out.

I gave her hands a squeeze because, above all else, she needed to know the rest—the most important part. "Please know, I never thought twice about whether I should keep you. You were a gift. You *are* a gift. The most precious thing in my life. I'll find the courage to face Mac and tell him about you, which is the fair thing to do. No matter what his response is... always know that I made the choice to keep you and love you."

She was silent, watching me, letting my words sink in. She'd always been a smart girl with a big loving heart, and knowing who her father was—and not having contact— would eat at her. She'd proven that by orchestrating a whole move to the same town as him without my having any knowledge.

"Did you love him?" she whispered.

And that was her real issue. She needed to know she was created by love—as if it made any difference at all.

"Almost from the moment I met him. Telling him goodbye was the hardest thing I'd ever done."

Her brow furrowed in confusion. "Then why...?"

I lifted a shoulder. "We shared first names only and agreed to keep our time together lighthearted and fun. A fling. I was young, starting a new career. He was older and getting over someone else, and I knew he wasn't ready to jump right into a relationship with me. The only thing I regret is that I didn't have a way to contact him to let him know about you." My voice broke as I finished, and then my girl pulled me into her arms and offered me the same comfort I'd given to her countless times over her life. And being the pathetic fool I was, I allowed my daughter to hold me.

"No matter what, I love you," I whispered into her neck.

"No matter what, I love you too, Mom."

I pulled out of her arms and sat back, cupping her face and stroking her hair. She really was the most beautiful girl in the world. "We'll decide when the time is right, but for now, I'm going to ask you to let this go. It's not the right time to bring this up. But thank you for showing me this picture."

Her eyes searched mine. "You just..." She paused and started over. "You look so happy in it. I just want you to be happy, Mom."

Oh, my sweet, soulful child. "I was happy. The day that photo was taken, we'd had a great day on the beach. It was the day before we were leaving, and we made the most of it. But I am also happy now. We have so much to look forward to."

"Will you tell me about him?"

I hesitated. This path, her questions, all of it... what good could come from it? She'd want to know everything about him. She'd want to meet him and try to know him. What if he wasn't open to the idea? What if he rejected her? She'd already been devastated by one other father figure. I didn't want to take the risk of her getting hurt more.

"Honey, give me some time to think it over. To get used to the idea that I have to see him on a regular basis. I'll tell him, I promise. Because he deserves to know. I never intentionally hid you from him. But can we just take things slowly for now? Get settled and get our bearings, and then we'll decide what to do."

The doorbell rang, ending the heavy conversation. I jumped up to answer it while Rosie cleared away the journal and photo, and then we stuffed ourselves full of pepperoni. She didn't mention it again, but somehow, I knew—things were going to change. I knew it, could feel it. And I couldn't stop it. I just hoped we'd all come out unscathed on the other side.

Chapter Six

Mac

The whole situation around the new chief was a thorn in my side, and something just seemed off about it. Maybe it made sense bringing in someone from the outside, given the amount of bullshit our department had been through in the past couple of years. The weird circumstance the former chief had left under—with allegations of favoritism—then the interim chief having to deal with the tornado and following months of recovery. Then the whole bullshit of the arson case.

That one still haunted me because I'd almost lost a good man. Finding Thoren nearly dead in that house, lying next to his twin, had almost broken me.

But the new chief was a different kind of wrinkle.

It was bad enough bringing in fresh blood to our station and not knowing if she had an agenda, but my personal connection, and my reaction to seeing her again... all of it was so damn confusing and complicated. The way she looked directly through me with zero reaction stung. I'd had to work damn hard to keep my face neutral. To appear unaffected—like my body didn't automatically respond to hers.

It sucked that she was so cold about our time together when I'd thought of her so often over the years. Asking for discretion like it had meant nothing. Like *I* meant nothing.

My footsteps echoed in the cavernous stairwell as I trudged up the flight to the chief's office, the sound pinging around the concrete walls and glass windows like my thoughts bouncing around in my head.

Why was it that in the last two years, I'd managed to avoid coming down to headquarters, yet this was my second visit in a week?

My gut rolled with anticipation, or maybe it was nerves.

Fuck that. I didn't get nervous about seeing the chief. I hadn't in over a decade, and I wouldn't now.

I paused at the doorway to the administrative offices, taking a moment to steel myself. It was just a meeting with the chief. How bad could it be?

"Hey, Cathy," I greeted the clerk sitting behind the desk, a mass of reports spread in front of her. Photos of her musician husband playing the guitar and her towheaded little boy sat off to a corner.

"Hey, Captain Collins. How's it goin'?" She glanced at me in greeting and then frowned at her computer screen and mumbled, "That's not right."

"Anything I can help you with?" I offered, willing to do anything to stall this face-to-face with Li—Chief Hawkins.

"Eh. I just can't get this inventory to balance. My numbers must be off somewhere." Cathy clicked her mouse and then turned to me with a smile. "Are you here to see the chief, or is there something I can help you with?"

I'd always liked Cathy. She'd been our administrative assistant for a decade and called herself the chaos coordinator. She handled our timesheets, our invoices, any certification records, and basically made sure we were taken care of.

"I've gotta meet with the chief on this arson case."

Cathy's eyebrows shot up her forehead. "You get some news?"

I grunted in response, because I had news, but it wasn't good.

"You can head in. She's free for an hour or so."

I paused at the open doorway, an odd, fluttery sensation filling my belly, making me regret skipping lunch when I'd had the chance to stop. Low blood sugar was a real thing. That's all it was. Definitely not nerves.

She stood facing the file cabinets along the back wall, her back to me, that glorious ass cupped in another of her skirts. I swallowed, hard.

Quit looking at her ass. She's your boss, dummy.

Rapping a knuckle on the doorframe to get her attention, I tried not to stare as she turned.

"Hello, Captain Collins," she greeted as she turned, surprise flittering across her features for a half second before returning to the ice princess.

But that voice. It did things to me.

"Hey, Chief, you got a minute? I've got news about the arson case."

She approached her desk, motioning for me to sit. I glanced behind her, waiting, as she lowered to her chair. Much like Cathy, she, too, had photos lining her desk. A teenage girl smiled from a frame.

"That your daughter?" I asked as I lowered to the chair across from her. What a stupid question. Why else would the chief have a photo of a girl in her office? I blamed it on how strangely drawn I was to the image of that girl. Her hair was different in the photo, but seeing it still reminded me of that stupid social media post of Kylie's.

"Your news?" she stated, voice sharp, cutting to the point. So she didn't want to discuss her daughter. Noted. But at some point, I was going to have my questions answered.

"After months of them hedging, I finally got the truth out of the deputy that was on guard the night Loren Watkins went missing."

She didn't need to know that I'd cornered the officer, or how effective a forearm to the throat was.

"This is our arsonist? Suspected arsonist?" she corrected.

I nodded and opened the file I'd brought with me, found the report I was looking for, and flipped it around, placing it on her desk.

"Loren Watkins. This is what we know about him, in summary. He set multiple fires, some of which had catastrophic results, then made it personal and laid a trap. Thoren almost died. We had the bastard caught when he got injured in the same fire Thoren got hurt in. Talked to a buddy of mine at the PD, and they are doing their own investigation, but it boils down to this... The guy they had guarding Watkins got distracted and left his post."

Her eyes shot to mine. Icy daggers glinted in the coldness of them. "Got distracted how?"

I couldn't tell if this cold attitude was directed toward me, or if this was just who she was now. If the passage of time had hardened her from the warm, caring woman I'd known into this ice queen. I glanced at the photo behind her and, for a heartbeat, wondered again about the girl in the photo.

Shifting my gaze back to the chief, I met her direct gaze.

"Apparently, there was an attractive female nurse that drew his attention."

"Unacceptable. Was it deliberate?" she fired back.

"Hard to say. I doubt it, though. Watkins is an opportunist. It's likely that the officer on detail just happened to have his back turned and Watkins snuck right out."

She shook her head in disgust. "And what happened to the officer?"

"I'm not sure. Couple days off, maybe?"

"We have photos of the crime scene. Do we have any of the suspect?"

"No."

She thumbed through the report, giving me a chance to study her. Her dark brown hair was pulled back with a clip, but even with the severe style, the curls I remembered were still visible, refusing to lay flat, begging to be released.

What a fucking stupid thought.

Curls couldn't beg. It was hair, for God's sake. And I was a fucking moron, remembering another time and place and imposing it on the woman before me, who was not at all the warm, effervescent person I remembered. That woman smiled easily and had eyes that twinkled, like she held a secret that was too good, and she wanted to share it with the world. She'd been playful and spontaneous.

This woman was cold and calculated.

"And what happened with Firefighter Watkins?" she continued, looking down at the reports, the folded pages caught with a manicured nail.

I recalled those nails scratching down my back. In fact, our last day together had left me with several marks. She'd teased me, telling me she wanted to leave me with something to remember her by. I'd laughed and given her a reason to remember me as well when she dug her claws in.

The snap of a paper brought me back to the present.

How come I'd gone for years not really feeling any kind of sexual attraction to anyone at all, and suddenly, I was as horny as a teenager?

Realizing she'd asked a question,I cleared my throat and shifted in my seat, trying to ease the discomfort at my fly. "He's since recovered. The building, though, was a loss."

She placed the folder on her desk and sat back in her chair, gazing at me with that cool expression on her face. "Can I ask you something and trust you to tell me the truth?" she asked after a long silence.

"Of course, Chief."

"Why is it that administration didn't deliver this news? Or the police chief when I met with him earlier this week? Why am I just now learning that there is an active investigation that one of my people was injured on?"

Something about the way she was claiming Thoren as hers resonated with me. Maybe the ice queen was making an appearance because someone she saw as "hers" had been wronged.

"Truthfully, it's probably because they don't know or don't care. But Mike Harrison, he's the fire marshal, will be your point of contact. I guarantee he will keep you posted on the details."

"So, what made you decide to come deliver this news to me in person today? Why not let the marshal handle it?"

Was she pushing my buttons on purpose? What the hell was she asking me? "Because I know he was headed out of town for a few days, and I thought you might want to know sooner rather than later."

Another one of those cool moments passed where she just sat and watched me. I'd survived boot camp and eight years of military service working with some of the most hardened motherfuckers on the planet. I'd done a year with PD before landing in the fire department. Her cool assessment ranked right up there with some of the best interrogators.

Or maybe it was just the effect she had on me.

I would not fall under the pressure of her gaze. Those beautiful dark blue eyes that were glacial, and yet, I remembered how they heated. How her lids lowered as she'd climaxed around me.

Motherfucker, why couldn't I keep my mind out of the gutter?

Like the pussy I was, I broke first. Yielding to her superior stare down, I glanced to the side and focused again on the photo. It drew me in, made me want to snatch it up and study it.

I needed to get the fuck out of here.

Wiping my palms on my pants, I leaned forward a bit and extended a peace offering. Not that we'd been fighting. I just wanted to offer her something. Anything.

"I figure you and I are on the same team, and I'm just trying to help. Bring you up to speed on things. When Mike gets back, I'll send him your way. In the meantime, I'll keep an ear to the ground and see if I can find out what the PD knows that they aren't telling us."

Her shoulders released ever so slightly. I hoped she'd been battling herself as much as I had.

"Thank you, Captain." The words were a relieved dismissal.

With no reason to linger, I left her office and made my way home, wondering why I'd even bothered to try to meet with her. She'd made it very clear she held no remaining interest, not that I could go there with her anyway, or would even want to, especially since there were rules prohibiting any kind of relationship between us. But still, there might have been a tiny part of me, buried somewhere down deep, that wondered *what if*.

Buster, my yellow lab, watched from his lounge spot in the yard as I pulled up to the house. He met me at the door with a chewed-up stick poking out both sides of his mouth.

"Hey, buddy." I gave him a good scratching behind the ears before tossing the stick toward the pond. A couple of tosses later, he was bouncing into the edge of the lake, his favorite thing.

We had an easy routine, a simple one. I liked it that way.

We played fetch, Buster would swim. We'd go inside and find some food, then settle in for some TV, or I'd finish a book, Buster at my feet. On my off days, we worked on projects, or we went to the lake and worked on my boat. A quiet life. It was a good life.

So why couldn't I get a certain ice queen and her little princess off my mind?

* * *

A week went by and, finally, things at the fire department were settling in.

Mike had come home and pushed the issue of the officer's negligence. We'd had a blessedly silent week of minor medical calls. I stayed away from headquarters.

So why couldn't I quit replaying all the times I'd seen Olivia Hawkins. The way her skirts cupped her ass. The way she wasn't afraid to hold a man's gaze.

More than once, I'd fantasized about that skirt, with her bent over the table in the conference room, and it bunched up around her waist.

A knock at the front door ripped me back to the present. I wasn't in the conference room with a certain sexy brunette who I had exactly zero business fantasizing about. I was nursing a lukewarm beer in the silence of my den on a Tuesday afternoon instead of taking advantage of my time off.

With a curse, I stood, dropped the beer on the counter on my way to the door, and grabbed my shop keys from the rung. I needed to get out of this funk and do something with the rest of my day.

The young girl staring back at me from the doorway stopped me dead in my tracks. With a backpack slung over one shoulder, she wore a vintage Eagles concert T-shirt, ripped jeans, and beat-up Converse sneakers.

Recognition was a lightning bolt, firing all my senses and zapping my brain.

There was no denying she was mine. She was the perfect combination of both her mother and me. She had her mother's luscious hair and facial structure, but those were my eyes that stared back at me, my nose on her face. She was tallish for a girl. Lanky. Just like I'd been. My heart stopped beating, breath caught in my throat.

This was not a joke.

This girl was mine. If you held a picture of me next to her at the same age, we'd be twins.

"Are you Mac Collins?"

I couldn't speak. Couldn't breathe, couldn't think, couldn't move.

Dumbstruck.

That was the word I was looking for.

Every-fucking-thing I'd ever known just flew out the window. Every lie I'd ever told myself about not wanting kids or a family slapped me in the face with the truth. An overwhelming sense of loss threatened to consume me. I had a child, a daughter. A living, breathing part of me that existed outside of my body.

As I took her in, that grief morphed into fiery-hot rage. All of my unanswered questions rose to the front of my mind.

How'd she find me?

Had her mother told her where I lived?

What did she know about me?

What did she want from me?

She began to fidget beneath my stare, wringing her hands and shuffling from side to side. I couldn't drag my eyes off her.

"You look just like your picture, only, like... old." She paused, her eyes going wide, hands stilling. "Old*er*, I mean."

She dropped her hands, huffing and looking down the expanse of the covered front porch. Her gorgeous cheeks bloomed an adorable pink as she studied the swing at one end.

I chuckled despite myself. "You had it right the first time."

I stepped onto the porch, letting the screen door slam behind me. Buster rounded the corner of the house and bounded up the stairs. Her eyes lit up as she dropped down in greeting, an offer Buster accepted with glee, his yellow tail wagging in delight at a new person to shower him with affection.

"Oh my gosh, he's so cute. What's his name?"

Obviously, Buster was a welcome distraction.

Without hesitation, she dropped right to her butt, burying her face in his neck when he stepped right into her, his version of a full-body hug.

"This is Buster. He doesn't understand the concept of personal space."

Her giggle as Buster showered her with doggy kisses tightened my chest as both instant affection and denial warred for dominance.

"He likes you." I stated the obvious, at a loss for what to say, finally dragging my eyes off her. Staring at her was freaking me out.

In the yard, a shiny new mountain bike lay on its side, answering my question about how she'd gotten here.

I studied the bike, trying to figure out where the fuck to start. Did I go full-on with my questions? She obviously knew who I was, so what the hell was she doing here? And why now?

Another giggle, combined with happy whimpers, drew my attention back to the rollicking crew on my porch. With a last scratch behind his ears, she made to stand. I reached over and grabbed Buster by the collar, pulling him away, and grasped her elbow to help her stand. She flinched at the contact, and I immediately dropped my hand and stepped back.

"What's your name?" I started with the obvious.

"Rosa Nell Hawkins." Her last-name confirmation was a solid punch to the gut. She continued, "You know who I am?"

I nodded. "You're Chief Hawkins's daughter, right?" *And mine.*

"Yeah."

She was still too nervous, too jittery to be confident, but I had to admire her for the sheer amount of brass balls it took to find and confront me. I needed to be gentle.

"It's nice to meet you, Rosa Nell. I'm Mac."

"Yeah, I know who you are."

"You, uh, you want to sit for a minute? That swing's real nice on a day like today," I offered, rearranging my face into what I hoped was an inviting expression. And damn if I didn't sound like some backwoods weirdo offering a kid a piece of candy.

Her head bobbed once, her arms wrapping around her slender waist as she checked me out without directly meeting my eyes. "Everyone calls me Rosie."

I took another step back and leaned against the porch rail, bracing my hands on the banister behind me and crossing my legs. Making myself the least intimidating as possible, needing her to feel safe and comfortable.

"It's a long way out here. Your mom know you're here?"

She eased onto the porch swing, shaking her head. Buster crowded her legs, begging for her to continue. Her hand landed on one of his ears, absently giving him head pats and ear rubs.

"No, I told her I was just going for a ride."

"She lets you just run wherever you wanna go?" The thought didn't sit well with me.

"No. I lied and told her I was meeting friends."

At least she was honest about lying. In some fucked-up way, I respected that. It was how I'd lived my youth.

"So, what made you lie to your mom and then ride all the way out here to the middle of nowhere, alone? Which isn't safe, by the way. How old are you, anyway?" The words came out stern, almost gruff.

"I'm fourteen. I wanted to meet you."

I had to hand it to her. She was forthright. And also the exact right age to be mine.

"You did?"

She swallowed, glancing out to the pond beyond the

house while she fiddled with a turquoise ring on her finger. Then she looked right at me.

"I saw an article online. You guys raised a bunch of money for a firefighter who had cancer."

That was totally not where I expected this conversation to start.

I waited and let her continue. "The guy who had cancer was the cousin of one of the girls at my old school. She was bragging about it in class and was really thankful. And then after he died, they reposted that article online, and I made the connection with the town. So, when we moved here, I figured maybe you'd want to know that, about the family, and I found you."

Okay. Part of that might've been the truth. Probably.

But I sensed there was more to this story that she didn't want to say out loud.

She was back to fidgeting, not meeting my gaze. "So I did some digging and figured out where you lived, then rode out."

Did some digging? How? Where? Definitely more to this story.

"Well, that's awfully nice of you to come out here to tell me. I appreciate that. I remember that fundraiser. He was a nice guy. We miss him."

She nodded.

I waited patiently. I could wait all day if it gave me a chance to study her.

"So, yeah. Anyway. I was just out exploring and realized I was close, so I thought I'd drop by." She stood and hitched a thumb over her shoulder. "I guess you have things to do, so I'll just be on my way."

She bent to scratch Buster's ears again. "He's a great dog. Before Mom was chief, she was gone every third day.

Who helps you with him when you're on duty?" She stood again, glancing into the house. "You have a roommate or something that helps you? A girlfriend?"

She was fishing.

I chuckled because she was so unexpected and mischievous. I didn't know her end game, but I appreciated the effort she was making.

I snapped my fingers to get Buster's attention and give her some space. He bounded over to me as if just noticing that I was available for attention. "Buster is a roamer. When I'm not here, he hangs out at the neighbor's house. We sort of have joint custody, though I do get stuck with the vet bills."

"So... no girlfriend?" The amount of hope in the words was surprising. I needed to steer us away from this conversation, but for some weird reason, I shook my head no.

"You headed back to town now that I've answered all your burning questions? It's a haul. You don't want it to get too late and cause your mom to worry." Plus, I needed to man up and figure out just how to address this elephant. Because Rosie being here meant she thought she knew me. And I thought I knew her, and yet, here we were, bouncing around this subject and not confirming anything or really talking about the real issue at all. I really needed answers from Olivia.

"Yeah, I guess I better go."

She slipped her other arm into the strap of her backpack and tugged the straps to secure it. I wanted to offer to give her a lift, but it wasn't a smart move to offer a fourteen-year-old girl I'd just met a lift. Any number of accusations could come from it.

I turned, bracing both hands on the porch rail as she bounced down the steps. She was so young and full of spirit.

She paused at the bottom to look around my property, her eyes wide and curious. Taking in my workshop, the deer feeder in the food plot beyond the workshop, the small pond in the distance. "You've got a really great place here. Any fish in that pond?"

I grunted in acknowledgment.

"You think I could come back sometime, and you teach me to fish? Some of the boys in my old school talked about it all the time. They'd go with their dads to the marshes and always had the best stories. I've always wanted to learn, but my stepdad wasn't into it."

How the hell was I supposed to answer this? The hope was back, and it killed me to even think of telling her no. If she knew who she was to me, and she was as brave as I first thought, why didn't she just ask me outright if I was her father? I felt like that's what she wanted to ask, but what if she didn't really know? I certainly couldn't be the one to tell her.

Plus, a stepdad? What was the deal with that?

Not to mention, I didn't want to piss off my daughter's mother.

I needed to tell her no and stay far, far away from this girl.

She turned expectant eyes on me, and I crumbled.

"If your mom says it's okay."

She beamed at me. "Thanks, Mac."

She gathered her bike, swinging a long leg over the seat and setting off down the drive that would lead her to the road and safely back to town. Except, people were assholes. And she was gorgeous.

The next thing I knew, I was opening my truck door and whistling for Buster to get in. She didn't need to be alone in my truck. But that didn't mean I couldn't follow her at a safe distance and make sure she got home okay.

She spotted me about a mile in when she stopped at a stop sign.

"Not trying to scare you, just following to make sure you get to town safely."

She grinned as she pushed off, yelling over her shoulder, "Thanks, Mac."

As she pulled into a nice townhouse complex in downtown, my heartbeat finally returned to normal.

I hoped her mom told her no when she asked about fishing.

I hoped she'd douse this curiosity she had about me.

I dreaded the whole conversation—the multiple hard conversations I needed to have—with my chief. But at the same time, I knew they had to happen.

Buster, who'd spent the entire ride with his head out the window and his attention on Rosie, barked a goodbye at the girl as we slowed to pass.

"Bye, Buster!"

Even my dog was already in love with her, but he loved everyone, so that wasn't saying much. No, it was my own reaction to her that left me feeling like I'd been hit by a bus. Gone was the dread and anxiety over the knowledge of her existence. In its place was a bone-deep acceptance and immense grief that I'd missed so much of her life.

The front door of the townhouse opened, and my chief stalked to the edge of the front porch, a stern glare leveled on Rosie as the girl passed by her.

"Shit." The curse rumbled forth, drawn from the deepest part of me. Seeing the two of them side by side was a fist to the gut.

I eased my truck to the stop sign beyond their complex and checked the rearview to find Olivia scanning the street. Part of me relaxed seeing Olivia as a concerned mother rather than as the cold woman I'd dealt with. The other part of me wanted to turn around, go back and demand to know why her daughter had had the freedom to venture so far out on her own.

Demand answers to so many fucking questions.

And yet I didn't want to betray this young girl who might be mine. I didn't owe either of them anything aside from common decency. But a strange sense of loyalty toward Rosie wormed its way through my chest. She'd made it a point to seek me out, so obviously she wanted to know me. I didn't want to be a total asshole and reject her or stick my nose into Olivia's personal business. She'd had the opportunity multiple times to clear the air between us. Why hadn't she? And why had she waited so many years?

I glanced to the back seat as I made my turn and found Buster looking out the back window. His huge expressive eyes met mine, and he whined.

"Yeah, I know," I said on a sigh. "I'm fucked."

He clapped a paw on my arm in solidarity, and I ruffled his fur. "Thanks, buddy."

Chapter Seven

Mac

"So are we all just going to be chill and act like it's not weird that, all of a sudden, Capt has drama?" Thoren stood at the sink in the station's kitchen, washing a salad. I'd almost managed to escape their inquisition by keeping us busy all day. But dinnertime meant a few moments of downtime, and now all bets were off.

A prickly sensation crawled over my skin. I hated being the topic of conversation, and I certainly didn't want to talk about Olivia and Rosie.

"I was trying to give the man a moment to absorb everything." Nate scowled in Thoren's direction, immediately winning brownie points for standing up for me. "But now that you've brought it up." Nate turned to me. "What gives, Capt?"

"You bunch of gossiping hens," Mo piped in from the recliners. "Learn to read the room. Capt doesn't wanna talk about this, evidenced by his even pissier than normal demeanor."

"Well, we weren't the ones seen following a pretty young girl on a bike through town yesterday," Thoren shot back. "Word to the wise. You really gotta watch out for those old ladies, Capt. They got a whole calling-tree chain and everything. Kylie said it's scary the amount of dirt they have on people."

I didn't even need to be in the room. They could have this discussion without me. I didn't want to think about anything, and I certainly didn't want to talk about my life issues, especially with them.

I was supposed to be their mentor, not the other way around. I was the "old man" of the crew—one of the reasons I was so keyed up to make it to retirement. Working around men young enough to be my kids and not being able to keep up... my time in service was running short. This career was hard on an old guy. And I certainly did *not* want to think or talk about the two new additions in my life.

"The kid came to my house." Dammit. The words vomited forth like I had no control over them.

Thoren spun to me, his eyes growing wide as he tapped the water off and set his bowl aside. "Whoa, Captain. Maybe let's go have a sit-down."

Nate came around the island. "You're looking kind of pale, boss." He ushered me to the table, his grip on my arm the only thing that kept me steady until I could sink into a chair.

Mo braced on the table, leaning over me like a father scolding a child. "Talk."

Oh, how the tides had changed.

I was the one who was supposed to issue orders.

How many times had we had debriefs in this same space? This was just another debrief. I let that thought wash over me and laid out what I knew. An odd sort of relief coming with every word.

"I still don't have all the facts," I admitted. "Don't know why they're here, if there's a reason. But the girl came by my house. Her excuse was that she knew someone from Landreau's family and wanted to thank me for that charity fundraiser we held when he was so sick with cancer."

These men had been there during the organizing and execution of that event. But I'd been the lead face for the department and had been tasked with all of the PR work. "She showed up at my house, riding a dang bicycle, of all things, and man, it was like looking into a mirror and seeing a young female version of myself."

"How do you feel about that?" Mo asked.

I swallowed. Hard. "I don't know. I'm conflicted."

"Man, I bet. That's kind of huge to find out you have a kid."

Especially when I'd resigned myself to being alone. Had given up on ever finding the right person to start a family with. Had given up on having a family of my own, even though it had been something I'd wanted from the time I left the military. Diedre hadn't been ready, and then she left me. And all those dreams of a family got buried. But I couldn't tell these men, these friends, about that. It was too close. Too personal. I could only nod at Mo.

"So... the daughter found you," Thoren prompted. At my nod, he continued, "Now you've got to have a chat with the chief."

"I know, I just don't know where to start. I'm mad. Confused. I have a million questions."

"Do you want to know this girl if she's yours? 'Cause it sounds like she wants to know you."

Did I?

I let the thought roll around in my head even as I lifted a shoulder. "Maybe?" Everything was happening so fucking fast. I needed time to process. To think.

"Fair enough. Just a word to the wise. Make sure you have this conversation sooner than later, because it sounds like the kid is invested enough to seek you out. You don't want to hurt her," Mo advised.

"Or," Thoren offered, "you could see what the kid knows and then approach the mom."

Nate frowned. "Or he could be a grown-up and do the right thing and face the challenge head-on. But whatever you do, you better do it soon. Before the old lady squad one-ups you."

And from there, they went round and round, each offering their own idea, each solution adding to the weight pressing on my shoulders. The kid didn't deserve my attitude—that should be directed only at Olivia. And it was time for answers. Just as soon as I found the courage to ask the questions. Because the answers could change my life, and I wasn't sure I was ready to face what they held.

The next afternoon, the crunch of gravel and Buster's happy yipping, followed by a high-pitched giggle, alerted me to company. I walked out of my shop, wiping my hands on a grease rag, to find Rosie wrestling with my lab, her bike and backpack discarded in the yard.

"Hey, Mac," she yelled, earning her a face full of doggy licks. She grabbed Buster in a headlock and kissed him back, sending a wild burst of energy through the goofball, which erupted in a case of the zoomies.

Rosie scrambled to her feet and bounced over to me. "Hey! Whatcha doin'?"

She looked as if she had not a care in the world. Like this was a normal situation, and it was common for a young girl to show up unexpected at an older man's house. It made me uncomfortable to be alone with her like this. I shook my head at her. "Shouldn't you be in school?"

She bent to retrieve the stick Buster returned with. "Dude, school got out, like, an hour ago." Buster took off on another tear, playing his favorite game with apparently his new favorite person. "I just came by to check on my buddy. I stopped by yesterday, too, but you were at work."

I narrowed my eyes at the wild child before me. What was she up to? "Your mom know you're riding out here by yourself?"

She shrugged, dropping to a knee to dig through her backpack. A knot of unease unfurled in my chest. What was Rosie telling her mother about why she kept stopping by, or was she even telling her mother the truth? I knew the appropriate thing to do would be to have a conversation with Olivia, but I wasn't quite sure it was the right time.

Rosie stood and handed me a drawing, an amateur rendering of the view of the pond. "I brought you something. It's not very good, but I'm just learning landscape techniques. I came out here yesterday to do homework." She held up a hand. "Before you start, don't worry, Buster protected me. Though, he did try to follow me home."

An unusual feeling rolled around inside me, something warm and sweet. I tamped it down, shoving it behind that wall I'd built so long ago. I wanted to get to know my daughter, but...

"Rosie, it's not a good idea for you to be out here alone,

let alone with a man you just met. You gotta be smarter than that. You're putting me in a bad place here."

Her face fell as she took a step back. That soft spot near my heart pinched.

She stalked over to her bike. "I didn't mean to make you mad. I was just dropping off that picture. I was trying to be nice. You don't have to be a turd about it."

I gripped the back of my neck in agitation. How the fuck was I supposed to deal with an ornery teenager, one with too much curiosity and not enough awareness?

"Thank you for the picture," I offered awkwardly.

"Whatever. It sucks anyway." She tossed a leg over the bike. "And so do you," she mumbled under her breath.

"Now, wait just a damn minute," I barked, halting her before she could get on her way. "Just because I'm looking out for you, trying to make you see reason, that calls for you to think I suck? If that's the case, so be it." I stepped in front of her bike and got her attention. "Better be tough if you're gonna be stupid."

"Okay, John Wayne wannabe."

I drew in a breath, looking for some patience. I had no idea how to talk to a teenage girl. Hell, I scared most men, but this girl was immune to intimidation.

"Rosie." I softened my voice intentionally. "I'm not trying to be an ass. I'm trying to look out for you. You are young and pretty, and there are some very bad people in this world who would love to hurt a pretty girl like you."

She side-eyed me like she wanted to believe me but didn't.

"Also, people like to think the worst, so it's best if you don't give them anything for ammunition."

Finally, her shoulders relaxed. "Yeah, I totally get that."

Something in the way she said it made me think she was

talking about more than being at my place. She looked out over the water and then back at me.

"Can I ask you a question?"

My bravado shriveled, but I wouldn't lie to her. Whatever she asked, I'd be honest. I nodded, motioning for her to continue.

"Did you ever have to move to a new place and make new friends? Why are people so shitty?"

I had a feeling this was going to be a complex conversation, one I had no idea how to navigate.

"Why don't we take a walk around the pond, and you tell me what's going on?"

A half hour later, we'd barely made it to the opposite side of the pond, having to stop and throw Buster's stick every other step. The sun glinted off the water under a bright blue sky. Buster's happy splashing at the shoreline had done its magic on both of our tempers, and we were having a real conversation. That warm, sweet feeling was back in my chest.

Rosie was relaxed and sharing about her shitty situation at school. "So anyway, by the time I realized what had happened, they'd taken my sketchbooks and snapped photos, and it was going around all over school before the day was out. People were making fun of me everywhere. And the girls who'd been so nice to me suddenly turned their backs."

"Sounds like classic mean-girl treatment. Get close to you to get what they want, then have no trouble hurting your feelings or setting you up." I had no idea if what I was telling her was bullshit, but it sounded reasonable.

"Exactly."

We walked in silence a little more, Rosie stopping to toss the stick to Buster again.

"I really dread going to school. I don't want to face these kids."

Now, *that* I could understand. Except, it was her own mother I dreaded facing. But during the course of our stroll, it'd become apparent to me that I was going to confront Olivia the next chance I got.

"I get it, kid. But you just be you. A lot of times when people are mean like that, it's because they're jealous. Do the teachers know what happened?"

She shrugged. "No. At least I don't think so."

"Do you think it would help if you talked to them?"

She shook her head. "I don't wanna be known as a tattletale."

"I get that, but is there one who might take your side?"

She kicked a rock. "Maybe my art teacher."

I didn't know what to say. Had no advice to give. And suddenly, I felt like stomping into the school and coming down hard on some punk-ass teenagers.

We walked and talked some more, and I found myself embroiled in the teenage angst of making new friends until, finally, the subject changed to more general topics, like what kind of boat I had and what kind of fish were in the pond.

By the time we made it back to her bike, her attitude was gone.

"Thanks for being here for me today, Mac."

"Anytime, kid."

I whistled for Buster to hang back with me, fighting the urge to follow her or offer her a ride.

Knowing that she'd come here again, I was conflicted.

Part of me was happy about it. I was glad she liked my space. Another part of me was holding back because what if Olivia found out—and she would, because I had to talk to her about this—and made it so Rosie couldn't come by anymore.

I felt guilty knowing that she was mine, especially with her probably knowing it too and both of us ignoring it. It was time to find my balls and confront Olivia because, after one afternoon, I was smitten with my daughter.

Chapter Eight

Olivia

Of all the things I'd anticipated with our new move, Rosie and I being called for a meeting with the principal hadn't been on that list. Principal Miller leaned heavily on his forearms, the stern expression on his face driving home the seriousness of the situation.

"She'll be suspended for the rest of today, Thursday, and Friday. She can return next Monday. But let me assure you, Mrs. Hawkins—"

"Chief Hawkins," I corrected.

"—this type of behavior will not be tolerated at Newman High School. Another offense of this caliber, and it will mean expulsion." He was a middle-aged man, starched shirt buttoned up to the collar, his comb-over failing spectacularly to cover the wide swath of scalp that gleamed under the fluorescent lights.

"You're sure my daughter was the only one involved in these drawings being passed around?"

"Your daughter was the artist, ma'am," he replied.

I glanced at Rosie, who'd been red-faced and silent during the entirety of this *discussion*. Just because she was the artist didn't mean she'd pulled them out and shown anyone, though. Something about this whole situation stunk. "Rosie, did you pass around dirty pictures?"

"What? No, Mom! You know I don't like showing my drawings." Her high-pitched wail reverberated off the stark cinderblock walls. And I *did* know that she was very private about her art, keeping her talent to herself so if she shared something with you, you knew it was special.

"Then tell me what happened. How these pictures, these drawings with your initials on them, came to be passed around the school."

Principal Miller butted in, "Mrs. Hawkins, we've already been through this with Rosa. She's given her statement."

I turned to face the idiot before me. "It's *Chief* Hawkins, Mr. Miller. I am simply asking if any other children were involved to better understand the whole situation, because this behavior is out of character for my daughter."

He puffed up his chest, obviously offended. "The bottom line is, we don't allow pornographic material in the walls of this high school."

This was going nowhere.

"Understood," I gritted out. Beside me, Rosie sniffled, and I knew there was more to this story, but this man wasn't going to listen. We'd just have to deal with the situation as best we could.

We completed the necessary paperwork, and then I marched her frustrating teenage behind out the door and to my SUV. The department vehicle had broken down on the way in that morning and had made me late. I'd just barely returned after juggling multiple meetings when I got the call to come get Rosie.

And to add to the list of super craptastic things, my mother called, saying she was putting my father in a nursing home because his dementia had gotten to be more than she could handle.

I slammed the door and took a few calming breaths before tackling the next thing on the list. The entire week had been a nightmare. My to-do list seemed never ending. Things were piling up and suffocating me, pulling me in multiple directions.

"Mom—"

I lifted my hand to cut her off. Deep breaths weren't cutting it. I needed a drink. And it was only noon. God help me, I didn't know what to do with her, with the school, with my job. I backed out of the high school lot and tried to focus.

"Rosa Nell Hawkins," I said through gritted teeth, "the next words out of your mouth better be 'I'm sorry, Mom.'"

"But Mom—"

"No buts. I want the whole story, but right now, I need a cool-off period. You're going home, and you're going to do all your classwork. You will not watch TV, and as soon as I get there, that phone belongs to me. The only reason I'm not taking the dang thing with me is because you need to have it in case of emergency."

Rosie flopped back in her seat, pouting. When we got to the house, she bolted up the sidewalk and slammed the door behind her before I could even climb out of the car. Fine. It was better if we didn't talk until we both had time to settle down.

I drove to the station, running through the endless things that I'd had to postpone because of that unexpected trip. Why was it that I couldn't seem to get caught up in this job? I'd expected to be busy, but there seemed to always be something falling through the cracks.

Cathy was on the phone when I walked into the office. I caught her eye as I passed, and her stunned expression made me pause. She turned to fully face me, saying, "Yes, sir. She just walked through the door. Can I place you on a brief hold?" With the touch of her headset, she stood, twisting her hands nervously, and I knew the day had taken another turn.

"What is it?" I demanded, my voice coming out harsher than I intended.

Cathy grimaced, the look so out of place with her normally chipper attitude. "Mayor Smith is on the line with a reminder about some conference that you must attend. It starts tomorrow. In Savannah. He said the organizer wants to know if you have your presentation ready."

I stood frozen. What conference? What presentation? It felt like a threat. Like a setup.

Behind me, the door opened, and I felt a familiar presence at my back.

"What's wrong?" Mac's grumbly voice was right in my ear.

And suddenly, I couldn't maintain my calm, cool, collected self. Not in his presence, anyway. I smoothed a shaky hand down my shirt, feeling a boulder of stress building between my shoulder blades. Crap was bubbling over fast, and I needed to get a handle on it. First, I'd figure out what Smith was up to. Maybe by the time I got done with him, I'd be able to face Mac. And then I'd figure out what to do about Rosie.

"Put the mayor through to my office, please. Captain Collins, if you'll excuse me."

I hurried to my desk as my line rang. "Chief Hawkins."

"Chief, I'm surprised I caught you." The mayor's jovial voice boomed through my ear. "I heard there was a little hullabaloo down at the high school today."

His manner was offhand, but something told me he was making a point with his fake friendliness. And why would he have knowledge of anything related to my daughter? Regardless, I was not about to confirm anything, because I didn't trust the man.

"My apologies for keeping you waiting, sir. How can I help you?" Thankfully, my voice didn't give me away.

"Oh, it's no problem. I was just telling your girl that I got an email reminder that the former fire chief was supposed to be delivering a presentation at the ACCG conference this weekend."

My girl? Cathy wasn't a girl. And she had a name. I clenched my fist and tried to keep my voice even. "What kind of presentation, sir?"

"Oh, I'm not sure of the details, but I can have my girl send your girl the email, and you can contact them."

I bit my cheek to keep myself in check. "Thank you. I'll let Cathy know to expect it."

"You know, Chief..." During his weighty pause, I imagined him kicking back in his big executive chair, his beefy hands folded over his belly. "Directors within the city government are held to a higher standard, and in this city, the actions of the family members are also under scrutiny."

Pinching the bridge of my nose, I counted backward from ten. This son of a biscuit-eater better not be threatening me because my daughter got railroaded at school. I was certain there was more to the story, just like I was certain there was more to this so-called presentation and his utter lack of communication about it.

Even though it went against everything in me to capitulate, instead of biting his head off, I played nice and made my voice sticky sweet when I said, "It's a great place to work, Mayor. It's obvious that the leaders of the community work very hard to make it successful."

"Yes, well. I'm just reminding you that we hold everyone to the utmost highest level of moral representation."

This self-righteous asshole. I wanted to ask, *as defined by whom*, but I figured that'd be pushing it. Instead, I steeled my voice. "Thank you for letting me know about the conference. Please do send over the information, and I'll make it happen."

I slammed the phone receiver down. It didn't satisfy the angry riot of emotion swirling through my system, and it didn't help the overwhelm that was edging over into anxiety.

But it felt good.

If only for a second. Because I already had too much on my plate and now, apparently, had to speak at a conference tomorrow.

I stalked out of my office and headed toward Cathy's desk. We were reviewing the presentation details, me scanning the email from over her shoulder, when I felt Mac come up behind me.

Why was this a thing with him? How did he manage to sneak up on me like that? And why did my body respond like it was the most natural thing to lean closer to his warmth?

He brushed up against my elbow, and I got a whiff of his cologne, then heard his deep rumble of "Got a minute?" And everything caved in on me. Feeling the weight of the world on my shoulders, I turned and met his eyes.

His expression shifted from hard to harder. The muscle

in his jaw ticked. Apparently, something in my expression gave away the level of stress I was trying to handle. He grabbed my elbow and ushered me to my office, shutting the door behind us.

He led me to one of the guest chairs, then crouched before me.

"Talk, Livvie."

Maybe it was the old nickname that broke through. Maybe it was just Mac being Mac. Whatever it was, once the truth started, I was helpless to stop the word vomit and was mortified to find my eyes stinging.

"It feels like Mayor Smith is trying to sabotage me. The police chief keeps avoiding my calls, and I know there is something up with the arson investigation. My mom called and had to put my dad in a nursing home today. And Rosie got suspended. And now I have to go out of town, and I don't have anyone to stay with her, but I also can't take her with me, because if the mayor finds out, he'll use it against me. And I have to give a presentation that I'm pretty sure is going to be used as a test for Smith to pass judgment on me, and suddenly, it feels like everything is falling apart and everyone is out to get me."

Through my diatribe, Mac's frown intensified. "Tell me about the Rosie part."

A huge sigh escaped as I deflated. "Apparently, she's been drawing some erotica, and it got distributed around school." I couldn't even believe the words as I said them, but I'd absolutely seen it with my own eyes.

The line of his jaw shifted as if he might be gritting his teeth. He looked positively furious. I just didn't know who or what he was furious about.

"She's suspended tomorrow and Friday. She can stay home during the day alone, but I'm not comfortable going out of town and leaving her. And she can't come with me, because this conference is closed, with no guests allowed because, apparently, there is some major political bigwig coming. I would've called my parents to come stay with her, but my mom just put my dad in a nursing home, and she's got enough on her plate. Plus, I don't have time to get Rosie there and make it back to the conference."

That was enough to bring on the threat of tears again, but I clamped down my emotions. Crying wouldn't solve anything, and right now, I needed focus and direction. I blinked rapidly, concentrating on the bare wall behind Mac until the feeling abated.

"What about her dad?" he asked softly, snatching my attention even as his words froze my insides, as the day took another unexpected turn. Now was not the time for this discussion, not that there ever was a good time to let a man know he had a fourteen-year-old handful of a daughter.

We'd only known each other that one week, but I'd been reminded of him daily over the years. Had regretted my stupid decisions and mourned the loss of that chemistry and connection we'd had. In the early weeks and months, I'd written him love letters, wishing I could find him so that he might know the wonderful child he'd helped create. Even as I'd married another man, Mac had still held part of my heart.

I should try to avoid the question, should find a better way to out this truth. But looking into the face of the man who'd meant so much to me, words failed me. I couldn't lie to him. As I stared into his deep eyes, the world tumbled and fell away. Instead of Chief and Captain, we'd tunneled into a space where we were Livvie and Mac, and the outside world didn't exist.

"Mac..." I willed him to understand the words I knew I needed to say but somehow couldn't force out.

His head dropped on a gust of breath as if I'd hit him across the chest. The full impact of the unspoken truth lay between us.

He knelt, bowed before me, his big shoulders nearly trembling. He knew about Rosie. Or at least he'd suspected. Reaching for him, covering his hand that gripped my knee, allowing myself to touch this man as if no years had separated us, felt as natural and right and necessary as my next breath.

Shame. Hot, blinding shame coursed through me, and I pulled my hand away. I had no right to touch him. No right to comfort, not when I was the cause of this pain.

I was the worst person in the world for not finding him, for denying him the child he deserved to know. I hated myself for all that he'd lost.

I waited silently, twisting the turquoise ring that matched my daughter's, needing the connection to her, because everything from this moment forward would change.

"She's got my eyes." He spoke to the floor, his voice guttural, raspier than I'd ever heard it, as if he'd had to push the words out.

My chin trembled as I whispered, "I know." Those eyes had been my constant reminder and endless torment of the man I'd fallen for so long ago.

"And the same sandy-blond hair I had as a kid." Maybe he was allowing me time to adjust to this truth. Maybe he was waiting on me to say something. Maybe he'd deliver another blow to the day. "She's come to visit me. Nearly every day for the past week or more," he said slowly.

I braced for the righteous anger that I deserved. Instead,

the quiet rasp of his chuckle skated across my frayed nerves, leaving behind a warm tingle. "She's given me every line under the sun about why she comes over. She says she comes to check on my dog."

"She's always wanted one." My voice trembled as I studied my hands.

"But she knows who I am. And she comes to see me, and it makes me think she wants to know me." Was that a tinge of hope in his voice?

"She does."

Silence filled the room while the truth of that sank in. I was terrified of where this could lead—with either of them hating me, what could happen if he tried to take her away from me. But denying them a relationship wasn't fair to either of them when they both clearly wanted one.

"Is that a problem for you?"

Any other time, with any other man, maybe it would've been. Instead, I shook my head. I couldn't stop this train, didn't want to.

"Then I have a possible solution to part of your issue. I'm off until next Monday. Why doesn't she go with me to my lake house. She can get out of town, get her bearings. You can do your conference. I've got plenty of room. It won't be a problem."

"I don't know, Mac. You guys don't even know each other."

"Then how about this, let's ask her what she wants to do. If she wants to hang here, then I can do that too. But let's ask her how she feels before just negating the offer."

He was so confident, so compassionate and considerate. Just as I remembered. And it felt good to have support offered without argument or negotiation. Although Tim had made it a point in the early years to be supportive, as our marriage began to fail, he'd stopped being as available for Rosie, something she felt. And here was Mac, with his calm, steady presence, making things less stressful without my having to ask for anything.

Taking this step and allowing him into our lives was dangerous. For one, I didn't want Rosie to get hurt. Two, that old flame had never really gone out, and every time I looked at Mac or even thought about him, it flickered to life a little more. But other than my messed-up emotions, I didn't have a reason to deny Rosie this opportunity to know her father.

"Okay, why don't you come for dinner, and we'll talk it over more."

We settled on a time, and Mac left, never discussing whatever had brought him in. He'd just witnessed me having an epic meltdown and stepped in. And, somehow, had made things better.

The next few hours flew by as Cathy and I worked on my presentation before she adjusted my schedule for the rest of the week to account for last-minute travel. I didn't have the time or capacity to think about Mac and Rosie again until I was driving home.

I should've been somewhat relieved over the latest turn of events. But deep down, I knew things would get worse, and my concern started to spiral.

"Why are you acting so weird, Mom?"

I hadn't yet told Rosie that Mac was coming over—or asked her about the apparently daily trips to his house—because I was too distracted with getting dinner ready and worrying over all the other things that had happened throughout the day.

The Mother of the Year Award was definitely not

coming to me if I kept putting off these hard conversations, though.

"We're having a dinner guest." I paused and forcibly relaxed my shoulders.

A knock sounded at the door. Rosie watched me, her brows drawn together like she was trying to figure out who, or what, to expect before going to answer it. Her subdued greeting was faint, followed by Mac's deep voice as they greeted each other in the entryway.

"Mom," Rosie called as she led Mac into the kitchen. I didn't miss the slight wobble in her voice. "Um, Mac is here."

I turned the burner off, giving the chicken and rice a last stir. "Good, he's right on time," I said matter-of-factly. "Grab some plates and let's eat."

Panic blossomed across my adventurous daughter's features. I gave her my best mom-eye, the one that said *you're busted*. The girl was snared in a web of her own design as she realized she'd been caught in her little game of sneaking off to Mac's.

"Hi, Mac," I greeted, watching the pot to make sure the rice mixture didn't stick. The evening was awkward enough without me burning dinner. "Please, come in and have a seat." I glanced in his direction. Mistake.

He was entirely too handsome standing there awkwardly in the doorway. He'd dressed for the occasion. His salt-and-pepper hair combed neatly, a fresh shave, new dark jeans, crisp light-blue button-down shirt, tattoos peeking out from his rolled-up sleeves.

My heart flipped over.

Mac had dressed for a date with his daughter and was nervous.

He surveyed the small table for four. "Where do you want me?"

The question was innocent enough, except my dirty mind had derailed at the sight of the most perfectly fitted jeans ever made. My mind flashed to a dozen different images of where I could want Mac. Pressed up against me, pinning me to the wall. Under me as I straddled him at the table. Leaning over me, his weight delicious and heavy bearing into me.

Heat scorched across my entire face. I gestured toward one of the chairs and croaked, "There's fine."

Rosie's hands shook as she set the table. I turned back to the stove, trying to both hide from my dirty thoughts and suppress the smile that threatened.

Did I like seeing my daughter so distressed? No.

Was it sweet that he'd shown up and was trying to impress? Yes.

Did my kid deserve a little stress after going behind my back? Yes.

I didn't even know where Mac lived. How had she found out?

My own nerves were back, fluttering in my belly. I still wasn't sure how this conversation was going to go.

An awkward silence filled the room, and I glanced over my shoulder. Mac had a hand on the back of a chair, watching as Rosie meticulously set the table, stiff-shoul-dered and avoiding his gaze as she laid out the silverware.

This awkwardness was my doing. I dug for the courage to face the two of them, face the long years of failure and guilt, and lay all of the truth out in the open.

"Okay, supper's ready."

They dropped into seats across from each other like

they'd been playing a game of musical chairs, and I'd just turned the song off.

"I wish I had a fancy serving dish, but we've not made it that far in restocking," I explained, spooning heaping piles of food onto their plates.

Mac waited until I'd taken my seat, then said, "This looks good."

It did, in fact, not look good. It looked like a soupy, cheap meal.

"It looks like mash. Mom, why is it so soupy?" Rosie complained, and just like that, things were back to semi-normal.

"It's a little... juicier than normal. I think I added the milk twice," I admitted. "In my defense, I was nervous and easily distracted. At least it didn't stick this time."

"Fun fact, Mom is a terrible cook," Rosie told Mac. "Except for breakfast. She rocks breakfast."

Thanks, kid. Nothing like a teenage daughter to spill the embarrassing stuff. "Since you fired the first shot, dear daughter, let's talk about your day at school. Why are you drawing pornography?"

Rosie immediately went into argument mode. "It's artistic depictions from romance novels. It's not erotica or porn."

Mac choked on a mouthful.

"It was enough to get you suspended, whatever it is, and it got me in trouble at work too."

Mac's head snapped in my direction, but I ignored him and added, "So walk me through everything that happened, Rosa Nell."

Rosie slumped in her seat, fork clattering to her plate, and heaved a beleaguered sigh like it was so hard being a fourteen-year-old kid. "My art class is doing this pencil technique. It's probably got some fancy name, but anyway, our homework was to depict a scene from a book. I did the homework from a Harry Potter book. But I liked it so much, I decided to see if I could draw something else. I grabbed a book from your stack and read it to pick a scene. So, if anything, it's your fault for reading books about horny blue aliens."

Oh. My. God. She did not just say that. I was going to die of mortification on the spot. Keel over right in my plate. Did my daughter care? Nope.

"So it's just as much your fault as mine," she continued, heedless of my last wishes. "But also, you know I don't share my drawings. I think someone snuck into my notebook and snapped pictures and then sent them to everyone."

I couldn't bring myself to look at the man next to me. He'd gone still, hadn't spoken a word. The words horny and erotic bounced around the room like they'd been blasted from a bullhorn, reverberating off the walls. He shifted in his seat, the rough denim of his jeans scraping across my bare skin as our knees bumped in the small space.

My chair screeched on the floor as I shot up. Jesus Christ, I was losing all capacity to function. "We forgot drinks. I'm thirsty." Yeah, no shit after the knee touch and talk about erotica, and I would not be thinking about the positions my daughter had drawn and imagining Mac.

"Yeah, I could use a drink," Mac said. Was his voice strained, or was it my imagination?

"Sorry. I got all nervous when you got here and forgot. And um, why *are* you here, Mac?" Rosie, bless her heart, stepped in, innocently dispersing the sexual tension and bringing us back to the whole reason for this dinner.

I stole a moment, hiding behind the freezer door, both to cool my face and to gather my wits. And my courage.

Mac was silent, and it was my place to start telling the truth. "I invited Mac so that we could talk through some things. I think you know what they are." I busied myself filling the glasses and passing them out. So much easier to have this conversation if I didn't have to sit under his laser-beam gaze.

But with all my stall tactics out of the way, I rejoined the table and looked my daughter in the eye. Best to just rip off the band-aid. "Years ago, Mac and I met on vacation. We had a fling, and I came home with a souvenir."

"Me." She knew this part of the story.

"Right. Except, Mac didn't know about you. And now that he does, we can move forward. And the two of you can decide if you like each other."

My daughter looked at Mac with her whole heart in her eyes. What would I do if I lost her in this process? She'd never gazed at me with that much love on her face. Just like me, she was gone for the man, probably from the moment she'd met him. Had I messed up so completely by not looking harder? Or continuing to look through the years? By not taking all the steps she had to find him?

"Also? I'm sorry," I blurted, heat rising in my cheeks. I'd raised Rosie to be honest in all things, so now it was time for me to own my mistakes. I gathered my courage and looked at Mac, then her. "I just need to say the words. I'm sorry. I failed you both, and I hope you can forgive me." I hated the wobble in my voice.

Rosie stared at me wide-eyed. It was rare that I let her see me as anything other than strong and capable.

Mac grunted like I'd punched him in the chest. "Moving forward, Liv."

And that was that.

"So, moving forward, does that mean we can be friends,

Mac?" Rosie asked with all the hope a young girl could feel lacing the word "friends."

"Yeah, Rosie. And we're gonna start with you coming to hang out, not in secret anymore, with me at my house at Lake Martin while your mom goes to a conference for a couple of days. If you're cool with it."

"You've got a lake house?" Her eyes lit.

Mac nodded and dug into the food on his plate. Rosie was right, it did look gross. And he was being such a gentleman, making a point to eat the meal I'd prepared.

"Bought it with my dad a long time ago," he told her. "Meant to be a place for us to fix up together, and then he and Mom would live there after he retired. Something we could keep in the family and pass down. Got plenty of space, so you'll have your own room."

"That's cool. Will they be there? I'd get to meet them?"

Sorrow clouded his gaze as he stilled and looked at her. "No, kiddo," he said softly. "They passed away before they could ever enjoy it." The muscle of his jaw clenched as he paused. "But they would've loved you."

Add another to the list of people I'd failed. More guilt burned through me.

Rosie pushed her food around on her plate. "That sucks."

"Yeah, it does," he replied softly. "This picture situation the one we talked about with the mean girls?"

"Yeah."

Mac nodded in understanding. They'd clearly discussed her feelings over the situation, something I was going to have to come to terms with. They were allowed to have that, even if I didn't like being left out.

"So," Rosie shifted gears again, "what are we going to do at the lake house?"

"I dunno. I've got some projects to work on, and you can help. Always got projects going over there. It's a work in progress."

From there, the conversation shifted to what Rosie would need for the weekend. Mac said he'd handle getting her, and before long, they were making their plans, while I sat by as an observer to this fast friendship they had formed.

All thoughts of suspension, schoolgirl issues, and dirty pictures forgiven and forgotten.

This was what moving forward looked like with him.

I decided I'd have to also let go of the issue with the school, because he'd helped her resolve the root issue. She was serving her punishment, and if art was her creative outlet, I wanted to support her. But I would make it a point to be more responsible with my reading material until I could have more in-depth discussions about sex. Not that I was a good role model for having responsible sex.

I played bystander while they made plans to spend time together, my heart cracking just a little in the process. And if I was honest, a little jealous, because their plans sounded like a lot more fun than a public-safety conference.

But by the time Mac left, I was at least comfortable with the idea of letting her go. And even more certain that them getting to know each other was the right thing, even if it was hard to accept.

Chapter Nine

Mac

For the second time in a dozen hours, I found myself pulling into Olivia's complex, a nice older community a couple of blocks from the heart of downtown. Prior to the tornado last year, the complex had large old trees as a barrier to the road, providing shade during the hot summer months. Now, the early morning light glittered off the metal roof. At least the grass had begun to grow back.

The neighborhood was relatively safe, and although their complex wasn't gated, we never heard of any bad things happening in the area.

Olivia met me on the sidewalk, her arms folded over her chest, with an expression that said she still wasn't convinced this was a good idea. I hadn't meant to make the offer for Rosie to stay with me, but the words were out before I knew it, and the more the idea settled, the less nervous I was about it.

The meeting and official introductions, not that they were really needed, had gone surprisingly well. After all,

Rosie had been sneaking over and hanging out with Buster for a week, and we'd gotten into a routine, so we weren't total strangers. Plus, I still had paternal rights, and technically, I could enforce them. And maybe that was what had Olivia on edge.

Once Olivia got past her nerves and loosened up, she agreed that Rosie coming with me was the best-case scenario. I tried to remind myself of all the positives as I climbed out of the truck, because now that it was go time, I was scared to death. Buster woofed from the back seat, aware that this was a new place he hadn't explored.

"Stay," I ordered, before closing the door behind me.

Olivia shifted, arms wrapping around her waist, looking like a concerned mother rather than the tough-as-nails fire chief. I couldn't blame her. She was sending her baby girl off with a virtual stranger.

Her worried eyes met mine. "You sure about this? Now's your chance if you've changed your mind."

I hooked a thumb in the pocket of my jeans to keep from reaching out to rub away the crease between her eyebrows and shook my head. "No take backs. We'll be fine. You go kick some ass, and we'll see you when you get done. You got the address, right?"

Olivia began nodding as the front door burst open, and a mass of bags and flying blond hair bolted for us. "Hey, Mac. I'm ready! Bye, Mom."

I caught up with Rosie, taking her bags. "That's not good enough. Try again." I didn't mean to, but it came out as a growl. I nodded to where Olivia stood watching, looking for all the world like this might be her last goodbye with Rosie.

Rosie stood frozen in place, eyes wide. We needed to get some things straight from the get-go. Even so, I didn't want to scare the kid before we even hit the road, so I softened my tone before I laid it out.

"When you leave your momma, you give her a hug and a kiss and tell her you love her. Always. Every time."

Realization dawned, and she turned and dashed back to Olivia, nearly taking her out with a full-body tackle. "Bye, Mom. Do good on your thing. I love you. I'll call you tonight."

Before I could even get around the truck, Rosie was in the passenger seat, loving on Buster.

I chuckled, feeling a little awkward that she'd just ditched her mom without a thought. I stuck my hands in my back pockets because I still didn't know what to do with them, aside from reaching for her, which I shouldn't do, no matter how strong the pull between us.

I was supposed to be making their lives easier. This was supposed to be helping. So why did it feel like I was kicking a puppy?

"I reckon she's excited."

The corner of Olivia's mouth tilted on a sad smile, her eyes glued to Rosie. "You could say that. After you left, she packed and repacked for two solid hours. I don't know that she's slept a wink."

"You sure you're okay with this? You seem a little upset." I kept my voice soft so that Rosie wouldn't overhear.

Watching her daughter with sad eyes, she nodded. "I wouldn't stop this for anything in the world. Look at her."

I was too caught up on the woman in front of me to drag my attention off her. I hated this defeated expression on her face, hated that she looked so melancholy, hated that I felt guilty for taking Rosie with me. Olivia was clearly going to miss the girl. Was this what parenting was like? Was this what I was in for? My whole world, wrapped up in the happiness of my child?

Olivia dragged her attention away from Rosie and Buster with a huge sigh and turned to face me. "You've got my number if you need me."

"I do. Same goes for you. You need us, you call. Otherwise, I'll have her call you tonight. Do your thing and don't worry about us. We'll be fine."

The drive to the lake house was two solid hours of Rosie singing along to Taylor Swift songs. After we'd unloaded the truck, she and Buster had an afternoon session of fetch. They'd both come into the detached garage soaking wet after a dive in the lake, and I'd banned them to the yard until Buster quit shaking, not wanting him to sling mud on the canoe I was refinishing.

Rosie had taken an immediate interest in my project. "What's that?" had been her favorite question, asking it over and over, and paying attention when I explained each part of the boat. Eventually, I put her to work, and she'd fallen into the same meditative state I fell into when working.

She stood across from me, sandpaper in hand, working over some rough sections, while I worked on rigging rope anchors. Her stomach growled, interrupting the late-afternoon silence.

I glanced at the time. We'd been at it for hours. "You wanna go get a pizza?"

Her head popped up over the edge of the boat. "Add this to the things-to-know-about-Rosie column. Pizza is my favorite, and I'm always down for some."

The corner of my mouth hitched up. She was such a smartass. "Go wash up. Meet me at the boat in five."

Her eyes grew huge with wonder. "We're taking the boat?"

I'd barely nodded in response before she bolted out of the garage, whooping the entire way to the big house, four-legged shadow in tow.

The lake house was my sanctuary. My dad and I had bought it on the cheap, intending on it being a retirement home for him and my mom, and then someday mine. But someday had come all too soon, and he never got to enjoy retirement or the lake house. I'd spent nearly a decade reno-vating and fixing up the small two-story house. It wasn't fancy or expensive, but it had a great view of the lake all year, and it came with a detached garage that I'd converted to storage space and a workshop.

I whistled for Buster, who turned on a dime, realizing I was headed down to the dock. Ten minutes later, we were cruising the big water of Lake Martin, headed for a pizza. Rosie was snuggled up to Buster in the back of the boat, laughing and happy.

My chest squeezed tight. This feeling growing inside me almost hurt.

Was this happiness? Being able to share one of my favorite things with my child? Showing her how to build things and answering a ton of questions? Experiencing a level of patience I didn't know I had?

Was this love?

And was it weird that it was so all-consuming and powerful when I'd only just met her? It made sense, though. How many times had I heard someone say they'd fallen in love with their child on sight?

Granted, they meant on first sight as a newborn.

But still. It was surprising that I was enjoying every

minute of being with her, sharing all my special places along the lake.

An hour later, we were stuffed full of pizza, with leftovers stowed in the hold, and headed back home when Rosie called out, "Hey, Mac, will you teach me to drive the boat?"

I nodded and throttled back, slowing us down as we neared a decent-sized cove with no boat traffic. "Yeah, come on."

It wasn't until she stepped up to take the wheel that I had second thoughts. How was I supposed to teach her without standing uncomfortably close to her? Thinking back on all the guys I'd seen teach their kids, it was natural for them to stand behind them and be their guide. But I couldn't do that. I sank into the chair across from her and gave her instructions.

"Okay, just ease that forward when you are ready."

Rosie white-knuckled the wheel with one hand and the throttle with the other.

"Relax your grip on that throttle, just lightly touch it. We don't want to go fast. Just inch it forward until we start moving."

She swallowed, gathered her courage, and nudged the throttle forward. The motor engaged, and the boat started moving. I kept watch on the direction, gave her some corrections to make, and guided her through making a turn.

The boat slowed as we came to the end of the lesson. "Good job, kiddo."

Rosie let out a whoop as we began a lazy drift and the breeze kicked up around us. "That was amazing! Can we do it again?"

"After you do the homework to get yourself a license."

We swapped places, and I steered us out of the cove, resuming the trek back to my house.

Rosie folded herself in the cocaptain chair, with a foot in the seat, arms hugging her raised knee. "How long will it take?"

Buster stretched out on the back bench. I'd never had a dog enjoy a boat ride like he did.

"I dunno. That's for you to find out," I replied, looking left over my shoulder and maneuvering us out into the big-water traffic. It was late in the day, and there were more boats now, more wakes to manage. Dark clouds were rolling in, and everyone who'd been out on the water was making the mad dash to shore. The problem was, we were headed directly into the ominous-looking storm.

"Those clouds look kinda scary." She took the words right out of my mouth.

"Yep."

"Are we gonna make it back in time?" Now her tone sounded worried.

"I don't know, we'll get there as quickly and safely as possible." Her mother would kill me if something happened to Rosie under my care. "I probably should've gotten her permission to even take you on this ride."

"Why? You're my dad. You have a say too."

And just like that, Rosie floored me. Because I wasn't her dad in any sense other than the fact that we shared the same DNA.

The crosswind picked up, and the waves got larger. Then the rain started, and visibility dropped, so I slowed further.

"Do me a favor," I yelled into the wind. "Reach in that compartment and grab a life jacket for you and one for Buster."

Rosie pulled them out and got them each buckled in safely, and I relaxed a tiny bit.

"What about you?" she yelled.

"I'll be fine, it just makes me feel better knowing you're protected." I'd be fine if we could make it to the other side of this torrential dump of rain; with any luck, we'd ride out the other side any minute.

A life jacket slapped my arm, flapping in the wind as Rosie held it out to me. "You gotta be covered too."

I glanced over to see Buster tucked under her legs and Rosie huddling behind her half of the windshield, trying to get out of the stinging rain. I slipped on the life jacket and fastened it as best I could one-handed. That tight feeling in my chest returned. Part fear, part pissed off at myself that I'd put her in harm's way. Part something else that she'd cared enough to make sure I was covered too.

We made it to our cove and pulled under the covered dock. The rain poured harder, and lightning flashed in the sky, thunder rumbling around us.

"Want me to get the ropes?" Rosie offered.

"Yeah, I'll keep us steady until you can get the first tie-down secured." I talked her through the loops to make, and together, we secured the boat. Buster jumped onto the dock and led our dash to the garage.

"Well, that was fun until the rain started," Rosie quipped, shucking her lifejacket and hanging it on a peg. She ran her fingers through her long hair—soaked, but no worse for wear. I thanked our lucky stars that the lightning hadn't started until we were docked.

"It got a little hairy there for a minute."

"No shi—kidding."

I cut my eyes to her. "Good catch."

"Mom doesn't like it when I cuss," she said matter of

fact, then tilted her head quizzically. "Which I don't understand because she'll let them fly when she doesn't know I'm listening."

I brushed the water from my hair with my hand, chuckling at this insight into Olivia. "She's just trying to be her idea of a good mom. You can't blame her. She's done a good job with you."

Rosie plucked at her wet clothes. "I guess I'm gonna go get out of these wet clothes. Thanks for the boat ride, Mac. I'll keep the stormy part out when I talk to Mom."

"Yeah, thanks," I said to her retreating back.

A half hour later, I figured I'd given Rosie enough time to get herself settled and chat with her mom and was just closing the shop when my cell rang. Not many people called me when I was at the lake house. Not many people called me at all anymore. There'd been a time when I'd hang with some of the locals, but over the years, they'd sold out and moved away. And I kept to myself mostly anyway. Occasionally, the guys from the shift would have a cookout or get-together. Sometimes I went. But my phone ringing outside of work was unusual.

"Hello?"

"Hey there, it's me. I was just calling to check in."

Olivia. Something hot rose in my chest, and I rubbed a hand over the spot. Damn pizza was talking back. Or maybe it was lingering fear from the race back across the lake. Had to be what it was and not the sound of her voice. "Hey yourself. Things are good here. You talk to Rosie?"

Mild panic settled in next to the heartburn. I absolutely couldn't tell her about having Rosie out in the storm. She'd lose her mind.

"Yeah, just got off the phone with her. She sounds like she's having a blast."

Relief was heady. Rosie had kept her word, and maybe it was wrong to keep Olivia in the dark, but I kind of liked having this shared secret with Rosie. No reason to worry her mom. "Things are going well so far."

"She's pulling her weight, right?"

Rosie helping me with the canoe felt a lot like the times I'd spent with my dad, making the dream of the lake house a reality. I'd done the work to the house after he died. But there were endless projects that I still wanted to do, always improvements to be made. Starting with finishing my sail-boat. And now I could share that with my daughter.

The heartburn kicked up a notch.

"Absolutely. So far, she's helped me on a project I'm working on. Who knew that giving a kid sandpaper would shut them up? But she's a lot like me; she gets focused and gets in her head. We took a boat ride for some pizza, and she chattered about everything on the lake. Wants to know everything about driving the boat."

Her low laugh came through the phone as sultry, though I knew she didn't intend for it to be so sexy. "She's obsessed with driving, period, right now."

"Well, I gave her some homework and told her if she'd study and get her license, I'd teach her to drive the boat. I hope that's okay."

Silence filled the line for a moment, and I had the sinking feeling I'd already fucked up this co-parenting thing.

"I suppose it is. It's just hard letting her grow up, is all. In my head, she's still six years old and barely learning how to ride a bike. And now she's ready to spread her wings and test her independence." A sadness tinged her words, and that ache in my chest grew. What would it have been like to know Rosie when she was six?

The storm slacked off a little, and I stepped to the doorway to find the lights on inside the house. Through the window, I could see Rosie in the kitchen. Realizing we'd left the pizza in the boat, I walked down to grab it so she could have it later.

"I'm sorry, Mac. That was terribly insensitive of me." Regret tinged Olivia's voice.

"It is what it is, Liv. Do I regret not having that time with her? Some. But then again, I'd never planned on having kids, so the loss doesn't feel as great." It was a half-truth. I could be mad and linger over what might've been. I could hold a grudge and make life hard on all of us. Or I could forgive Olivia and embrace Rosie and let the past live in the past.

I'd done enough living in the past. Spent over a decade wondering what might've been if Diedre had stuck around, if we would've had kids. Started a family. If my parents hadn't died so soon after she left. If they'd been able to have more kids so I wouldn't have been left alone in the world after their accident. But living in the past had gotten me nowhere.

"Moving forward, Liv."

We needed to get off this dark stuff and get back to easy, so I steered the conversation to get her to tell me about her presentation.

She'd done well, like I knew she would. In the end, the conversation turned again, and we talked until I noticed that the clouds had dissipated and the sun was beginning to set. We'd talked for over an hour, and it'd felt like just a few moments.

"Well, I better get in here and make sure she's not cooking something up in the kitchen. I learned the hard way that Rosie is no cook."

Olivia laughed. "At least she gets something from me."

"I'll check in tomorrow. Have fun at your conference."

"Tomorrow will be another long one, but Sunday should be a short day. I'm hoping to be done by noon."

"You should come to the lake. And have some time with Rosie." *And me.* The thought came unbidden but not wholly unwanted. There'd probably never be a time that I didn't want Livvie.

"Thanks for everything, Mac." Her voice held a smile as we hung up, and I pictured what that smile would look like aimed at me. And that tightness in my chest grew a little more.

Chapter Ten

Olivia

By the end of the second day of the conference, I was tired of dealing with multiple levels of misogynistic bullshit. Of the entire attendees, I was one of only a handful of women, and by the time the cocktail hour had ended the first night, I had been propositioned no less than five times.

Not wanting to be subjected to that again, I decided to skip the second-night cocktail hour. I made my exit from the last seminar session and headed toward my room, glancing back over my shoulder at every turn to make certain no one followed me to the elevator.

The door pinged, and I stepped inside, breathing a sigh of relief, only for a hand to appear between the doors at the last minute and halt their closure.

A large man joined me, his too-wide smile and lingering gaze I attributed to the alcohol I could smell on his breath. I stood with my back ramrod stiff and kept him in my peripheral view.

"Chief Hawkins," he started like he hadn't been leering at me. "Paul told me you'd be giving a speech. Good presentation considering it was such a last-minute addition. Shame they canceled the other talk, though, to have you present, but Paul can be a persuasive guy when he wants to be."

And just like that, I had my confirmation that Mayor Smith had set me up for failure. They'd already had the schedule set without me having to do all that work. And he'd... lied about the whole thing. But why? Why was he sabotaging me?

I felt no need to respond to this revelation and stood watching the digital readout of the passing floors. He took my non-reply as encouragement, though, and stepped closer, boxing me in.

"You know, there's a whole lot I can help you attain if the fire service ever becomes a bore for you. I know plenty of higher-ups at the state level. I'm sure I could get you an interview." His fingertip traced the skin of my forearm, damp and unwelcome.

I jerked away and just barely stopped myself from throwing a punch. "Excuse me, sir. You do not have permission to touch me. I don't want your damn interview. Matter of fact, I don't want anything from you. Not your interest or your favors. Nothing."

The elevator pinged on my floor, and I stepped off, head held high against his stunned reaction. The door closed on his outraged declaration, something about Mayor Smith and my regrets, but I didn't care. No job was worth the type of harassment and favors this crowd offered.

I swiped my keycard and entered my room, wanting nothing more than a shower. It was these types of men, the ones who thought every female was beneath them and served only to warm their beds and man their kitchens, that made my blood boil.

I'd spent my entire career fighting bastards like this one. And to know that Mayor Smith had set me up just made it worse.

I was beginning to think the bullshit wasn't worth it. Why have a dream job where people didn't respect you?

The men and women who worked for my department deserved better than someone who would cow to this type of political pressure. So just like I'd always done, I'd put on a brave face, shove the misogyny aside, and do the job they'd hired me for.

As it was, I still had some missing inventory to find and an arsonist to catch. And apparently, the police department was relying on my new fire marshal to handle the majority of the investigation, so I'd give him my full support.

I checked the time, and since it was early yet, I gave Marshal Harrison a call to get a status update. That done, I felt better and relaxed some, allowing my thoughts to turn to Rosie and Mac. I called Rosie and chatted with her, and her exuberance over the old sailboat she and Mac were restoring made my heart ache. I wanted to be there, experiencing this with her.

It was a Friday night. I could have all weekend with my daughter versus a golf tournament and useless seminars. I'd already fulfilled Mayor Smith's scheming demands, so I checked the schedule for the next day. A photo of the jackass from the elevator was next to the session information. With that knowledge, my decision was made.

Twenty minutes later, I was in my car with my phone GPS—because my piece-of-shit vehicle was absolutely void of any niceties like Bluetooth or navigation—showing a five-hour drive to get to the lake house, to retrieve Rosie and relieve Mac of weekend kid duty. I cued up my favorite true crime podcast on my phone and headed west.

With an hour of travel left, the rain started. And then the roads grew narrower and darker, with minimal streetlights. My high beams were no match for the sheet of rain that pounded around me. I flipped the radio to a local station when the setting became eerily similar to the location of the episode playing.

Occasionally, lightning would flash and illuminate the dark country road. But the rain just kept pouring down. And I was well and truly creeped out.

Without any warning signs, the road curved sharply, and my tires squealed as I slid. With sweaty palms, I maneuvered the car back to a safer, slower speed.

Mac better have a stiff drink available when I got there.

I cringed. I should've called when I left and given them a heads-up that I was coming early. But I didn't, and now I was afraid to take my eyes off the road to make the call.

Finally, my headlights illuminated his mailbox number, and I turned into the drive. No lights were on inside the house, but Mac's truck out front was all the confirmation I needed. I cut the engine and took a long, deep breath to calm my nerves.

By the time I made it to the door and huddled as closely to the house as possible, my clothes were drenched. The T-shirt I'd changed into before leaving clung to my body. I knocked a second time before the door was wrenched open to a very surprised Mac on the other side.

Lightning struck nearby, creating a loud crash.

With a yelp, I ducked.

Mac's strong hand gripped my elbow and tugged me into the small entryway. Right up against his firm chest.

In the split second our bodies were pressed against each

other, I was instantly transported to another time, when we'd made a mad dash through the rain and sought shelter in each other. We'd been happy and laughing and ended up kissing and peeling our wet clothes off each other before making love the rest of that rainy day.

A shudder ran through me as I pulled away from his heat. I was not here for this. I was not here for him. I needed to remember that. Even if his lips looked ultra-kissable.

"Surprise," I said weakly.

"What are you doing here?" That full-body collision had him looking as stunned as I felt.

From beyond the hallway, my daughter's voice rang out, "Mom!" followed by her running footsteps.

Then I was bear hugged and smashed even closer to him by Rosie.

"What are you doing here?" she squealed, the delighted surprise in her voice bouncing off the walls.

I didn't know what to do with my hands. Under any other circumstance, I'd lay them on his chest, maybe snuggle into him. As it was, I was highly aware that our hips were pressed together and his big hands were on my waist, and Rosie was the bulldozer pushing me into him.

Mac's lake house, from what I could see beyond his shoulder, was an older home. Unadorned cream-colored walls made the small entryway feel brighter than it should. Wood floors led down a short hallway. I took all of this in as I awkwardly tried to hold my body away from Mac's. No doubt I was soaking him with my wet clothes.

He reached around me, patting Rosie's back. "Hey, kid. Your mom's probably freezing. You want to give her some room?"

For the briefest moment, the almost hug surrounded me in his warmth, and my body responded immediately. I wanted to burrow into that warmth, breathe in his woodsy smell, melt into him. Instead, Rosie let me go, and I stepped back, plucking at my now see-through shirt. I turned to hide the fact that my nipples were hard. It was just because I was cold, not because I'd been rubbing against Mac.

"I decided that I'd head out a little early from the conference."

With mischievous twinkling eyes, Rosie turned to Mac. "Mom's skipping her classes."

"Sounds like it. Don't get any ideas," he warned.

"Gah, you're just as bad as she is," she huffed, turning on a heel and leaving us alone again.

Mac ushered me down the hallway to a kitchen that overlooked a large living room. Tall windows lined the far wall, probably overlooking the lake, though it was too stormy to tell. Rosie sprawled on a big comfy sectional sofa, using a yellow Labrador as a pillow. The dog, obviously in heaven, lay there with an eye on me, tongue lolled out, almost smiling.

"You got bags in the car?" Mac asked. He stood at the counter, arms braced, wet patches dotting his dark-gray shirt. The tattoos that covered his forearms drew my attention. What was it about really good forearm porn?

I realized belatedly that he'd asked me a question. "What?"

"Bags," he repeated, the corner of his mouth lifting in a smirk. "Are they in the car? I'll go get them when the rain lets up."

"Oh, I wasn't planning on staying. I was just going to grab Rosie and head home."

Mac frowned. "You aren't going anywhere in this weather."

I opened my mouth to argue.

"Nope. Putting my foot down." His voice was gruff, full of authority, and a total turn-on. And now was not the time. "There's no reason for you to be on the road," he continued, despite my turmoil. "I have plenty of room for you to stay. Besides, you already skipped out of the conference. Might as well enjoy the rest of the weekend."

The corner of his mouth tipped up, and my ovaries flipped. I'd recognized in the few weeks that I'd been on the job that he was usually stern, almost hard. That ghost of a smile did things to me.

"I can't put you o—"

His hand shot up, stopping me.

He held my gaze and shook his head. "It's not safe, Liv. I'd rather you not be on the road if you don't have to be." His soft request tumbled my insides until all that existed was the desire to hear my name in that voice again. His stare held me in place until it became clear I was not going to win this argument. He was braced and ready for a fight, taking up all the space in the room. All the air. A memory of his focused intensity flashed bright and hot, and I had to lick my lips to keep from gasping.

Heat grew in his gaze as if he could read my thoughts. His eyes dropped to my lips, and I felt them on me as if he'd physically touched me.

"Okay." The simple word came out so breathy and soft, I had to break the lingering eye contact before I completely crumpled. "If you're sure it's not a problem," I said more firmly, "my bag is in the back seat."

Mac gave a nod and stalked out of the room. I let my gaze wander over his wide shoulders that nearly filled the hallway, and his firm ass in cutoff sweatpants. He really had kept in great shape over the years.

A giggle drew my attention.

"He's hot for an old guy, right?" Rosie stage-whispered.

Heat crept up my cheeks. "Rosa Nell." But I had to stop at her name because I didn't know what else to say. "Watch yourself, young lady," I finished weakly.

Mac braved the unrelenting storm and brought in my bag, ushering me to the other spare bedroom. I changed and explored the house more, noting the decided absence of decorations. Only a few photos here and there. But no trinkets or personal items. As if he'd been there but hadn't ever settled in.

"You've got a nice place, Mac. Thanks for letting us stay," I said, joining them on an old blue L-shaped sofa. Mac stretched out across the shorter end, and Rosie had her legs curled up in the middle of the larger section, Buster lazing between them. Outside the large windows, lightning continued to flash as the storm lingered.

"Thanks. Dad fell in love with the place when he saw it. Now it's just me here, mostly."

I didn't know how to respond. The thought of Mac spending most of his time alone made me sad. With nothing left to say, the subject dropped.

The evening passed, and the whole time, I tried not to notice the way Mac's thighs bunched any time he shifted or the way his biceps bulged when he folded his arm behind his head.

But despite me actively avoiding checking out his body, my gaze seemed to be drawn there. Especially when he and Rosie had an in-depth conversation after realizing they had a shared love of old-school westerns. Curled up next to her on the couch, I sat as an outsider, witnessing my daughter fall a little bit in love with her father.

Despite my fear of her being hurt, it was sweet that they had so many similarities. What would our lives have been like if he'd been in it all along? And now that he was here, would she choose him over me? The thought sank like a stone, settling somewhere in the pit of my stomach where it rolled and churned.

Between the drone of the old black-and-white western —I didn't even know the name—and their hushed conversation, the long, stressful week caught up with me, and my eyelids grew heavy. I drifted somewhere between a dream, where this was our family, and reality, where I was chaperoning my daughter as she got to know her father.

She had endless questions for him, and he answered every one, his deep voice wrapping around my dreamlike state, bathing me in safety and comfort.

I didn't want this.

I was scared to death that things would go wrong because I knew we couldn't relive the past. I didn't want to find him so attractive. I didn't want my daughter to be so obsessed with him. I didn't want my career to take me away from her and push her to him.

But here I was, rolling with the punches.

Everything was mostly going my way now—new job, new place, wonderful kid. Maybe if Tim and I had been able to make things work, I wouldn't feel like such a failure. But I couldn't even regret it too much, because seeing her with Mac drove home how tense and unhealthy that relationship had become.

I was so tired.

Tired of thinking, of being in charge, tired of waiting on the next challenge and facing it alone.

But I wasn't alone right then.

Rosie had Mac, and in a way, I had him too. He was definitely stepping up to the challenge of learning to be a dad, whether he'd wanted it or not. I sank into the comfort of that thought and closed my eyes, drifting on a wave of their voices and low TV background noise.

A warm finger brushed across my forehead, followed by a gentle hand on my shoulder.

"Hey." Mac's voice was extra rough in my ear. "Why don't you head to bed?" A cascade of goosebumps broke out over my skin. Mmm, Mac. Bed.

My eyes popped open, darting around the room as I tried to get my bearings. The television was off, and a single lamp broke the darkness. Rosie tottered down the hall, yellow lab in tow. Mac was in the space where Rosie had been earlier. I sat up, loopy after what must've been a deep sleep.

"She stole your dog" popped out of my mouth.

"He'll find me once she goes to sleep. That's what he did last night, anyway." He sounded like he didn't mind so much, and I clung to that hope because I didn't want him to be upset with her.

I hugged the blanket that someone had thoughtfully covered me with. The moment felt intimate and right in so many ways. Somewhere deep in my heart, a little piece of me that I'd kept protected and sheltered began to unfurl. That split second of thinking Mac would join me in bed woke a desire I'd not experienced in a long time. Not since before the divorce. Not a desire for sex, just for... companionship. I didn't want to sleep alone, didn't want to be alone. I was lonely. Had been lonely for so many years.

"Mac..." I started, my voice thick with sleep.

"Liv, just let things be for a while. We don't have to know the answers, and we don't have to make any decisions or solve any problems." The intense set of his jaw was the only indication that he felt more than he was admitting to.

His hand brushed my hair softly. "Get some rest. We can sort things out tomorrow."

He pushed to stand and stretched, the hem of his shirt riding up, exposing a tanned strip of his stomach. He dropped his arms and padded across the room to the back door, checking the locks. My eyes were glued to his every move until he disappeared down the hall, toward the front door, breaking my trance.

This was not good. I couldn't keep my eyes off him, nor keep my thoughts out of the past. I didn't know how this whole thing would go, but I didn't have a good feeling about it. I rose, folded the blanket, and headed to my room. I felt him come down the hall behind me, his presence warm and solid. At my door, I paused and looked over my shoulder to him.

"Thanks for everything, Mac."

A muscle in his jaw ticked as he silently regarded me. With a single nod, he walked into his bedroom. The soft click of the latch catching nearly shattered me.

Chapter Eleven

Olivia

The next morning, I found Mac on the back deck watching the sunrise. The storm had cleared during the night, leaving behind a gorgeous, clear blue-sky morning. A long wooden walkway stretched from the house to the lake, broken by a large deck decorated with comfortable-looking outdoor furniture and a raised fire pit. Two more wooden walkways led off the deck; the one to the left went to a covered pole barn, where a modest-size boat was anchored. The walkway to the right led down to a floating dock. The backyard was landscaped with large rocks bordering a small grassy area, not a huge space, but enough for a dog to romp around.

Mac sat in one of the chairs, his long legs stretched out in front of him, casually rubbing the ears of the yellow lab that seemed to be watching the sunrise with him.

The morning birds sang, and the sun gleamed across the glass surface of Lake Martin.

The peacefulness of the place seeped into my bones, and I released a level of stress I didn't know I'd been holding on to.

I walked as softly as possible to not disturb the stillness, but the boards creaked beneath my weight. Mac turned his head my way, a soft smile on his lips. Gone was the intense glare and subtle jaw tick. Just a peaceful man, taking in a peaceful morning. He was so rugged and handsome sitting there bathed in early morning light.

"Morning," he greeted.

"I see you still enjoy sunrises." I smiled at the memory of the week we'd spent together, sometimes watching the sunrise after a night of lovemaking and then napping under a cabana during the day.

He nodded. "Looks like it's going to be a beautiful day. I was thinking we might take a boat ride."

That sounded amazing. I hadn't been on a boat in forever. But still, I didn't know if I should. "I should really head back to town. It's not right for me to stay here."

"Right. The fraternization thing. We need to talk about it. Liv, it's going to be difficult to navigate the rule, with me working for you, and Rosie being ours. It's been on my mind since I found out about her. But the rule got the last fire chief fired. Of course, he was sleeping with the summer intern. Still, they've been looking at all relationship connections since then and making people switch departments."

"What happens if they can't switch?"

"Someone has to leave."

Dread settled in the pit of my belly. I didn't want to leave the fire department, and I didn't want Mac to leave either. His gaze met mine, understanding and maybe regret passing over his face. Then his gaze dropped to my lips, and just like before, the look was almost palpable.

I wanted another chance to know what he tasted like. Wanted to see if we'd burst into flames from a single kiss like we had so many years ago.

Mac cleared his throat. "Tell me about the conference." From there, the conversation chased away the peaceful feeling of the morning and left a sour taste.

I told Mac about my suspicions of the mayor and then watched his eyes grow stormy as I mentioned the man in the elevator. "I don't know if he's just out to get me, but I'm concerned about the mayor finding out we had a past relationship, and how that would be handled with their fraternization rules."

"I get you're concerned, Liv. But look, you're already here. There's no rule that says we can't be friends. Hell, the whole shift is like one great big family. They do everything together. This is no different. Why don't you hang out today, take a day off. We can figure the rest out later. Besides, there's a great burger joint I want to take Rosie to."

The smart option would be to head home with Rosie, but part of me wanted to stay and enjoy the ride.

"Okay, Mac." I let the grin spread across my face. "Let's take a boat ride."

* * *

"Oh my God, Mom, this burger is amazing," Rosie gushed around a mouthful. Grease dripped down her fingers, and a trail of cheese clung to her chin. Twin spots of ketchup marked her cheeks like dimples.

I laughed at my daughter. It was glorious seeing her happy and in her element. We'd taken a short boat ride, where Mac had taught Rosie more about driving and even let her take the wheel in the less crowded areas. Her connection with Mac had grown deeper, and it was evident that they were truly enjoying spending time together. It was weird being the third wheel to my daughter and her father, but here we were.

Mac had his chair tilted back on two legs, taking long pulls from his soft drink, eyes twinkling above the straw.

At the table next to us, a woman stood abruptly, the chair screeching across the concrete patio. Her wild eyes skittered across the restaurant, just as a bloodcurdling scream ripped from the adjacent beach area.

A man ran into the waist-deep water, then rose with a small child limp in his arms. Mac and I sprang into action. I snatched my phone, already dialing 911. We reached them as the man laid the child on the ground. Mac checked to see if the child was breathing as the distraught man, probably the boy's father, by his reaction, kneeled next to him.

I dropped to my knees opposite Mac, doing my best to channel his calm, collected front as the operator answered, "911, what's your emergency?"

Mac checked for pulse and breath, and I fought to keep my voice steady. "We are at Larry's Dockside Bar. A child was just pulled from the water. Nonresponsive, not breathing, no pulse. We need an ambulance."

Mac looked at me. "You start compressions."

A woman pulled the father away to console him. I motioned her to me as I spoke both to her and the operator. "I'm Fire Chief Olivia Hawkins, and this is Captain Mac Collins. 911, I'm passing my phone to..."

I looked at the woman, who replied, "Glori."

"Glori is going to stay on this line while my partner and I get to work."

Mac and I fell into a rhythm, me counting to thirty in a

steady cadence. I didn't think. Didn't otherwise react. Just worked the compressions against his rescue breathing.

"Switch," I gasped after five rounds.

Mac gave his breaths and moved to take over compressions.

We paused for assessment. Began again. Over and over. Breath, compression, assessment. Until a bag dropped by my head and I felt a presence at my side. Reality began sifting back in. Mac and I moved out of the way to let rescue personnel take over. I sat back on my heels, trying to catch my breath.

"I don't know how it happened." The young father, calmer now and able to speak, stood with a police officer. He sliced his fingers through his hair, pulling at it like he wanted to rip it out. The whites of his eyes were still too large, his voice tortured. "I turned around for just a second to empty the cooler. He was playing in the sand while my wife took a load to the car."

The medic closest to me hit the child with AED paddles and paused. "I've got a pulse," his partner responded, and they continued working the child. Nearby, the parents broke down in each other's arms.

Mac and I assisted the medics, helping them load the child for the waiting ambulance.

As they lifted the stretcher, the boy began to cry, and my knees went weak. If not for Mac's arm snaking around my waist, I would've hit the ground. Instinctively, I took a step closer, wrapping my arm around him and gripping the shirt at his back for dear life.

He shifted against me, pulling me closer.

Mac and I clung to each other, and across from us, the parents mirrored us as the crew placed the child in the ambulance.

"Mom?" Rosie's voice cut through the chaos of the scene, high and tight and more than a little scared. I pulled away from Mac and scanned the area to find her huddling on a bench. "Is he going to be okay?" she asked as I wrapped my arms around her, fully aware that at any point, I could've been, could be, that mother.

"I don't know, honey. But we did the best we could." I tried to reassure her, even if I was having trouble processing it myself.

"Is it always like this? This terrible?" Her voice shook with uncertainty.

"Sometimes." Mac's voice was more gruff than normal, as affected by the scene as the rest of us. "I've never had an emergency while on vacation, but sometimes things happen. It's not... expected when on duty, but it's almost as if you're more prepared. Dealing with an emergency is almost second nature. You just do it. When it happens off duty, the instinct to act is still the same."

Mac stood behind Rosie on the other side, his large hand landing on her shoulder. The contact seemed to free her, and she bolted around the bench and into his arms, where she burst into tears.

"You have the worst job in the entire world."

Mac wrapped my baby girl in a bear hug like she'd been the one who might have been lost. The vision of them grew blurry as I fought back tears. That whole scene could've been so much worse. He raised his head from her hair and held an arm out to me. I stepped into the awkward embrace, sandwiching Rosie between us.

Finally, Mac said, "I'll tell you like I tell my crew. We aren't responsible for the calls, for the emergencies. We are a small part of the solution, and we do our very best, every time. Sometimes things work out for the best. Sometimes they don't. But we know we've done everything we could to help. And that's what brings me peace."

In that moment, I didn't know what was sweeter. Holding my baby girl, us both being held by this man, or his simple philosophy. The only thing I knew for certain was that I didn't want the day to end.

Chapter Twelve

Mac

"You have a beautiful family," a generic voice said, breaking through the tender moment with my girls. Genderless, faceless, nameless. It didn't matter who said what, because I was caught up, drawing in strength from having Rosie and Livvie in my arms.

I preached to my guys all the time about processing calls, and we worked regularly to debrief together, especially after the more traumatic ones. But it hit me differently now that I knew I had a child of my own.

It was irrational, probably a little extreme. And I realized how much I'd been lying to myself about wanting a family. Because holding these two in my arms felt good. It felt right.

And even as I knew I was already half in love with them both, I was scared to death.

One, or both of them, could be taken away or could choose to leave me in a heartbeat. I'd been there, done that, and it sucked.

I needed to not be so all-in so early. I needed to hold myself back some because I didn't want to hurt like I had so many years ago when Diedre left me.

Of course, it *had* been Olivia who had put me back on the path to healing. So it made sense that she was the reason for me coming back full circle.

Still.

This was too much, too soon. There was still so much to deal with and go through, and there was no way Olivia and I could pursue any kind of relationship, even though it seemed that Rosie wanted us together more than anything.

I had to stop this train.

I gave them both a last squeeze and pulled away from the embrace. It felt like ripping out my own soul.

"Okay. That was an experience." I tried to sound light, but the words fell flat.

Rosie wiped her eyes as Olivia pulled her under an arm.

They looked good standing together, tear-stained cheeks and all.

I gave up the act and held out a hand to them. "Let's get out of here."

The boat ride back was much different from the ride over. I didn't make any special stops or take any detours. We just made a straight beeline to the house.

At the dock, Rosie automatically helped me secure the ropes. A twinge of pride swelled at how naturally she'd picked it up, and then she and her mom went to the deck and spread out in lounge chairs.

I went to my garage and hid behind my canoe.

I didn't want to have these feelings.

This pride.

This intense longing to know everything about my daughter. Or her mother.

This sudden consideration for another person in my life was frustrating and confusing and way more than I bargained for.

It had been just Buster and me for so long, I'd come to accept it. I was used to it. Throwing in another person—or people, actually, because Rosie came with Olivia and vice versa—was upsetting my life, and I didn't have the emotional or mental capacity to process all the changes.

I was deep in the zone when a small shuffle sounded at the door. Staying focused on the layer of stain I was applying, I tried to ignore it. Buster tunneled his way into my line of sight, crawling between my legs and laying his head on my thigh. Since he'd ditched me the moment Rosie had climbed in the truck, I knew who I'd find at the door.

Dropping the pretense of work, I balanced the application sponge on the top of the can and gave him my attention.

"Are you mad?" Rosie's voice was small, hesitant.

I focused on Buster so I could avoid looking at her. Because apparently, I was a sucker for my daughter.

"No." My voice sounded gruff to my own ears. I sounded mad. I sounded like an asshole; I knew it and still couldn't stop it. But she deserved better than a clipped response. On a sigh, I continued, "I'm processing a lot right now, kiddo. But I'm not mad. There's nothing to be mad about."

"I get it. It's been a dramatic day. And you've had to do it with us crashing your space."

I hated that she sounded so withdrawn and defeated, and I'd done that to her by hiding from her.

"Listen." I hesitated, making sure to choose the right words. "We've all had a lot to adjust to. It's going to take some time to figure out our new reality. Plus, I think I deserve a little bit of understanding here. You've known about me a hell of a lot longer than I've known about you."

Sadness leaked from her. Sweet, stubborn, foolish teenage kid. Even standing in the doorway looking like I'd kicked her puppy. Could she not be so adorable?

"I don't want to be a burden, Mac. I just... want to know you. That's all."

The chin quiver broke my resolve to keep my distance. I drew her into my arms because I wasn't a total asshole, and when I saw tears, I wanted them to stop.

With her face buried in my chest, and my arms around her slight shoulders, I knew my life was never going to be the same.

The retirement I'd been looking so forward to was suddenly in jeopardy. All the plans I'd made were suddenly in limbo. Every decision I'd ever made to move me toward the early retirement that was within my grasp was now threatened... possibly put on hold. And it didn't sit well.

My father had died three months before he was able to retire. I watched the man work his fingers to the bone. He'd looked so forward to moving to the lake house and never gotten to enjoy it. I'd been so determined not to follow in his footsteps.

I was on track to have everything paid for and be able to retreat to this place permanently, and I was ready. I didn't recover from the all-nighters like the younger guys did. My body ached daily from the wear and tear of hauling heavy equipment and being on the go all the time. It was harder to come down from the adrenaline rush of going from a dead sleep to flat-out sprinting to the truck.

Still, my plans weren't her burden to bear. It was my decision, my choice to make on how I handled this going forward. All she'd asked from me was time spent together. I gave her a reassuring squeeze and pressed my lips to her hair.

"You're not a burden, Rosie. We'll figure it out." Maybe it was odd that I'd fallen so hard, so fast for this girl, but the truth was, I had. We'd figure out the rest later.

We left the garage and headed to the house. Rosie wasn't completely back to her normal cheerful attitude, but she wasn't crying anymore either, so I took it as a win. Olivia was at the table when we arrived, muttering to her laptop with a frown.

"This can't be right."

"Mom talks to her computer all the time. Just some FYI for you," Rosie informed me. She picked up a ball and dangled it in front of Buster's nose. "Come on, buddy, let's go play."

Buster followed her like a lovesick fool. I'd have to come to terms with losing my dog.

"What's wrong?" I asked Olivia, reaching for a beer from the fridge, noticing the distinct lack of real food. Rosie and I had stopped at the grocery store on the way in, but we were running low on supplies.

"We have a whole set of bunker gear and a SCBA unit missing." Olivia scrolled through a document and noted the totals again. "There's some other stuff, too." She rubbed her forehead in exasperation. "It just doesn't make sense."

I wanted to tell her that it would be okay, but I knew she was under an enormous amount of pressure from city hall, and having missing inventory when she was trying to justify budget spend was a big deal. I opened my mouth and closed it, because anything I could say would just be a platitude, and she deserved better than that.

My phone chimed on the counter. Hers rang at the same time.

Our gazes met and held.

Knowing that it couldn't be good that we were both getting a call at the same time, and also knowing that we didn't need to appear to be together, I swiped mine off the counter and headed out the door.

"Go for Mac," I said into the phone without checking the caller ID. I sank onto the front porch rocker, watching Rosie and Buster.

"Captain, are you at the lake?" Thoren asked, worry seeping into his tone.

"Yeah, why? What's up?"

In the yard, Rosie giggled as Buster made a flying leap and nearly tackled her to get the ball from her hand.

"He's back, sir."

I stilled.

Thoren's brother. The guy who'd set fire to numerous structures and almost cost me a couple of my personnel.

"Talk to me," I demanded.

"I got another calling card, similar to the ones he'd left before."

Loren had left several clues behind in his rampage against his brother.

"But, Captain... this time he left it in the station."

My beer bottle thunked to the chair arm.

"How the fuck did he get in?"

"I don't know, sir. But he also left a note. Bastard basically threatened the entire department. And..." His voice dropped a notch as if he didn't want to be heard. "He threatened the new chief."

Fear crawled along my spine.

"What?"

"I know, it's weird. But he called her a c—"

"Don't even finish that sentence," I growled. Olivia was mine. I'd be damned if anyone threatened her.

On the line, Thoren cleared his throat. "Sorry, sir. Anyway. We did a drive-by, and she wasn't home. But PD is going to keep watch throughout the night."

"Why is he targeting her? What does she have to do with anything? She wasn't even here when all that went down." I couldn't make it make sense in my head.

"He states, 'Tell the …c-word, to back off' in his note. I guess she's making some waves with the investigator's office and he's aware?" He ended on a questioning note.

I needed to warn Olivia.

"Okay, I know she had a conference thing to go to," I hedged. "So she's probably still out of town. I've got her number. I'll make sure she's aware. But PD still needs to continue with the drive-bys just in case."

"Okay, Captain."

I hung up, assuring him I'd talk to Olivia immediately. For a split second, I sat frozen, watching Rosie play with Buster. Then I whistled and motioned for her to come inside.

Her long hair bounced around her as she raced Buster to the house.

I didn't know who Olivia had pissed off, but somehow, she'd landed squarely in the crosshairs of a very bad guy. He probably assumed, like most people did, that it was just her and Rosie. That she was an easy target.

But what he didn't know was that Olivia was as stubborn as the day was long and as hard-nosed as any person he'd ever met. If she was making waves, it was because someone, somewhere had fucked up and was trying to hide it.

He also didn't know that Olivia had me on her side.

And I'd make sure she and Rosie were safe. Even if it meant moving them in with me.

* * *

"Absolutely not." Her voice rang loud and clear through the kitchen. The high color on her cheeks and the way her fists lay clenched on the table, not to mention the firm set of her jaw, was enough to terrify most people.

But I wasn't most people, and I wasn't taking no for an answer. Gone was the pleasant boat ride, the emotional aftermath of the restaurant, and now a fuming woman sat across from me mere minutes after receiving the news that Loren was back on the loose and she was a target. I wanted to wrap them both in bubble wrap and then hit something. Hard.

"This is the most ridiculous thing I've ever heard. I'm not about to sit by and let some punk-ass threaten me and my daughter and let him run me from my own damn home." Her voice rose with every word, echoing off the bare walls of my lake house.

"Chief—" I was back to calling her by her title because I'd needed to put that distance between us.

"That's right, Captain. I am the chief. And what I say goes."

She was wrong there.

"Olivia," I barked, needing to get her attention, allowing fear to take control. "I'm not your damn subordinate in my own fucking house, so listen up. I'm not taking any chances. You've read the file, but you weren't here when Thoren almost died. You didn't console his girlfriend while we waited. You weren't the one running in to save him from that fire. I've been on the waiting side too many times recently. I'll be damned if I sit by and let you put yourself in harm's way."

"That bastard is bluffing. He's not coming for me." The fire glinting from her eyes would be a beautiful thing under other circumstances. Seeing her all worked up and pissed off did things to me. But I tamped that ridiculous thought down because now was not the time to be thinking of how beautiful Olivia Hawkins was.

I shook my head. "You don't know that, and I'm not taking chances. Think of Rosie. Hell, think of me. If I ever meant anything to you, if she means anything to you, you will trust me on this and let me at least provide you a safer place. Some backup."

Some of the fire went out of her at my words. Her shoulders relaxed to the point that she almost looked defeated.

"If I hide, it will make me look weak. I can't stand looking weak." Her voice was soft, vulnerable.

I pulled out the chair next to hers and sat, placing a hand over her fisted one. "It's not weak to accept help. It's not weak to be safe," I offered. "You and Rosie come to my place. Let me take care of you. Let me be the man my daughter needs me to be."

All my pride bled away as I practically begged her to understand.

She studied our hands for a moment, and then finally, *finally*, she turned hers over in mine and linked our fingers.

"Okay, but we will have to sort this out so that city hall doesn't turn this into something they can use for grounds for dismissal."

I wanted to reassure her and tell her it would all be okay, but I couldn't bring myself to lie to her. So I just squeezed her hand and silently prayed that it would.

Chapter Thirteen

Olivia

"This is ridiculous," I muttered under my breath as I tossed a couple more items into the bag. I'd been muttering the words over and over the entire ride home from the lake house. It was finally Rosie who trumped me into agreeing because I didn't want my daughter to be in danger, and if being with Mac meant she might be a fraction safer, Mac's was where I'd take her.

All my frustration wove tightly around the fact that spending time with him had royally messed with my head. Independent woman? Yes, thank you. Horny and attracted to the silver fox that fathered her daughter? Also yes. Trapped in a situation that meant one of us could lose our jobs if something came of this attraction?

I shook my head because now *I* was being ridiculous.

I was more upset about what might happen if I was forced to spend time with Mac, and how that absolutely could not happen, than I was about being targeted by a killer.

Why?

Because just the minimal amount of time that we'd spent at the lake house had shown me that Mac was still as amazing as I'd remembered.

And everything he did made me want him more. Which was impressive considering I hadn't had much of a sex drive in the past few... years, it seemed.

Being told she's "frigid" would do that to a woman.

Old shame resurfaced at the memory of Tim and me trying—and failing—to talk through our intimacy issues. In the end, it had just been easier to forgo sex than to deal with the problems that came with it.

To him, it didn't matter that my mind wouldn't shut off, ever. Even when we were in bed. *Especially* when we were in bed.

He'd go down on me, and I'd start thinking about a grocery list.

Maybe part of it was that he just wasn't a very skilled lover. But the other part was that I just couldn't get out of my head long enough to enjoy sex.

And then my body had begun shutting down almost, and my doctor told me that if I didn't use it, I'd lose it— meaning the ability to lubricate—and that just made things worse.

The last time we'd tried, Tim had made some snarky comment about my dryness and gave me an unceremonious squirt of cold lube right on my vagina without putting forth any effort to make the act even remotely romantic. Sex became a forced transaction between us, and I resented the hell out of it—and him.

I pulled the vibrator I'd purchased after the divorce from the bedside table. It was rather tame looking compared to the others in the store, but the clerk had called it the tried-and-true go-to. In the two years since the divorce, I'd tried to use it a couple times, had even proven to myself that I could at least experience sexual sensation again.

And absolutely none of that had anything to do with me packing up to go stay with Mac. Even if I felt a flutter of activity low in my belly at the thought of maybe using the vibrator in his house, in sheets that smelled like him. I dropped the vibrator back into the nondescript storage bag in my drawer. And instead, I picked up the small bullet that I'd gotten at the same time and buried it in the inside pocket of my suitcase before I could change my mind.

I zipped the bag and rolled it out to the door with Rosie's. "Are you ready?"

"Almost."

The front door opened, and Mac's head and broad shoulders poked through. "This stuff ready to load?"

I hummed my assent, turning away so he couldn't see the heat burning my cheeks.

Where was my badass attitude? My woman-in-charge mindset?

I was a horndog with zero focus, and he had really great forearm porn.

The real issue was the threats being made against me, and what that meant.

I took a fortifying breath, calling on the focus and intention that had gotten me through the last fifteen years. I could handle the threats and the way the mayor seemed to be sabotaging me. And I could handle staying with Mac for a few nights.

* * *

By the end of the third day, I could admit that I'd been lying when I convinced myself I wouldn't be affected by pretty much constant interaction with Mac. The first night had been mildly awkward on my part, because despite my trying, I couldn't forget about the toy hidden away in my suitcase, and watching Mac be all kinds of capable was a total turn-on. The second night had been equally as awkward, because being in Mac's space while he was on shift just felt wrong. But the third day had been rough.

At work, it was easy to make it through the day without wondering what he and Rosie were doing after school.

Not.

If I stopped to check my phone for a message from him once, I'd done it a hundred times.

By the time I finished up my reports for administration and made it home, the sun was hanging lower, and the late-summer evening was starting to wind down.

Mac and Rosie were on the far side of the small pond in a little boat, fishing poles in the water. Rosie held hers down and out in front of her while Mac showed her how to cast. He demonstrated, and then she took a turn. Her sound of frustration echoed across the water.

I chuckled to myself because he didn't know what he was getting into trying to teach the world's worst sport how to do anything. My child was headstrong, just like me.

With them on the water, I had plenty of time to duck inside to change and get dinner started. I opened the door to the fragrant smell of spices and something in the kitchen. My nose led me to find a slow cooker on the counter, and I lifted the lid. Rosie's favorite meal to make, probably the only meal that she could make—roast with potatoes and carrots—bubbled.

I checked the meat and realized we'd be ready to eat soon. They must've put it in right after school.

A tiny sliver of unease ran through me as I glanced at the two of them on the water.

Not even a week had gone by, and Mac was stepping up... or stepping in.

Already, he'd proven to be the one she was drawn to. They had the same contemplative look and some of the same mannerisms.

And now, he had my normally pristine, diva-ish daughter on the water, teaching her to fish, of all things. I shook my head at my own absurdity. Was I jealous of my fourteen-year-old daughter?

I pushed the troublesome thoughts aside. After changing out of my uniform, I poured a glass of wine and went out to the porch to wait for them.

Buster saw me and took off running, clearly over being left alone on the bank.

This was another thing I was getting used to. Having a dog. I could see where the draw was because he made a good companion. But it was a first for me. I'd never thrown a tennis ball more in my life.

I pitched the ball to him a couple of times and pulled out my phone to check emails. On impulse, I zoomed in and snapped a photo of the two fishermen—fisher*people*, I mentally corrected.

Mac was looking at Rosie, pride etched on his rugged features. Rosie had her arms extended and was intensely concentrating. The whole scene was idyllic and sweet, and it made my heart ache just a little.

The sun was just beginning to set when they docked the boat and made the trek to the house, Rosie hopping along to his steady gait.

Really. The man had no business being so attractive. But from this distance, it was safe for me to notice the way his long legs ate up the ground, the muscles of his thighs playing peekaboo with every step he took. He was steady and sturdy, and I understood the pull my daughter felt to him.

I stood to catch Rosie as she ran up to hug me, face the slightest bit pink from being in the sun. "Hey, Mom! Mac is teaching me to fish."

"Looked like you were having a good time." I gave her a peck on the cheek, smoothing a hand over her unruly hair. Times like this, she let her little girl shine. I'd take it over the surly teenager she could sometimes be.

She ruffled Buster's fur and bounced inside. "I'm going to wash up and finish dinner. Did you see that I cooked, Mom?" The door closed behind her before I could respond.

A deep, masculine chuckle sounded behind me, the effect sending a shiver down my spine and straight to my lady parts. I looked over my shoulder to see him lean a shoulder against the post, his eyes cast down near my ass. Was he checking me out?

I turned to face him, and his gaze tracked up my body like a visceral touch.

"Hey, Chief. How're things at the firehouse?"

He said it like he needed reminding of our situation. Like he was establishing the boundaries between us.

But the heat in his eyes as they met mine told a different story. For a moment, I wished I could bounce into his arms like Rosie had to me. I licked my lips in anticipation of what it would be like to feel that body against mine.

His gaze grew darker, and he pushed off the rail, stalking toward me. I was frozen to the spot, my breath shallow.

Like he'd read my mind, he got closer, close enough I could feel the summer heat coming off him.

"I'm gonna go grab a beer." His arm brushed mine as he reached for the door, and then he was gone. That... was not what I was expecting.

I blew out a breath. *Whew.* He still had whatever it was that made me want him. And I absolutely could not think like that.

Taking a moment to gather my wits, I sank into my rocking chair and picked up the wine glass, draining the last few drops. I sat back with a sigh.

Twilight was one of my favorite times, right after sunset, when the world felt almost suspended. I nudged the rocker in motion with a toe and let the peacefulness of Mac's place sink into me. Of course he'd have two houses on water, two houses situated to enjoy both the sunrise and sunset.

And if I could get past this feeling of want, this little forced vacation could be relaxing.

Suddenly, it hit me. I was feeling things, sexual things. I wanted him. My lips turned up at the realization that maybe I wasn't broken after all like my ex had made me feel. I let the what-ifs run through my mind.

What if I'd leaned forward when he'd drawn close?

What if I'd pressed my lips to his and explored that delicious-looking mouth?

What if I'd brushed his chest as he passed by, or reached out to trail my fingertips across his waist?

The door creaked open, and the man himself stepped through.

What if I wasn't his boss?

It was this last thought that sobered me as he settled into the chair next to me.

He passed me a cold beer and said, "Rosie says supper will be ready in seven minutes."

"That's a very specific time frame," I noted.

The corner of his mouth turned up, his lips full and inviting, and I should not notice his mouth at all.

"She might be preparing you a surprise." The twinkle in his eye did it for me.

"Mac..."

"I'm glad you're both here." He spoke over me. "She's a good kid."

Well, if his admission didn't just stop my arguments right in their tracks.

I recalibrated by saying, "Looked like you two had fun out there."

"Yeah, I'd forgotten how much fun a lazy afternoon of fishing could be. I suppose I owe you a huge thanks for letting me get to know her." He met my gaze then. "I know it can't be easy for you. I'm just letting you know I appreciate it."

Dammit. He had to stop being so amazing.

Why couldn't he be a jerk like Tim?

And how wrong was it to be wishing a crappy father on my daughter? I needed to check myself because this wasn't healthy for anyone.

"She is a good kid. Thank you for noticing. And thank you for spending time with her. As you can tell, it's made her very happy."

Silence filled the void between us.

"She's not the only one, Liv. I'm also glad you're here." He drew a long pull on his beer, my eyes drawn to the spot where his throat flexed as he swallowed.

I didn't know what to say. No one had said anything like that to me in so long. Made me feel appreciated and seen.

Buster nudged my hand, his soppy head leaving a trail of dog hair on my hand. "Ew..."

Mac chuckled, low and sexy, and called, "Buster, come."

Buster took two steps, stopped directly in front of me, and shook off his swim. A shower of doggy-scented pond water sprayed over my legs.

I squealed and drew them back, and Mac busted out laughing. A rich, deep, delicious sound that was worth its weight in gold. His big hand swiped down my leg, and he froze, hand just above my ankle. In slow motion, it seemed, his eyes went to my lips, and his fingers tightened on my ankle.

Every nerve in my body sat up and took notice. Warmth pooled in my belly. I was a breath away from sliding my leg through his hand, urging him to move it north. To touch me. Remind me again of how good it was between us.

"Supper's ready," Rosie called from inside, startling us both and breaking the spell.

Mac stood and offered me a hand to join him. I slid my hand in his and held my breath as I stood, coming so close it wouldn't be anything to press my chest to his. I watched him swallow. Watched his jaw clench. And watched him take a step back to open the door for me.

I also didn't miss the reflexive way his hand fisted as he let go of mine.

I didn't know if I was going to survive staying here, but I was beginning to think going up in flames might just be worth it.

Chapter Fourteen

Mac

Friday afternoons into early evening were an interesting time in late August. With school back in session and vacations completed, people were restless. And the citizens of the city of Newman weren't any different. Traffic in town increased as folks cruised through, looking for their next stop, especially on Friday game nights. Teenagers, and those reliving their teenage years, had a nice one-way, two-lane drag to see and be seen.

Station One, headquarters, located right off the square in downtown, was an old cinderblock building painted a neutral off-white color. The huge parking pad and painted brick retaining wall made the perfect hangout spot for the crew to do some people watching.

"Hey, Captain. What's up? What are you doing here? You get bored out at Four and miss wall-sitting?" Firefighter Cal Roberts, the one guy who always managed to skip his turn at buying rounds at the bar, hitched a leg on the wall so he was half sitting, half standing.

I shifted the toothpick in my mouth. Biting into it was supremely less satisfying than lighting a cigarette.

"Just came by to drop some paperwork off." And possibly see the chief before she headed out, since I'd be spending my night at the station. It was little comfort knowing she'd at least be at my house, though she and Rosie would be alone.

Not for the first time did I feel every one of the long nights ahead. Usually this dread was because I was tired already and knew I faced a long night of calls. But even if we had a blessed zero-call night, I would be awake worrying about the two females at my house. A regular day job held more appeal than ever.

Cal's lips tipped up in a knowing grin as he waggled his eyebrows. "You sure that's all? Word is there's a certain person staying at your house." His eyes flickered up to the area where Olivia's office would be.

This was exactly the kind of bullshit we didn't need.

People assuming and making more of this than it was.

I plucked the toothpick from my mouth, shifted my stance, and let my best glare loose. "You realize that she's been targeted, threatened by the same asshole that put Thoren in the hospital?"

The smug expression on his face faltered, so I drove my point home. "And this same perp killed, excuse me, *allegedly* killed those kids in that fire earlier this year." I stuck the toothpick back in my mouth, planted my hands on my hips, and looked at him like the dumbass he was. "If you've got something you want to ask me, here's your chance. Otherwise, you need to quit making assumptions."

"Sorry, Capt."

I grunted in acknowledgment of his apology and crossed

my arms over my chest, forcibly shifting my focus to the passing traffic.

The problem was, he wasn't wrong.

I was making more trips downtown than I had in the entire year before she'd come on board. Granted, they were all valid reasons. But still.

Obviously, people were talking.

And where gossip went, attention went, and she had enough on her from administration already, without these bozos adding to it.

A beat-up older-model red Toyota cruised by, a bevy of female voices and loud rock music pouring through the open windows. As they passed, the driver honked the horn multiple times. Cal, like an idiot, tossed up his hand.

"Mistake," I muttered, watching as the car hit the left lane to make the loop back through town.

"What? I'm just being friendly."

I shook my head. He'd learn.

Not five minutes later, the red car hit the lane closest to the station, the passenger leaning halfway out the window. "I've got a fire... in my pants!"

I chuckled quietly. "See what I mean? That's trouble, with a capital T, cruising around in that car."

Cal's smirk returned. "Yes, sir, it is."

Tones dropped, echoing from our radios and through the speakers in the bay behind us. We listened to the call-out for Station Four, and I headed to my pickup. The address was familiar.

I beat the engine to Francis O'Malley's house to find a frantic Leah Miller on the front porch waving at me. Leah was the fiancée of Fire Marshal Mike Harrison, and Mrs. O'Malley had become the adopted grandmother of their group. On occasion, I'd spent time with the sweet elderly lady. She was an incorrigible flirt, loved a good romance novel, and was a staunch supporter of the annual fundraiser calendar.

"Mac. Thank God it's your crew. Maybe you can deal with this stubborn old woman."

I mounted the steps two at a time, noting the pinched lines at Leah's eyes. Regardless of her frustration, she was concerned for her friend.

"What happened?"

Leah led me down a long hallway of the older house, the wood floors creaking in places and our footsteps echoing off the high ceiling.

"She fell. Swears she didn't hurt herself, but she can't move. She called me to come help her up. I called 911 when I got here and realized how bad it is."

"You hush your mouth, missy. It's not that bad."

I rounded the doorway to find Francis splayed on the floor, leg jutted at an awkward angle. A hip dislocation at best, broken at worst.

"Hey, Mrs. O'Malley."

"Hey yourself, Mr. December. And it's Francis." She tried to smirk, but pain laced her features.

"Looks like you took a little spill." I kept my tone gentle, conversational, but my instincts kicked into overdrive. At her age, a fall like this could lead to so many more life-threatening problems. I needed to assess her more thoroughly, but I'd wait for the others before trying to stabilize and move her. Chances were, she'd pass out from pain if I tried.

"Aw, I got tripped up in these silly slippers. This hard floor isn't very forgiving. I just need a little hand up, if you don't mind."

I dropped to a knee beside her and placed a staying

hand on her shoulder. "Just hang tight until the others get here, to be on the safe side."

"Well, don't get yourself all dirty on my behalf. Leah, get the man a chair, for heaven's sake."

From the doorway, Leah made an exasperated noise. If I didn't get her out of here, these two would start bickering, and keeping Francis calm was key.

"Actually, I need Leah to go make sure the guys know where you live. Leah?" I looked over my shoulder and gave her a pointed look. "Can you go wait for the ambulance for me? I'm gonna hang here and keep Mrs. O'Malley company."

Leah's expression softened and she nodded. "Okay."

"Now, you're not going to have to cut my clothes off me, are you?" Francis sounded almost hopeful. "Because I don't want you cutting my good bra. Just unhook it like a good boy."

I froze, suspended in shock. Pretty sure my mouth dropped open as I stared at my elderly patient. Under any other circumstance, I would've been able to hold my composure, remain stoic and professional. But Francis had always had the ability to both take me by surprise and make me blush.

Leah made a sound of disbelief. "No one is cutting any clothes off. Behave, Francis."

"Leah, medics," I reminded her and then continued my assessment.

"You seem to be tolerating the pain pretty well," I stated. Francis really was in a good state considering the circumstances.

"Probably that edible I took this morning," she replied with a wry grin.

The medics arrived and packaged Francis, and together,

we lifted her onto the stretcher and loaded her in the ambulance.

In the meantime, Leah gathered bags, her voice echoing down the hall as she made a series of calls, first to Mike, then to her best friend, Kylie, and then to Jordan, Nate's girlfriend.

This community of friends, this family they'd built, was unexpected. It was good that they had each other in times like this, and I was fortunate that they included me from time to time.

We met out on the porch, and I walked Leah to the ambulance. Francis was loaded, Nate and Thoren hanging out at the open back doors, watching over the old woman like nervous parents.

"Bye, sweetheart. We'll come check on you later. Jordan's on her way already," Nate called before closing the doors. They each took a step back as the bus pulled away, and Leah sidled up to Thoren, who threw an arm around her shoulders.

"Is it broken?" The concern in her voice turned Thoren's head.

"Most likely."

Standing by like this always made me feel like the worst kind of interloper. I should be used to it by now, but this patient was special, and the situation hit the group hard. They all loved this old woman, and it was a damned good thing she had them in her life for situations like this.

A little seed of something unpleasant planted itself in my mind. If I were in her place, who would even know to come look after me? The guys didn't call me daily to check in on me. Sure, if they needed something, they knew to call because I was always there for them.

But what if the roles were reversed?

Would anyone come take care of me in the hospital? Or was I in for a long, lonely life in my senior years?

Shoving those thoughts aside, because wallowing never did anyone any good, I ordered, "You guys get back in service. Thoren, see if Mike is available to take Leah."

"I already talked to him, sir. He's in the middle of an interview. He said he'd meet her there later."

I sighed. I couldn't in good conscience leave her to drive there alone. She was too upset. So even though the command unit was supposed to be city personnel only, I said, "I'll drive Leah over."

The drive was mostly silent until I pulled under the awning at the hospital. Leah reached for the door handle and paused, before looking back at me. "I've always thought you were the best kind of man, Mac. You don't have me fooled. You're this gruff meanie on the outside. But I know there is a heart of gold under that rough exterior."

What was I supposed to say to that?

"I don't know why some good woman hasn't snatched you up. But I hope you find someone who will take care of you as well as you take care of others."

Then she was out of the truck and disappearing through the sliding doors of the emergency room waiting area, leaving me with a tight chest and a throat I couldn't swallow through.

Images of Olivia and Rosie flashed in my mind. What would my life have been like if Olivia and I had kept contact over those years? If I'd been able to raise my daughter? If I'd had a family of my own? Would I still feel like an outsider, a fraud, in this found family?

The fire brotherhood was out of my reach even in the normal day-to-day. Sure, we pulled together when shit hit the fan, but largely, it was me calling on my crew when bad things went down. I got it. It was hard to be friends with the boss.

But what would it feel like to have someone care about me? To check in with me daily like these people did with each other?

The thought left me unsettled.

I picked up the phone to call home. Hearing Rosie's voice might settle some of this unease. I was supposed to be the mentor, though. Not the other way around. I was being ridiculous. It was too soon to feel this invested, to need Olivia and Rosie like I did. I hadn't had a family in so long, I was grasping at the closest straw. This feeling, this want, was just my tender heart being stupid. I laid the phone back in the truck seat, shifted into gear, and drove back to the station.

Chapter Fifteen

Olivia

"The courthouse was originally built in 1904 and renovated in 1975."

It was Friday afternoon, and I'd been invited to tour the historic landmark with Fire Marshal Harrison and City Manager Bloom. Bloom was giving me a history lesson, while Harrison asked the technical questions.

"And there was no damage when the tornado came through?" I asked. I'd done my research on the EF4 tornado that blazed a mile-wide path through the three counties, covering nearly thirty-eight miles.

"None," Bloom replied. "We were very fortunate. Four blocks north, and this building would've been destroyed."

The massive structure covered an entire city block. The exterior was red masonry, and a massive copper dome housed the clock that chimed every hour. The interior had a high ceiling and wood-paneled walls, polished to a shine and reflecting the sunlight coming through from all four entrances. An ornate dual staircase led to the second-floor courtroom, with historic wooden pews and more wood panels.

"This old wooden interior is a tinderbox if a fire ever gets started in here," I noted.

Harrison nodded in agreement, making a note on his ever-present clipboard.

"The records indicate that the sprinkler system was updated?" Harrison asked.

Bloom hesitated before saying, "Yes."

Harrison stopped writing and looked at the city manager. "You don't sound very positive about that."

"Problem is, there's a narrow passageway into the clock tower, and we've had trouble getting water to that area."

"That's why we have our brave men and women of the fire department." Mayor Smith's voice echoed off the marble floor. "You don't need to worry, Cornelius. Chief Hawkins's crews can handle any disaster." The round mayor turned toward a slim bespectacled young man following him. The guy sported a press badge.

"Henry, meet Chief Hawkins. First lady fire chief we've ever had. Henry here is an intern for the newspaper, doing his first big article about the city government," Smith bragged.

Henry's face turned pink under the attention. "It's nice to meet you. Chief Hawkins, I was hoping to meet with you to discuss any agendas you might have for the fire department."

Timid, a little bit like a fish out of water, Henry offered me a surprisingly firm handshake.

I smiled at him. "My main agenda is to improve our equipment and safety gear."

"Now, Chief..." Smith gave me his politician smile. The placating one that I hated, all the while looking at the men around me with an expression of *forgive her ignorance.* "You know we try to do the best we can with the limited funds we have. But, by all means, feel free to update what you can within the current funding amount."

Tension rippled through my shoulders. They'd spent all my money before I could even get started. I clenched my jaw to keep from spouting out all the ways the department's budget had been mishandled previously.

"Fire Marshal Harrison, do you have any updates on the arson case?" Henry asked.

Harrison made another mark on his clipboard. "Nope."

"Oh, come now. Give the boy a kernel of information," Smith demanded. I wanted to step on that shiny polished boot of his and tell him to stuff it. He didn't get to boss my staff around.

"Marshal Harrison's investigation is ongoing and not for public record at this time." I forced an icy current into my tone. Every time I was around the mayor, I could literally feel my blood pressure spiking.

Smith glared at me. Offended that I blatantly disobeyed his demand.

"Well, this is your notice to get prepared. I expect a public announcement next week. The citizens need to be aware of what's happening in their community."

Smith gave handshakes to the men, ignoring me as he ushered his young charge toward the staircase and presumably the historic courtroom.

"Thanks for the deflection, Chief. The mayor's office has been pushing me on this case."

"Why?" Bloom, who'd remained silent and out of the attention zone while the mayor had been busting my balls, asked.

"No idea, other than Smith's push to be in the media

spotlight. Small-town paper is one thing. But a story like this will bring the Atlanta news stations down and give him some camera time."

I scoffed. "Why in the world does he want our crime in the spotlight?" More ridiculous posturing and grandstanding.

Bloom sighed. "I don't understand why he thinks he's the face of the city anyway. We have a media relations person for that."

Harrison raised a brow. "Sounds like the mayor needs to take a step back and let people do their jobs."

Bloom gave a half snort. "He's just mad because he got out voted in hiring the chief. He wanted to give the job to someone else."

Clarity was a beautiful thing. "Let me guess. His choice was a buddy of his."

Bloom gave a singular nod. And just like that, I had my answers. I was fighting a losing battle with Smith because I wasn't one of his good old boys.

From the courthouse, I dropped Bloom at city hall, and Harrison at headquarters. Finally alone, I rolled my shoulders, trying to shrug off the aggravation that was dealing with the mayor. I just had to keep my head down, keep working for the good of my department. With that in mind, I pointed the car toward Mac's and planned for a girls' night with my daughter.

Mac

I pulled up to the house on Saturday morning after running calls all night to find Olivia had parked in my normal spot, forcing me to pull into the yard or take a chance on blocking her in.

Why this irritated me, I couldn't tell.

I expected Buster to run and greet me, then remembered he was probably holed up in bed with Rosie.

Damn traitor.

All I wanted was to go inside, grab a shower, and kick back on my couch with a good book for a little while. Then maybe I'd go work in the shop. I didn't want to face Olivia and her sexy body. Or Rosie and her perky, sometimes-pesky teenage attitude. I didn't want to talk about Taylor Swift or boys or fishing. I wanted some damn sleep.

I opened the truck door and landed in a puddle, mud kicking up my pants legs and seeping through my shoes.

Dammit.

I trudged up the porch, stomping my feet to shake off some of the mud.

The screen door squeaked as I pulled it open. I needed to fix that today.

I juggled my work bag and travel coffee cup to pull my keys free. They slipped out of my hand, and when I stooped to pick them up, coffee poured all over me.

"Son of a bitch." My voice blasted the quiet of the morning.

Fuck, I was tired.

I managed to get inside without dropping or stepping in anything else and left everything by the front door.

From there, I headed straight to the couch. To hell with the shower. My joints gave a sigh of relief as I stretched out and pulled the blanket over me.

Somewhere in the swirl of a deep dream came quiet feminine voices, the jangle of Buster's dog collar. I rolled over, pulling the blanket over my head to block out the light. The screen door squeaked, and then blessed silence. I sank into blissful sleep again.

The mouthwatering smell of bacon pulled me back from the depths of a dream where a certain curvy brunette lay spread on the deck of my boat, sunning herself.

The clink of utensils, followed by the sizzle of something hitting the pan sounded from my kitchen.

I stretched with a groan and got a nose full of doggy kisses in the process. I wiped my face with a hand and then gave my best boy a head scratch. "Hey, buddy." God, my voice was scratchy.

I cleared my throat and sat up, blinking away sleep.

The house looked the same, but it felt... different. There were smells and sounds to replace the normal quiet solitude. I stood with a good, long stretch and followed my nose to the kitchen.

Rosie flipped something in a pan while Olivia supervised. Their bond was sweet. It was in the way they met each other's gaze, with soft smiles and gentle shoulder bumps. A deep longing to be in the middle of that scene bloomed in my chest. I wanted to be on the receiving end of those sweet smiles, those soft touches.

I hated to interrupt but also didn't need to stand there creeping on their sentimental moment. An image of standing on the edges of Thoren and Leah's conversation about Mrs. O'Malley flashed in my head. Was I always going to be on the outside looking in? But this felt different. This felt like they were mine. And I was theirs, and we were sharing a life. What would it be like to have Rosie and Olivia chatting and making my house a home long term?

I needed to respect their intimacy and go back to the couch. Maybe pick up my book or find a show to watch.

But I couldn't drag myself away. I was inexplicably drawn to these two, so instead of doing the right thing, I interrupted my house guests. "Morning."

They turned to me, and the happiness radiating from them sucked the breath from my lungs. I had the two most beautiful women in the world in my kitchen, and neither were truly mine.

Olivia's expression fell as she took me in. I should probably wipe the scowl off my face.

Rosie broke the silence first with a giggle. "It's noon, sleepyhead." She rolled her eyes at Olivia. "And you thought I was bad."

Olivia faked a smile and ruffled Rosie's ponytail affectionately. "Those are ready to flip." She turned to me. "Long night?"

I scratched the back of my head, wondering if she could see the balloon filling my chest. "Yeah. We ran thirteen calls from midnight to eight a.m."

She nodded to the table, avoiding looking at me directly. "Well then, have a seat. Rosa Nell has prepared a treat for you." Her smiles with Rosie had been as radiant as the sun shining through the windows, wrapping around my heart and replacing the thick sludge in my chest with something so light and sweet, I couldn't dare to even think of it. Now that happiness was gone after one look at me. And all I wanted was to see it again.

So I sat.

Olivia brought me coffee, and Rosie served up a plate of the best-looking French toast I'd ever seen. My mouth watered. "This looks amazing, sweetheart."

They both froze for half a second. And then fixed their own plates and joined me at the table.

"Not a bad brunch, is it, MacDaddy?" Rosie said around a mouthful.

The forkful of food I was shoveling into my face froze, suspended in mid-shovel.

"What did you call me?" All the blood drained from my head.

"MacDaddy."

"You can't call me that." The words stuttered out.

"Rosie, you can't call him that," Olivia echoed.

"Sure I can. It's who you are." Rosie was the picture-perfect image of nonchalance, alternating between forkfuls of toast and bacon. "You're Mac, and you're my daddy." This was said around a mouthful of bacon, and though her words were mumbled, they rang loud and clear. My fork landed on my plate, and I struggled to breathe. There was no way in hell this child could call me that. Now, her mom... yeah, I didn't need to go there.

"Rosie, honey. I don't know if Mac is ready for that just yet. You guys don't really know each other that way yet," Olivia said, her voice rigid as she tried to be the voice of reason. I couldn't tell if she was mad or just had her guard up, but suddenly, between the stilted facial expressions and now the tone in her voice, it felt like she was wearing her ice-princess armor against me.

Rosie lifted a shoulder at her mother's advice, still scarfing down food, oblivious to the riot she'd unleashed inside me and the tension brewing between me and Livvie. I kept my expression impassive but couldn't manage to stop the tremble of my hand as I reached for a sip of coffee. I really could stand to add a shot of something stronger to this cup.

"It's the truth, though. 'Sides, he already feels like more of my dad than that ass Tim ever did."

I couldn't stop the tug at the corner of my lips. My girl was always pushing her mother's buttons.

My girl.

"Plus, Mac doesn't mind, do you MacDaddy?" Rosie

drew the words out, making the nickname sound ridiculous. But there was no way she could call me that; it sounded... wrong. All kinds of wrong.

I cleared my throat twice, trying to make an audible sound. "Rosie, kiddo." I kept my voice gentle, because as much as the name made me uncomfortable, I didn't want to hurt her feelings. It was ironic that I was feeling this sentimental and emotional, that I was even considering her feelings when any other time in my life, I'd just say what I needed to say. Regardless, she was an impressionable young woman, and I needed to handle her with care.

"Sweetheart," she prompted.

"You can't call me sweetheart, either."

Rosie blushed, eyes dropping to her plate. "No, that's what you call me."

Now I was the one blushing, because I had and hadn't even realized it at the time.

"Okay, time-out." I lifted my hands in surrender. "Your mom is right. We need to chill on this a little."

Rosie's head flew up, wide, accusing eyes aimed at her mother. I'd heard all the warnings of teenage girls' mood swings, but witnessing the switch from gentle, happy teenage girl to instant brat was shocking.

"But," I continued, and her eyes darted back to me. Her brattiness quelled just a bit. "It's also true that we have this weird... I don't know, easy friendship starting."

The words were lacking, and I knew it. I just couldn't do more in the moment. It would open me up too much. Give away too much.

I still didn't know how much Olivia was on board with this relationship thing, or what it would mean for us. And hadn't it been just this morning that I'd been frustrated with having to share my space?

"So, what does that mean?" Rosie prompted when I stayed silent a moment too long.

The longing in her voice pierced the last wall I'd built, the little bit of my heart that hadn't been ripped out and trampled on years before.

"It means you're my daughter. We're spending time together. Getting to know each other. I'm here for you. And all you have to do is be a kid, and trust that whatever happens, *all* you have to do is be a kid. Your mom and I will take care of you. You don't have to force labels or nick-names, or categorize what we are to each other."

Rosie's expression changed, confusion flittering across her pretty face as she sat back, absorbing my words. Olivia spun her mug on the table, peering at it as if it had all the answers to all the problems we faced.

I leaned back, allowing them both time to think. I looked around my kitchen, noting that towels I'd never seen before hung on the oven door. And a wooden plaque with the word *Home* stenciled in the center now sat in my kitchen window, next to a potted plant with dainty yellow flowers pointed toward the sun. In place of the old, worn coffee tin, there was a new container on the counter holding my spatulas and spoons.

All around my kitchen were little touches of them making my space nicer, homier.

They'd even cleaned up the mess I'd dumped at the front door when I got in.

"You guys went shopping for more than groceries this morning," I said, that bubble of appreciation swelling in my chest again, making it hard to breathe.

Olivia sat straighter and seemed almost... embarrassed. "We wanted to do something nice as a thank-you for letting us stay here."

I'd been to their house and had seen what they'd started over with—next to nothing. What they'd done for me, when they still had so much to furnish in their own space, humbled me.

"It's nice. Thank you."

Rosie shared a long look with her mom, sharing some secret. I wanted to know all their secrets.

Olivia dragged her gaze away and focused on me again. "You're welcome." Her voice had lost that casual ease and was tense again. "It's not much, but we appreciate you looking out for us."

"So, does this mean I can't call you MacDaddy?" Rosie clarified.

"Yes," Olivia and I said in unison.

Rosie rolled her eyes and pushed to stand. "Y'all are no fun. All right, I'll go with Mac, but I reserve the right to call you old man, or maybe even old fart, every once in a while."

I chuckled because she was stubborn if she was anything, and that trait came straight from me.

I cleared the brunch mess while the girls went to drag in more bags. When they turned to make a second trip for even more, I wondered how much damage they could do in such a short period of time.

Then I whistled for Buster and headed to the shop.

An hour or more passed before a rustle at the door drew my attention. Olivia stood in shadow at the open door, her curves highlighted in the perfect way to make my mouth instantly dry. I didn't know what it was about her—maybe it was my memories making this attraction to her that much more—but whatever it was had my pulse kicking up.

She strolled across the shop floor, her gaze roaming around the space, taking it all in.

I dropped the tool I'd been holding and grabbed a rag. Wiping my hands, I turned to face her.

"Sorry for the interruption," she began, crossing her arms, that instant barrier forming as if she needed that protective wall to hide behind. "Rosie is enthralled with her YouTube videos, and I thought I might have a moment to chat with you privately."

I gestured to a stool by the worktable. "Have a seat. What's on your mind?"

Her gaze flittered around the space, landing briefly on the place where I did my woodworking, then the wood stove in the corner, before she straightened and drew her attention back to me.

She cleared her throat, and I almost felt sorry for her. She sat so stiffly, so ramrod straight, I could probably bounce a quarter off her shoulders. Whatever was on her mind must be really bothering her.

I drew a stool close to her and sat, my legs splayed wide on either side of her, and leaned my arm along the wood table behind her.

"Talk to me, Liv."

Those gorgeous eyes that had drawn me in the moment we met held mine. She turned slightly, her hips brushing the inside of my thigh. I had to work to not lean closer.

Her hand rose to cup my cheek, fingers dancing across the hair at my temple. "This is a good look for you. Really suits the whole MacDaddy, silver-fox vibe." She watched her fingers play, while I had a hell of a time trying to catch my breath at her touch.

"She cannot call me that." *You could, though.* The thought reverberated in my brain, and I couldn't let it go. I had to stop this train. Her eyes dropped to my mouth. And then she licked her lips. She was so close... I could lean just the slightest bit and kiss her.

As if my desire willed it, she moved just a fraction toward me.

And that was all it took.

My lips landed on hers. She spun fully into me and met me there. I was already halfway to the point of forgetting everything except this woman and her glorious mouth.

I wrapped my arms around her, pulling her close, but it wasn't enough. I needed more. I stood, slipping my hands to her hips, and lifted her, setting her on the waist-high workbench. Stepping between her parted legs, I lost myself to her.

How long had it been since I'd felt anything close to this fire Liv and I shared?

Her fingers gripped my hair, tugging me where she wanted me. The table put her at the perfect height for me to grind into her, the hardest part of me pressing into the softest part of her. There was no time lost, no space between us, nothing but irritating clothes stopping me from absolutely burying myself in her.

My hand snaked up her neck, where I spread my fingers to feel her pulse while we kissed as though our lives depended on it. Like all the years lost to us meant nothing. She kissed me back with a fever that lit my soul on fire.

Open-mouthed, with dancing tongues and racing heartbeats.

With one hand, she cupped my head, pulling me into her as the other skated down my back like she, too, couldn't get enough.

I was ready to take her right then and there. Damn the dirty shop, the sawdust, and the tools scattered around. None of it mattered. All that mattered was this moment, with this woman. It was so right. Her in my arms. Tasting her. Dry humping her in my workshop.

With a hand to my chest, she pushed me away, both of us breathing hard. That little niggle of doubt at her backing away sent me into a free fall. I didn't want to fall. Didn't want the crash that I knew would come.

But it was too late. I'd lost my heart the moment I laid eyes on her again.

I rested my forehead on hers and closed my eyes, sinking into this bliss. "Liv, what's going on."

"I don't know what's going on," she whispered.

"But something is, isn't it?"

She nodded.

"But is it a good thing?" I shouldn't have kissed her like that. No good could come from us being together because, in the end, it would mean me having to give up my retirement or her having to quit her job. Or her leaving. "You've been kinda tense. And beyond the job thing, until just now, I've gotten the feeling that you didn't want to be here. Is it so bad staying in my house?"

Something in those words must have struck a nerve because she stiffened in my arms and pushed me away.

"Besides the fact that I'm being threatened, the job thing is key, Mac." She slipped down from her perch on the worktable and brushed off her pants, avoiding my gaze. "We both know that, because of our jobs, a relationship beyond co-parents can't happen. Aside from that, yeah. I'm a lot stressed about all the other bullshit happening around me. Smith, this arsonist. Trying to make changes in the department on a shoestring budget. So yeah. I'm kinda tense."

Old, ugly memories of another rejection surfaced with her words. Another woman who pushed me away, left me standing alone with my heart in my hands.

In a way, I was grateful for the rigid stance Olivia had. It'd make keeping the distance between us a little easier.

But no matter how hard I tried, she was under my skin, and I had to learn to deal with it for the sake of Rosie.

"Anyway, I came here to thank you for being so gentle with Rosie this morning. She's trying really hard to please you."

I sighed and let go of the repressed memories that tried to surface, of the confusing mix of frustration and heat that Olivia so easily fueled, and focused on my daughter. "I know. I probably came off as a jerk. I didn't mean to. I'd been up all night and was exhausted when I came in."

Olivia nodded her acceptance at my apology. "Understandable, and that's what I told her."

Her hand reached out toward my chest, pausing, hovering just near my heart. "You're a good man, Mac Collins. And you already have her heart. I'm asking you to have a care with it." Her fingers tapped lightly on my chest, punctuating her words, before sliding away.

It was all I could do to stand and watch her walk away, knowing she took the half of my heart that Rosie didn't already hold with her.

Chapter Sixteen

Olivia

Try as I might, I couldn't get past that day in the workshop. The next week, things remained stilted between Mac and me. The almost brushes in the hall, him usually shirtless, were becoming unbearable. I'd even thought about busting out the bullet vibrator I'd stashed in the front pocket of my suitcase, but I was scared he'd hear the buzz and figure out my secret. Until one morning I was over being sexually frustrated and snapped at him.

"Put a fricking shirt on, for Christ's sake! There's a young girl in this house."

Unfortunately, I'd hurt myself in the process, because he did, in fact, begin wearing a shirt, and he also began avoiding me more. Stealing away in his bedroom, the one I had to pass on the way to my guest room. And somehow, the distance grew more charged; the more I avoided him, the more I noticed him.

I was definitely not touching myself while replaying

that kiss in my mind. Or the way he lifted me so easily, placing me where he wanted me. And I absolutely was *not* thinking about how incredibly turned on I'd been—until he brought up me being tense. I'd been damn proud of myself for not stumbling as I basically ran away.

His words had hurt. I knew I was tense. Hell, after all that I'd been through, anyone would be.

The thing was, Mac calling attention to my stress was too close to how Tim used to make me feel. And I wasn't going to try for a second chance to prove to him that I wasn't frigid or tense. I'd gone that route with Tim, and it had blown up in my face.

"Mom?" Rosie slid in beside me while I was putting on makeup the Friday after that thing that didn't happen in his workshop.

"What's up?"

"Are things okay with you and Mac?"

I focused on my mascara. "Sure, honey," I lied. I hated lying to my daughter, but I also didn't want to get her hopes up on a "ship," as she called it, between me and Mac. "Why?"

She shrugged. "It's just felt kinda weird around here lately. It's like y'all keep avoiding each other. If one of you comes into the room, the other leaves."

"We're fine, honey. I'm sure Mac is ready for us to get out of his hair, and I'm ready to get back to our place."

"Why?" Her eyebrows shot to her forehead, her chin jerking back in shock. "You don't like it here?"

"Of course I do." Truth was, I loved Mac's house. It was peaceful and quiet, and I found myself relaxing more and enjoying my time with Rosie while leaving the work behind. But... "It's a great place, but we can't stay here forever. We need to make a plan."

"Has that bad guy been caught?"

"Well, no."

"But it's safe for us to suddenly leave? I thought the whole reason we were here was because of him?"

She had me there. "No other threats have been made. The police think it's safe to assume that he was just doing it for attention." I didn't know how I felt about that. I didn't fully trust the PD investigation's lead and was waiting on confirmation from Harrison before I put my daughter in harm's way. I'd trust my guy over the police chief and mayor any day. It'd been months that the PD's lead investigator had been searching for Watkins, and why he suddenly felt like things were fine left me unsettled.

Rosie leaned against the counter, shoulders slumped, looking positively dejected.

"Do you think Mac would let me come stay when we move back to the townhouse?"

My heart squeezed at her request. Losing a little piece of her was a knife to the heart. Still, I couldn't blame her for wanting to be here, to be with Mac. And I wouldn't deny her the opportunity, no matter how much it hurt me.

"I'm sure he would love that, honey." It was the truth, because for every step away that Mac and I took, he and Rosie grew closer.

"Now, run and go get ready for school, or we'll be late." I shooed her away so I could have a moment to let the tears brim.

Then I shook it off and went to face my next challenge of the day.

* * *

"Chief Hawkins, this budget request is ridiculous." Mr. Bloom was sounding more and more like Mayor Smith, and neither of them were supportive now that I was settling into my role. "The city manager's office cannot present an increase this large."

He shoved the document away, the spiral ring scraping against the conference table. He'd probably scratched the glossy surface of the ostentatious table.

I'd come to hate the conference room at city hall and the man sitting across from me. He and the mayor represented every man who had ever pushed me down and held me back. Every time I'd come here, they'd acted like I was beneath them.

"I respect your position, Sir. However, please note the chart on page two of the section titled Support." I flipped the pages in my own report and began reading out statistics. "The proposed budget merely represents an increase from the current budget. However, if you look at the reference years, the proposed budget is in fact equivalent to that year. I am requesting for our budget to be restored to the former level. I noted during my research that the grounds and beautification division increase last year is the exact amount that was removed from the fire department. Certainly, the citizens will appreciate their fire service as much as having flowerpots lining the downtown sidewalks."

Across from me, Bloom's face grew red. I'd done my research. I knew that he was the reason for the transfer of the budget and that his wife's florist supplied all the flowers and had won the contract for maintenance. That deal was worth quite a bit of money, especially for a florist who had been small time and operated mainly from their household until they were "lucky" enough to win the city contract.

"You'll notice that most of the increase is all local match

on grant funding that I'm seeking to secure. Which means more bang for our buck." I had zero faith he would understand without a clear breakdown. But calling out the grounds contract had earned his attention, and he began flipping through the rest of my proposal. I didn't want him to be the same "yes man" that I'd met in every administration I'd worked in.

"Sir, if I may be frank, I don't want us to be adversaries." I tapped the document in front of me. "I want an advocate, a supporter, an ally in making the fire department the best it could be for the citizens. I've spoken to Public Safety Foundation. I've made a few connections. And I'm willing to work hard to find the funding we need. But the simple fact of the matter is, if you restore our budget, we can work toward improving our ISO rating, which will mean lower insurance costs for the citizens, which means they are happy with the leaders they've elected to govern their community." The reelection of said leaders, I left implied.

"Thank you for your proposal, Chief Hawkins. The budget team will review, and you'll be allowed a chance at rebuttal if they determine any changes need to be made."

He ushered me to the door, and I clipped down the hall, not knowing if he was on my side or not.

"Hey, Chief, here're your messages." Cathy handed me a stack of Post-it notes once I got back to headquarters. I flipped through them, heading into my office.

Between the notes and the blinking voicemail indicator, I had hours' worth of calls to return and a late night ahead of me.

My head was throbbing and my eyes burned as I pressed play on the last message.

"Stop the investigation, you stupid cunt."

The message was less than three seconds long.

A blip, where time seemed to stand still.

And when reality returned, the hair on the back of my neck stood and my heart thundered.

"Cathy!"

She barreled around the door.

"Get Harrison on the phone and let him know his arsonist left me a voicemail. Find out what buttons he pushed."

I picked up the phone and dialed the back line I had for the chief of police. "Chief Dennis, I received a message from the subject of our arson investigation."

By midafternoon, it was determined that the call had been placed from somewhere in Oregon. More than a day's drive or a half day of air travel away. The PD determined that due to the distance, it was an empty threat. So when Rosie called and asked permission to stay the night at her friend Shae's house so they could binge-watch their latest TV series after the football game, I agreed. Mainly because Shae's father was a police officer. I didn't mention the call to Rosie, but I did update Shae's dad.

By the time I pulled up at Mac's, exhaustion lay heavy in my bones. Nighttime had fallen, and a chorus of summer bugs serenaded my journey up the porch steps. Buster greeted me when I pushed through the door.

I dropped my things on the table and kicked off the blasted high heels right inside the front door. I normally tried to keep my things tidy and organized, especially since we were guests at Mac's. But tonight, I just couldn't find it in me to care.

Dim lamplight illuminated the den, spilling over and throwing the kitchen into shadows. I rounded the corner and lost the last of my capacity to function.

Mac lay on the couch, one arm behind his head, propping him up, and one leg stretched out, the other bent, resting against the back of the couch. He'd been reading a book.

The whole vision of him was so mouthwateringly sexy, I couldn't help myself. I gave in to temptation and let my gaze linger on his bare feet, his faded jeans. The white unbuttoned shirt that fell open, exposing his bare chest.

The book that lay face down there.

The reading glasses he held in his hand, propped on his hip.

The tousled salt-and-pepper hair.

The smirk that played on his lips.

He shifted, causing a ripple effect on his abs. The sound in the back of my throat was involuntary. If a man, any man, but especially this man, wanted to turn a woman on, all he had to do was exactly what Mac was doing.

His pose was relaxed and casual, but the message in his gaze was pure seduction.

"Rough day?" His gravelly voice was deeper, more intimate. And despite how I normally tried to hold things together, in this moment, I wanted to sink between his legs on the couch and rest my head on his chest and just let him hold me.

As it was, all I could do was nod.

He swung his legs around in a slick move that brought him to sitting and held out a hand to me. "Come here."

I stumbled over and stood stupidly, waiting on his next direction.

He scooted over, patting the couch. "Sit."

I did, and he reached down, taking my ankle in his large, warm hand, spinning me so that I had no choice but to recline in the warm space he'd left.

His thumb pressed into the arch of my foot as he began to massage. A deep moan of satisfaction rose involuntarily.

In all the years I'd been married, Tim had never rubbed my feet for me, but it was probably the most caring thing a person could do for another. At this moment it was, anyway.

I closed my eyes in bliss as Mac rubbed one foot, then placed it gently in his lap and began on the other. When I was suitably relaxed, the massage inched up toward my ankles. Then my calves. I immediately tensed at his touch.

"Relax, Olivia. You don't have to be in charge here." Mac's low voice washed over me and settled right between my legs. "You don't have to think. You don't have to do anything, except let me take care of you."

I took his advice. When thoughts of the day tried to creep in, it was Mac's hands that I focused on. His comfy couch supporting me, his presence calming me. The evening was warm, the house quiet.

Eventually, the day's worries drained away, replaced by a new thought.

"Why the change of heart?" The question came out soft, so soft I wasn't sure he'd heard me.

Mac continued his assault on the muscles in my legs. "Change of heart?"

I twitched as he hit a tight spot on my calf. Immediately, his hands were there, gentler but still firm. And so warm. As if his body heat were seeping into mine through his fingertips.

"Yeah, last weekend you called me tense and basically rejected me." My tone was teasing, but only to hide the scary truth. His rejection had hurt.

"Liv, I didn't reject you. Trust me. I want nothing more than to be right here with you, with my hands on you. Even if it's to soothe tired legs after a long day. I've been avoiding you all week because I was afraid I couldn't control myself."

Oh.

Oh.

His hands made a long sweep from my knee to my ankle.

"Besides," he continued, "you were the one who walked away."

Something in those words struck a chord, and I realized that I'd hurt his feelings as well. My eyes shot up to his face to find his eyes glued to where his hands warmed my skin.

"Sometimes I'm too cold and closed off for my own good," I admitted.

Another long sweep, this one deeper, slower, hitting all the little muscles of my calves. I groaned in pleasure.

"Who told you that?"

As focused as I was on what his hands were doing, I didn't even stop to weigh my words. "Tim called me frigid. You struck a nerve when you called me tense."

"So we're both in the wrong," he pointed out. I began to nod, but he continued, "What I can't figure out, is what he meant by that."

I blushed to the roots of my hair. "You know what he meant."

"But I need to hear you tell me."

I swallowed my pride and admitted, "Things weren't that great between us in the bedroom. I always had trouble... getting ready, physically."

"Tell me more about you having trouble 'getting ready.' You mean you couldn't get wet?"

I was going to die of embarrassment. I pulled the blanket from the back of the couch and covered my face.

For being such a badass lady boss, I was a coward when it came to the personal stuff. "Pretty much."

"Did you use lube?"

God, this was mortifying. "Not at first. We'd try... I'd try to be sensual and in the moment, but the harder I tried, the more embarrassed I'd get. Sometimes he'd get impatient and lick his fingers to have enough lubrication."

"What about other times? What happened then?"

"I eventually got some lube and he'd use it. He always grumbled about the fact that we needed it."

Mac rewarded my honesty by squeezing my feet. "Look at me, Livvie."

I flipped the blanket off my face and found Mac's heated eye on me. Watching him watch me was a total turn-on.

"That says more about him than it does about you. It means he wasn't doing something right."

"If you say so." I closed my eyes, trying to avoid this turn of the conversation.

"I'm right, and I know I'm right. And I'll tell you how I know." His long fingers ran up to my knee and back down. "See, if he was paying attention to you, taking his time with you, he'd know what gets you there. When you're in the zone, like you are now." His fingers inched up over my knee to my thighs. I sucked in a breath and held it, because his hands on me felt so damn good, and I was afraid that any little movement would make him stop.

"Poor Olivia," he teased. His sexy voice doing ridiculous things to my insides. "So touch deprived, even the thought of my fingers slipping higher, under that sexy, tight skirt, is driving you wild."

He was so right. I barely kept from squirming under his

touch, imagining how it might feel to have his hands on more of me. The man was a damn sorcerer, and he knew it.

"Just like now, you're holding your breath, enjoying every minute of this and praying that I won't stop. Look at you, breathing hard. Trying not to move. Afraid one tiny flinch will make me stop."

A long, slow sweep down to my knee, and an equally slow sweep up, this time inching under my skirt, his hands splayed wide, grazing my sensitive inner thighs.

"Breathe, Liv." His voice was ragged, as if this slow seduction was as torturous to him as it was to me. Still, I sucked in a ragged breath and blew it out slowly.

"That's my girl. Just like that."

On his next sweep down, I shifted my legs apart, inviting him to explore further. My foot grazed his crotch, drawing a hum of approval.

Eager to feel more, to be closer, I inched down the couch, my skirt riding up my thighs. The slide of the silk liner added to the dreamlike state Mac had me in.

"Look at you." His words came on a breath, low and seductive. As if he were talking to himself. "You are still the sexiest woman I've ever laid eyes on. And with you here, so soft and ready. Makes me want to worship you."

Emboldened by the desire in his voice, I pressed my foot to the solid length behind his zipper and gently rubbed, making sure I gave him the same pressure he was giving me. Mac made me feel sensual, adored... wanted. Taking his time to explore and, just as he said, to worship.

This time when his hands slipped up my legs, he didn't stop. The heat of them slid all the way up my thighs to the crease of my hips. The tips of his fingers flirted with the seam of my panties, his thumbs inches away from my aching core. I rocked my hips, seeking his touch. Delicious desire unfurling low in my belly.

Marveling at how turned on I was, I let myself sink into the moment. Into being free and open and willing. I was a goddess under this man's hands.

"You've always been so beautiful. I love seeing you like this. Hot and needy. Ready for my touch." His fingertips traced the line of my panties where they met my leg.

"You want me to touch you here, baby?"

I rocked my hips again in answer. Unable to speak, unable to think beyond what he was doing to me.

And then he gave me just what I needed. Shifted so that his lips met my inner thigh as he pressed a finger over my core.

"I can feel how wet you are through the fabric." His voice was lower, almost guttural. "It makes me want to taste you. Would you like that, baby? My lips on you, my tongue in you?"

"Oh God, yes," I gasped.

He pulled away, and I voiced my dissent, opening my eyes to see him rise onto a knee. He pushed my skirt to my hips and pulled my panties off in a long, slow drag. Every scrape of the material sent a rocket of sensation through me. I spread my legs in invitation and begged, "Mac."

His shoulders grazed my inner thighs as he lowered his body.

And then his mouth was on me, kissing the most intimate part of me like a starving man.

I cried out my pleasure, sinking my fingers into his hair. But I needed more. I rocked my hips toward his eager mouth. His tongue circled my clit, and then he gently sucked, and still, it wasn't enough.

"Mac, I need... more."

And just like that, he slid a finger inside me, then another, pumping in, hitting that glorious spot that made my toes curl. It had been so long, and he felt so good, and that delicious weight in my belly spread through my body, curling my toes, making my fingers clench in his hair as he took and took and gave and gave.

My orgasm blasted over me, stealing the breath from my lungs and forcing my back to arch, my every response drawn out by this patient man who, even after all this time, knew my body better than I did.

Chapter Seventeen

Mac

Olivia combusted. Her reaction to my touch was just as hot as every memory I'd ever had. Her legs quivered around me, her tight cunt gripping my fingers as she shuddered her release. I ground my aching dick into the couch.

If she was this responsive to my hands, I couldn't wait to sink into her. Her hands on her breasts, the way her body arched, seeking more, her soft skin, her cries of pleasure so rich. Young, and so fucking beautiful it made my heart ache. I wanted to worship this woman for the rest of my life.

And like a fucking teenager, I came in my pants.

I kissed my way up to the small patch of hair, as far as the skirt would let me move, and then eased my way up her body, pressing my deflating cock into the soft warmth of her. Braced on an elbow above her with our bodies aligned perfectly, I relished in the feeling that we were made for each other.

Her legs wrapped around my waist, her arms looped around my shoulders, and she pulled me in for a kiss.

"Mac, I want you," she said against my lips.

"I know, baby. I want you too, but you're gonna have to give me a minute or five to recover."

She pulled back, confusion written all over her face.

"It's been a while," I admitted, then lowered for a kiss so I wouldn't have to meet her eyes.

She ran her fingers through my hair, sending shivers down my spine. I sank into the sensation and lowered my face to her neck, placing gentle kisses from her jaw to her shoulder. Suddenly, she stilled.

With a tug of my hair, she pulled my head up so she could look into my eyes. "Did you...?"

"You're just as hot and taste even better than I remembered. I couldn't stop it—wouldn't have wanted to even if I could. You're amazing."

A low chuckle started, quickly morphing into girlish giggles. The first time I met her, her smile, the laughter in her eyes, is what drew me to her. I didn't care that she was laughing at me in possibly the most embarrassing moment of my life.

Instead, I froze so I could memorize her. Her giggles eventually subsided, and she lay smiling up at me. I couldn't help but run my fingers across the curve of her face, tracing the soft tendrils of hair that curled there.

"There she is," I whispered.

I kissed her gently, because I had to, pouring all the feelings I'd carried for her for so many years into the kiss. All the years between us disappeared. And in my heart, we were back to a younger version of ourselves, only this time, much older and wiser.

I pulled away so I could get more of that light in her eyes.

"Mac..." Her voice was soft, wondrous. "What's happening?"

I slid my arms under her and tightened my hold. She wouldn't get away this time. No matter what, I wasn't letting her go.

"I've done some foolish things in my lifetime. But I think the worst was all those years ago, when I let you get on that boat and leave that island. Seeing you again, smiling, laughing, holding you, kissing you... it's like I've finally come home."

Her eyes glistened as she stared up at me. For half a second, my heart clenched. What if she didn't feel the same way?

I dragged myself out of her arms and stood, pulling her with me, my jeans sticking to me uncomfortably. She noticed my awkward tug at the denim and stepped in close, slipping a hand into my waistband.

"Come on, MacDaddy," she teased. Her voice, low and seductive, went straight to my cock. "Let's get you out of these clothes. You're a dirty boy." She gave me a sexy wink and led me by the waistband to her bedroom, walking backward with a devious look in her eye.

I slid my hand to her waist, spinning her around, molding my front to her back and grazing my lips against the smooth column of her neck. "You know, when Rosie called me MacDaddy that day, all I could hear in my head was your voice saying it."

The muscles in her neck flexed as she tilted her head, allowing me better access. I traced the length of it with my tongue, then closed my teeth around the taught tendon.

Her sharp inhale was fuel to my fire.

I undid the buttons of her blouse slowly, taking my time at each one, unwrapping her like the finest gift I'd ever received. Peeling the blouse off one soft shoulder, tracing each new inch of skin revealed with my tongue.

I uncovered the swell of her breasts, revealing the scalloped edges of a lacy bra. "You always wear lingerie under your uniform?" I murmured.

She nodded. "Always. I work in a man's world, but I want to feel like a woman."

I pulled the shirt off her arms, trailing my fingertips up her arms, finding my way to cup her breasts through her lacy bra. Cupping them, molding them, relishing how perfectly she filled my hands. "Fuck, that's hot. All badass and buttoned up for the outside world. But a wet dream covered in satin and lace for me. I can't wait to taste these," I murmured into her ear.

I moved on to the zipper of her skirt. The soft, slow rasp as I lowered it a punctuation to what we were doing.

This was more than the start of a fling. This was two people, two hearts, that had found each other after too long drifting alone.

With a soft moan, she pressed her hips back, her hands guiding mine as I pushed the skirt down her hips. Meeting me, letting me know she was in this with me.

Grazing my palms up her body, I cupped one around her breast, teasing her nipple with my thumb as I slid my other hand down the smooth expanse of her belly, sliding a finger into her. "Fuck, you're so slick. See, baby, there's nothing wrong with you."

I withdrew my fingers from her body and spun her by the hips.

Her heated gaze ran over my torso as she brushed the shirt from my shoulders, trailing her fingertips down my stomach. "I thought of you so much. No one has ever touched me or made me feel like you did."

My abs bunched under her touch. The smallest caress from this woman, and my body reacted. She owned me.

I held my breath as she undid the button-fly of my jeans. With each slow unfastening, she pressed her knuckles into me, giving me pressure, stealing my ability to function as I waited.

"Liv," I gasped as she pulled the fly open. Sliding her hands around my hips, she pushed my jeans down as she sank to her knees before me. My hands landed in her hair, while hers made a slow exploration up my legs. Memorizing me. Her touch every bit as thorough as mine had been.

By the time she took me in hand, I was hard as a rock for her.

"Looks like you recovered nicely," she quipped, and then sank my whole dick into her mouth. Taking me deep— so deep I could feel the back of her throat. Fuck, she stole my ability to speak, to think.

"Jesus, I like the look of your lips around my cock," I growled out, taking a fistful of her hair in my hand. "My dick has been hard for weeks knowing you're under my roof. The thought of you naked, showering... *fuck*." I pumped hard into her mouth, unable to control myself. Dammit, I was too close, already.

"I'm like a horny teenager around you, Livvie. Zero control," I said, pulling out of her mouth. I cupped a hand under her chin, lifting her to stand. "I need to be inside you."

I couldn't stop touching her, kissing her. She wrapped one leg around my waist, moaning into my mouth like maybe she was as lost as I was.

With my tongue in her mouth and my hands on her

ass, I lifted her up, ready to haul her to the bed. Ready to bury myself so deep inside her, I'd never want to see the light of day again. One step toward the bed, and I kicked her suitcase, scattering the unpacked contents across the floor.

I broke the kiss with a curse. "Ow, fuck."

"Oops." She giggled. My buttoned-up queen giggled like a schoolgirl.

I dumped her on the bed, ready to claim her, but a shiny object caught my eye. "Well, what do we have here?"

"Oh my God." Her huge eyes took in the bullet, the most gorgeous flush staining her skin all the way down her chest. "I cannot believe that, of all things, is what fell out of that suitcase."

I flipped the switch on, and the bullet roared to life. "You been in here using this to get off every night, while I've been across the hall using my fist?" I shook my head. "We're such fools. We're gonna have some fun. I can think of at least a dozen ways I wanna use this on you," I said, letting my gaze roam over her naked body.

I turned the bullet off, tossing it onto the bed. "But first, I want all of you."

Her arms encircled my neck as I rose over her, lining the head of my cock up to her entrance. Pushing in the slightest bit. "God, it's hot when you get all breathy like that." I pulled her leg back, bending it at the knee, opening her to me, and thrust.

"Mac," she cried, her hips rising to meet mine.

I dropped to my elbow and took her mouth. The way her body took mine... I froze, breaking the kiss. "Fuck, Livvie. Condom."

Her hand cupped my jaw, pulling me back to her mouth. "I've got us covered. And I haven't had sex since my divorce and got tested after I found out he was cheating. I'm clean. If you're clean, then it's go time."

"Fucking go time, then." I pulled out and slammed back into her, loving the way she cried my name.

The harder I thrust, the more she cried out, over and over. The long, slow glide out, the hard thrust in. The way her breasts bounced as our hips met, the way her hips cradled mine. The slap of skin on skin. The cries she made. Pressure built at the base of my spine; I wasn't going to last. I slowed down, shifting her leg and rolling my hips into hers, changing the angle.

"Oh God, baby, don't stop. I'm so close."

Instead, I palmed the bullet and pulled out. Rolling off her and pushing my back against the headboard, I grabbed her under the arms and slid her up my body. Her legs straddled my hips as she rose over me.

I gripped her hip, guiding her where I wanted her. "I need to see you fall apart, baby." I cupped her jaw, drawing her mouth to mine. "Now kiss me while you put my dick in you."

Olivia

Making love with Mac was everything I thought I'd remembered and more. His filthy mouth. His caresses that were rough and gentle at the same time. The way his body owned mine. He made me forget that there was anything beyond me and him. The outside world didn't exist.

My legs slid over his hips, and all I could feel was open. Open to anything he demanded of me. His tongue slid into my mouth as I took him in hand and gave him a stroke. A groan of pleasure rumbled from his chest. I wanted more of that groan. More of Mac. I notched the head of his cock at my entrance.

"Take it," he said against my lips.

I waited, savoring the rush of knowing this man wanted me as much as I did him, drawing out the pleasure for both of us.

I rotated my hips, exploring just how far I could take this before he took over and fucked me into oblivion. I'd already had one orgasm. Two wasn't on the agenda for me, but if I worked it, maybe I could make him lose control. He sat up, capturing a nipple in his mouth, sucking and biting. His hand on my hip flexed, guiding me, gripping me. I sank lower onto him, edging us both.

With a growl, he bent his knees behind me, caging me in, and thrust his hips up, driving so deep into me that I cried out.

"That's better." His words were a deep rasp against my skin. His hand slipped between us, and something icy cold landed on my clit. Before I could register what it was, the buzzing clicked on.

I cried out again.

"Now ride," he growled.

I rotated my hips, chasing the high that his body promised. It was just out of reach.

"Fuck, but you're gorgeous." God, I loved the way his voice skittered over my skin. "Take the bullet. Let me watch you come while I'm buried deep inside you. Get there, Liv. I can't hold back much more." His words alone were almost enough, and if I hadn't come already, they probably would've sealed the deal.

But I didn't want him to hold back. I wanted him feral.

I pushed him back against the pillows, loving the way his abs bunched as he drove up into me, meeting me thrust for thrust. Sweat beaded on his brow, and his jaw clenched as he fought for control, his gaze sharp and focused on me, my breasts.

I took the bullet from him and circled my clit. "You wanna watch this?" My voice came out low and husky, desire dripping from every word.

His eyes dropped to where we were joined. The muscle at his jaw ticked again. He was so close.

I leaned back and widened my legs, giving him a better view, then circled my clit, making sure to slide it down through my folds so he could feel the vibration too. His mouth dropped open on a gasp.

His eyes pinched shut. "God damn, I can feel you clenching around me. So fucking good." He sounded like he was being tortured in the best kind of way. Wet slapping noises filled the room, combined with his deep grunts of pleasure.

He rolled his hips, hitting that spot deep inside of me. "God... Mac," I gasped. "Right there."

"Let go, baby. I've got you," he said, and with the combination of the bullet and his hip roll into that magic spot, an orgasm shimmered to life, tightening in my lower belly, coiling deep inside me.

I slipped the bullet in a slow circle once more and got the same outstanding hip roll. So much pleasure it was bordering on pain.

I removed the bullet and slipped my arm behind me, leaning my body onto his legs. Reaching down, I ran the toy down his balls, to the firm area just behind them, and pressed in.

The fingers at my hips dug in as Mac exploded under me. The clench of his muscles against my hand trapping it there as he thrust into me with a guttural roar.

I shattered around him, dropping the bullet onto the bed and collapsing into his chest.

His arms enfolded me as we melted into a tangle of roaming hands and soft kisses. We're finally back to everything we were before, only this time, it's better. This time, it comes with the promise of a future. Because after all we've been through, I'm not letting this man go again.

Chapter Eighteen

Mac

I lay propped on my side, watching the most beautiful woman in the world cross the room. Naked. Highlighted by the glow of the full moon shining through the window. My lips tipped up in a smile I couldn't contain. The graceful way she carried herself did things to me.

With a matching smile, Olivia braced a knee on the bed, leaning over to plant a kiss on my lips. Hovering over me in the semidarkness, she was a goddess. Smart, strong, capable, confident. Utterly gorgeous.

"You are breathtaking," I said, cupping her face to pull her in for another kiss.

Maybe age had made me a sentimental fool, but I cherished this moment. Being with her, making love to her. Hell, just having her in my house made life so much sweeter.

As she tucked her back to my front, I wrapped my arms around her, enjoying the feel of her, and buried my face in her neck.

This time meant everything in the world to me. In a

matter of minutes, every other thing, retirement, the lake house, the boat. All of it meant nothing. She mattered. Rosie mattered. Having a family mattered.

Because what was life if you didn't have someone special to spend it with?

Her arm covered mine, and she ran her hand down, humming her pleasure as she linked our fingers. I pressed another kiss to the spot just behind her ear, the one that made her shudder the slightest bit.

"What's on your mind, Mac? I can tell you're thinking deep thoughts." Her voice was quiet, intimate. I ran our hands from her waist, across the soft mound of her belly, up between the valley of her breasts to her collarbone, where I splayed my fingers, loving how the base of her neck fit perfectly in the V of my thumb and forefinger. Her fingers slipped down, encircling my wrist.

"You know," I began, keeping my voice soft, "I never knew I was lonely until you came back into my life." I pressed another kiss on her soft skin because I needed the pause. The thick emotion building in my chest made it hard to speak. "But you came and brought Rosie, and the two of you lit all the dark, lonely spaces with your light."

She squeezed my wrist, drawing in a deep breath. Curled around each other like we were, every move she made brushed against me. "I wish I'd found you all those years ago. I wish I'd never left you," she admitted.

We lay silently, lost in the past for a long moment. "I wrote you letters." The intimate admission came softly. "In a journal I kept. Rosie found it. I don't know that she read it. But that's where she found the picture of us."

"You know how I found out about her?"

"How?"

"She posted a picture of us on TikTok. The one from

the last day we spent on the beach and went sailing. We look so happy in that picture. She posted the photo wanting help finding her dad."

Olivia went still in my arms.

"I didn't know how to react, how or where to start to find you. But I'm glad I had the time to mull it over and come to terms with the idea of having a kid, because it took me a while. And then that day you walked into the conference room... felt like the earth shifted."

She lay quiet in the circle of my arms. Then I felt it, the slightest shudder. I didn't know if she was laughing or crying.

"I can't believe she did that, the little turd."

Laughing. Thank God.

I released a breath.

"I had no idea she'd even found the journal until after we moved here. Long after Tim and I split. She must've been planning to find you for a while."

I growled at the sound of another man's name in my bed.

"What's that for?" she asked.

"You don't say another man's name while you're in my bed. Whether or not I'm grateful to him for taking care of my girls until we found each other or not."

She shifted her arm around to pat me on the butt. "There, there, MacDaddy. It's okay, you're a big boy. You can handle it."

"Not the point, Liv."

She chuckled, obviously unaware I spoke the truth. "Somewhere inside me is a jealous caveman that wants to club you over the head and declare you as mine."

"That's weirdly cute. Not the clubbing part, but I kind of like that you want to claim us."

"Why wouldn't I?"

"Because it's just not something that we're used to. T—he who shall not be named—was present. We cared for each other in the beginning, and he stepped in and took care of Rosa when I needed help the most. But looking back, it was a surface-level feeling."

She turned in my arms to face me, running the palm of her hand over the scruff of my jaw. Her eyes searched my face in the moon's glow. "It wasn't the big, scary feeling that still runs deep between me and you."

I smoothed the hair at her temple, allowing her words to sink deep into my heart.

"I feel it too. It terrifies me, but I don't think I could live without the two of you anymore. I know it's fast, but I think I loved you then and never stopped. I don't regret anything, except that I didn't ask you to stay with me or come back with me. Or have some way to find you later."

Her mouth met mine, and we sank into each other, the kiss turning heated and slippery until we were both breathing hard, both content to make up for lost years of just kissing.

She nipped at my bottom lip and pulled away, scooting down to place her head on my chest. "Where do we go from here?"

I trailed my fingers down her back, thinking. "Well, if you're up for it, you and Rosie just stay here. With me. We live our lives together, and God willing, ride off into the sunset together." I hadn't meant to ask so soon, but it felt right. Now that they were here, I didn't want them to ever leave.

The skin of her back was warm under my fingertips, even though I could feel the little goosebumps my touch caused.

"I don't know, Mac. There's so much on the line. You've got your retirement plans all laid out. And we can't be public about this, because I know the mayor will fire me on the spot for having a relationship with you. One of us is going to lose in the job aspect."

She was right, and that had been my problem with starting something with her all along. But... "Just know, I'd rather have you and have to work the rest of my life than to have a job and long for you. You're more to me than any pension or title. We could be flat broke, living off beanie weenies and ramen, and I'd prioritize you over a job. We'll figure it out."

She kissed me long and sweet. "You sound like some lovesick young fool."

I chuckled. "I know." I trailed my fingers across her skin. Her being here with me was everything. "I don't have the answers, Livvie. But I'll be searching for the solution for both of us to get what we want."

"Although," she continued, her tone turning light, "I might be getting the better end of this bargain. Sometimes, things get heated between me and Rosie. Somedays I can't do anything right."

"I'll take her fishing on those days," I promised, laughing at the image of the two arguing over something ridiculous.

"Speaking of"—she glanced at the clock—"I should probably check in on her."

With a few more lingering kisses, we got up and dressed, her in my shirt, me in a pair of pj's that she insisted I never take off because she liked the way they hung on my hips. We met in the kitchen, where I made us a sandwich for a late dinner, and she called Shae's dad.

"Hey, Damien. How're things going."

I went about making gourmet PB&J's, not paying much

attention until she said, "Yeah, no other word other than he was somewhere out west. But I appreciate you being diligent, just in case."

She ended the call, and I pushed her sandwich across the counter to her and then braced myself. "What was that about?"

I tried to keep the irritation out of my voice but didn't quite manage. I had an inkling I was in the dark about something, and I didn't like it.

"What? Oh, I got a message from the arson suspect on my voicemail at work today."

Red-hot rage flashed through my body. I tried my best not to blow my top, so my voice came out deeper, more ominous than I intended it to. "And you didn't lead with that when you walked in the door tonight?"

Liv visibly prickled at the change in my tone. "Excuse me. I don't like the tone you're using on me right now."

"Get used to it. This is my what-the-fuck tone."

Her spine stiffened. "You don't get a pass to use it on me because we fucked."

Ego blow right to the gut. Diminishing all that passed between us to a simple fuck fueled my rage.

"It was more than that, and you damn well know it. I wouldn't go feral over some random hookup. Now spill. What do you know that you haven't told me."

We met each other glare for glare. Finally, she tipped her chin up and, in her calm, cool business voice, she said, "I had a voice message at work from the arsonist. I turned the message over to the police chief, who had it run through their system. They believe him to be somewhere out west."

"How does that work? How can they tell he's out west?" I didn't trust technology at all, and certainly not when it meant my ladies might be in trouble.

"I don't know. I'm trusting what the investigators tell me."

"I don't trust anyone when it comes to your safety. And you let Rosie go off tonight?" My voice was rising the more frustrated I got.

Olivia eyed me for a minute and then stated coldly, "Only because Shae's dad is a police officer."

"And you didn't think to talk to me about it? To let me in that you and *our daughter* are in danger?" I pushed off the counter and turned to pace the floor, gripping the back of my neck because I needed something to grasp on to in this moment. Something to help me come to terms with the fact that this asshat was now making it personal with Olivia. "How did he get your information? Why's he making you a target?" I made another lap. "And what about Rosie?" I'd need to make sure she had a second detail watching her, and I could ask the school resource officer to be extra vigilant.

"Mac."

Better yet, I could just take some annual leave and guard them myself, or find this motherfucker and settle the situation once and for all.

"Mac."

But what I would not do, the thing that had me spinning in circles, gripping the back of my neck like a damn ninny, was sit back and let someone else handle the situation.

I spun again, ready to figure out exactly what the first step would be, when Olivia stepped in front of me, blocking me. I stopped before I plowed into her, and realized my chest was heaving. Her arms slid around my waist, her front pressing into mine as she met me full-on, burrowing into me.

"Mac, honey."

It was the soft *honey* that did it. Had me lifting my arms to return her embrace.

"It's okay," she offered, like she was trying to calm a frightened animal. Because that's exactly what I was.

I inhaled and hugged her close, my mind still spinning with fear.

"Take a moment to breathe. We are okay. It's going to be okay."

"But I can't protect her if she's not here." I admitted the crux of the problem.

Olivia pulled back and met my gaze. "Welcome to parenting." Her palm cupped my jaw, and she leaned up to kiss the beast. "You're a good man. Gonna be a great dad."

Like an ice-cold bucket of water to the face, her words stopped the panic.

"Is this what it's like? This all-consuming fear that something bad might happen that you can't stop?"

"Not always, but sometimes. Others, it's the sweetest moments that you'll ever experience. I believe you've already had a few of those."

"How do I do it?"

"Do what?"

"How do I live with my heart beating outside of my body?" I choked out.

Her gentle smile of understanding helped calm me further. "You just grab it by the tail and hang on. We aren't guaranteed another tomorrow. So we cherish each day for the gift that it is. And hope that you chew your cereal the right way so that she doesn't turn on you."

I didn't totally get what she meant by that, but I figured it had something to do with mothers and daughters.

"Does this mean we're a family?" It was a stupid question, but one I desperately needed an answer to. Because now that I'd found them, I couldn't lose them again.

"In our own little weird way, I guess. Don't worry, MacDaddy. Everything is going to be okay. Rosie will come home and be sassy, and you'll forget all about this bittersweet moment. Just keep doing what you're doing."

She caressed my cheek and gave me another reassuring kiss, then pulled away. "I'm going to let Buster out, and then let's have a movie night."

I enjoyed watching the hem of my shirt bounce with every step as she walked away. I needed something to occupy my mind, otherwise, I'd have us back in the bed for another round, and I knew if I did, I'd lose even more of my heart to her.

Someone had neatly stacked my mail on the counter, and I pulled it to me and sorted through the sales ads and political cards. Mostly trash until I reached an envelope from the bank. The monthly mortgage statement for the lake house.

Before Olivia, the monthly notice had been motivation for making it to retirement. The constant reminder of the balloon notice waiting for me.

The lake house was the last thing I had of my parents. I'd planned to sell the Newman house and use my leave-time payout to settle the lake house mortgage, and then spend my years fulfilling my father's dream.

Just another reason we couldn't let this relationship get out and threaten our jobs. I looked up to where Olivia left the room, praying that somehow, someway, I'd be able to come up with a solution that would solve everything.

Chapter Nineteen

Olivia

Mac and Rosie spent the afternoon out on the pond fishing again. It was becoming their habit. I decided it was their time to bond and turned down the invite Mac issued and promised to make them a late picnic.

Knowing Mac was a big old softy had me smiling as I spread the blanket out in the grass near the small dock.

My mom called as I got things organized. I'd been trying to connect with her for a couple of days. "Hey, Mom."

"Hello, dear, it's good to finally hear your voice."

"I know, yours too. How's Dad?"

"Well, Dad has settled in well in his new place. He's been a little confused but seems to be accepting it. I still feel guilty that I can't take care of him here, but I'm not strong enough to physically help him. Plus, you know how he loves to chitchat, and there are plenty of people to talk to every day."

"I'm sorry I'm not there to help." It grated that to chase my dream to make him proud, meant that I couldn't be there while they went through this.

"Stop, dear. You know your father is proud of you. You are following your dream, and that's what he always wanted for you."

"I know. I just miss you guys and feel like I'm missing so much," I admitted.

"Hush now. Fill me in on how things are for you and Rosa Nell." Just like she always had, Mom quieted my fears.

I talked her through all that had happened over the last month. How Rosie was doing in school, our new place, my job. Eventually, I got the nerve to break the news of Mac to her.

"So... we had a thing happen," I started.

"What kind of thing? A good thing? A bad thing? Quit being vague and spit it out. I know whatever it is, it's important."

"Mom, Rosie's dad is here."

"What?" she exclaimed. "Tim followed you? I thought you left to start over?"

"Not Tim, Mom. Her real father."

"You mean the guy you had the fling with?"

"Yeah, that guy."

Silence descended for a moment. "Well?"

"He's still just as great as he was then," I marveled, watching him paddle the boat from the far side of the pond. He splashed the paddle, a spray of water arcing over Rosie. She laughed, the sound vibrant and light, echoing through my heart.

"You sound happy, sweetheart. How'd you find him?"

I couldn't stop the smile that spread across my face. It felt huge and right. "It's a long story, but Rosie actually found him through social media. And yeah, I am." My smile fell. "But I'm also... hesitant. I guess having a failed marriage did a number on me. I just want to be smart. And try to keep things in check for Rosie in the process. Although, she's pretty much already head over heels for him."

I wanted to be all-in with Mac. He was a great guy. But Tim had also been great when we started, not that there was any comparison between the men. Mac was Rosie's dad, and despite what happened between us, he wanted to be in her life. Tim had left Rosie, just as he'd left me in the end. I didn't want to put my girl through that again. I needed to take a step back and reevaluate.

"You deserve it, sweetheart. Things have definitely taken a turn for the good for you and Rosie, then." Mom's voice was gentle and loving, and hearing it made my heart ache that we weren't closer.

"I guess. We've been through our share of hard times. It's nice to enjoy the sweet for a bit." I lay back in the sun, enjoying hearing their voices carry on a low hum across the water. His deep chuckle and her high-pitched giggle providing the most delightful background music.

"He's good to Rosie? They are getting along?"

"Actually, they are two peas in a pod. They are just coming in from fishing right now. I've got a picnic ready for them."

Mom didn't answer, so I continued, "I think you'd really like him, Mom."

More silence.

"Mom?"

A sniffle caught me by surprise. "I'm here, sweetheart. I'm just glad to hear you happy, even if it's guarded." Her voice quavered, and I imagined the tears welling in her eyes. Then she cleared her throat and said, "Well, I'm going to let you go. I've got to get some cookies out of the oven and run them to your dad."

We hung up, and the bittersweetness of hearing her voice, yet being so far away, was hard. But she was right—Rosie and I were where we needed to be. I closed my eyes and waited for my two favorite people to get off the water, soaking up the stillness of the moment. They were rare and cherished.

Sometime later, a soft finger brushed my cheek. "Wake up, sleeping beauty." Mac's voice was low and for my ears only.

Earlier that morning, we'd decided we'd have to come clean to our daughter about the change in our relationship. We'd argued over the best way to handle it. Mac wanted to come right out and admit that we'd slept together, but I preferred to approach things a little more conservatively. That didn't go over as well and added to whatever had been haunting his gaze when he'd finally come to bed. I would've thought he'd been right behind me after I took Buster out. Instead, he went out to the porch with the excuse that Buster needed some "front porch time." As best I could tell, he'd just sat on the front porch rocking for a while. And when he'd come to bed, he'd been so focused on me, I let it go.

I opened my eyes to find a thoughtful Mac gazing down at me. I couldn't tell if he was mad at me for having reservations or if there was something else on his mind.

I didn't know if I wanted to kiss away whatever was bothering him or demand that he spill. Guess we had some more trust issues to deal with.

Giving him grace, I rose on an elbow. Maybe if I showed him I was here, now, with him, he'd open up. "Where is she?" I whispered.

"I sent her to the shop to wash her hands."

"What about yours?"

A wicked gleam lit his eyes, and the corner of his mouth tilted up. "I washed at the spigot by the dock."

"Why didn't she?"

"Because I didn't tell her about it so I could have a minute to do this..." His hand slid along my jaw, his thumb brushing my cheek before he pulled me closer and laid the hottest, deepest, most soul-cleansing kiss on me that I'd ever experienced.

"I've been wanting to do that for hours," he growled against my lips, then went back for more.

Helpless to do anything else, I draped my arm over his shoulder and pulled him closer. He deepened the kiss, exploring my mouth like we'd never kissed before. Like he couldn't get enough. *I* couldn't get enough.

"Uh, you guys know I can see you, right?" Rosie called from a few feet away.

My eyes popped open, and Mac and I both froze, lips still pressed together. "Jeez, Buster, give them two seconds alone and they are eating each other's faces. You're not a very good chaperone."

Mac kissed me once more, a punctuation on the situation. Making his statement that he and I were... *something* more than we'd been. He shifted onto a hip beside me, braced on an arm, with one knee raised. The ultimate cool.

I, however, was embarrassed and fidgety while trying to find the words I needed to explain to my impressionable teenager that I was starting a relationship with him.

"Okay, squirt, here's the deal. I like your mom, she likes me. It's a thing, and it's happening."

Rosie dropped to her knees on the blanket across from us. "Squirt?"

"Yeah."

Her nose wrinkled as she pondered. "You can't do better than that? It's so... basic."

Beside me, Mac's deep chuckle reverberated in his chest. "I'll see if I can come up with something more appropriate."

My head swiveled between them while I still searched for the ability to make words.

She plucked at the petals of a yellow flower. "I've been thinking. I kinda like princess. Or..."

"Buttercup?" Mac added.

Her face lit up. "Yeah, Princess Buttercup, like from the movie."

"What movie?" Mac asked.

Rosie and I both spun toward him in shock. "You've never seen *The Princess Bride?*" we asked in unison.

Mac shook his head and reached for the ball Buster had dropped on the blanket. After tossing it, he said, "Looks like I know what we're doing on date night with my girls tonight."

I was staring at him; I couldn't help myself.

"So, you guys...?"

I turned to find Rosie addressing her question at me. I couldn't tell if she was happy or concerned or nonchalant, or even what her question was. But now was when she needed my honesty. "Yes. Mac and I are..." Hooking up wasn't the right word, nor was trying things out, because we'd been there and done that, and she was the result. Continuing wasn't the right word either because we'd never been together before. "We're... becoming. We're starting out, figuring it out as we go."

It was clunky. But it was real.

Mac's hand landed on mine, giving it a squeeze. I

turned to find him gazing at me with the softest, sweetest look in his eyes and leaned forward for a kiss.

"Okay, but bleh. Don't, like, be kissing all the time, please." Rosie snagged the ball from Buster and tossed it again. "Can we eat now? I'm starving."

And just like that, the issue was settled. Mac and I were becoming an *us*. And Rosie was fine with it, supported us.

We enjoyed lunch, and then the inquisition started.

"So, MacDa—"

"Don't call him that."

"Don't even think about it."

Mac and I warned at the same time, although I could feel the heat of my blush and was positive that Rosie saw it too.

"Bleh—again. I don't even wanna know." She shuddered with her eyes squished closed. Wait. Had she been in my books again? "Anyways," she continued like she hadn't just smacked me across the face. "What I wanted to ask is… how did you guys meet? I mean, I know you had a vacation hookup, but I don't know your story. Mom always said she'd tell me when I got older, so I want to know your story."

She gazed at me first, waiting.

At the rate this day was going, my cheeks were going to be permanently red. Maybe I could claim a sunburn. Regardless, I cleared my throat and kept my promise to my daughter. "It was after college. I had just graduated from the fire academy, and I treated myself to an island vacation as a reward before I began my career. I walked into this cute little bar-hut on the beach. I got there later in the afternoon; the sun was high, and the sky was so blue it almost hurt. The little bar was tucked up in the shade of some palm trees."

Unsure of which details she'd want, I babbled on. "I

walked in and saw Mac sitting there hunched over a beer, looking sexy and brooding and kind of lonely, with his back to the ocean, and I thought, 'What a shame. A man like that should be enjoying the ocean.'"

I plucked at the blanket as I spoke; it was hard being this open about my feelings. But I wanted to keep my promise, and Mac also deserved to know, because I'd never told him about the moment I first laid eyes on him.

"I wanted to know him instantly, but I was nervous. It took me a few minutes, but finally, I gathered the courage to approach him. Just as I was headed his way, he turned, and our eyes met, and it was like my soul recognized his. And then he smiled at me..." I swallowed thickly and blinked the moisture away. Meeting Mac had had a profound effect on my life, but reliving the moment of meeting him was still one of my most beautiful memories.

He lifted my hand and pressed a kiss to my knuckles, where his lips lingered, his eyes closed as if my words had moved him.

"Aw, Mom, that's the sweetest," Rosie gushed before turning to Mac. "Okay, your turn, big da—"

"Nope."

"Not that either."

Mac and I spoke in unison again.

He cleared his throat and sat up a little straighter, letting go of my hand. I crisscrossed my legs in front of me and waited. His long leg was still stretched out, his knee still raised, but now he draped an arm around it, clasping his wrist. His posture almost closed off.

"My story isn't quite as happy," he started. "I wasn't on vacation—or I was, but I wasn't supposed to be alone. I was supposed to be on my honeymoon."

Rosie gasped and I blanched. I'd known he was sad when I met him, but not that.

"It's for the best, really. Worked out in the end." He winked at me.

"Anyway"—he looked out over the water—"my fiancée left me, stood me up, rather, at the altar. Turned out, she liked the idea of being married but couldn't deal with the stress of being married to someone who might potentially put his life on the line. I decided to take the trip anyway. I'd been there less than twenty-four hours and was starting to feel like the worst kind of loser, sitting at the bar, drowning my sorrows and heartache. I couldn't bring myself to find anything beautiful about the place and was considering leaving early. When I turned and saw this pretty young brunette in a yellow dress."

I sat up. "I didn't have on a dress."

The corners of his eye crinkled as he shot me a grin. "Oh, that's right, it was the tiniest yellow bikini I'd ever seen. So bright and full of sunshine... the most beautiful woman I'd ever seen." He looked back at Rosie and winked. "She's still the most beautiful, but her daughter gives her a run for the money."

Rosie blushed, her shoulders inching toward her ears in embarrassment.

"Anyway, I'd gone there to get over the heartache of losing a woman I thought I'd spend my life with. I came home having gotten over her, but the one who blasted her memory stayed with me. We tried to be smart about it, so we thought. No last names, no personal information. Just a week of having fun together, sailing, laying out in the cabanas. Late-night dinners, long walks while talking about the dreams we had. All future talk. And it helped pull me out of that funk and focus on moving forward."

I leaned forward and ran my palm down his arm, needing to touch him.

"You guys are so mushy," Rosie cooed. "And also, that's the most ridiculous thing I've ever heard. Not having a way to stay in touch. Anyways, so it was supposed to be a casual, fun fling. But both of you got more than you bargained for." She paused, considering. "I guess that's the truth of the saying hindsight is twenty-twenty."

The wisdom and ease of the teenage mind.

"And now you've got me, and each other. And what happens next?"

I bit into my sandwich and considered. And once again, Mac beat me to the punch. "Well, I'm hoping that instead of moving back to the townhouse, that you and Liv will stay here. And we can take things slow. And learn each other."

The bite nearly stuck in my throat as I swallowed. But finally, after a drink, I managed to choke out, "Would that be okay with you, sweetheart?"

Her head tilted side to side as if she were weighing her options.

"So... go back to that loud place, where I didn't know anyone and spent my afternoons inside alone. Or stay here, where I can hang out with Buster and fish?" She looked at us like we were both ridiculous for not knowing her immediate answer. "What do you think?"

Buster, who'd been oddly still, jumped up and dashed right through the middle of the blanket to chase a squirrel. Rosie and I squealed as the wet dog splashed by us.

"Ew, he stepped in the food," she cried.

The rich timber of Mac's laughter rang through the afternoon. The sound was so foreign, it held me frozen while Rosie jumped up, shaking to get yucky lake-water dog hair from the remains of her lunch.

He laughed until tears formed in his eyes and he was doubled over. That sound touching a sweet spot in my soul. Finally, he stood, offering us a hand. "Come on, how about we go get an ice cream instead."

And just like that, we moved into something that looked an awful lot like being a family. And I was terrified.

Chapter Twenty

Mac

Nick's Frozen Custard shop was a local favorite, and on any given evening, there was a line out the door, flowing down the sidewalk toward the fish fry restaurant. Red Adirondack chairs were arranged in a circle in one area, picnic tables with red umbrellas in another, and matching red rocking chairs dotted the front sidewalk, all standing in bright contrast to the stark white building.

The store was newish but was an obvious hit since it was always packed.

It wasn't until we pulled into the ice cream shop parking lot that I even thought about being out in public with Olivia and Rosie and what the implications and ramifications might be.

"Is this okay?" I kept my voice low so only Olivia could hear it as we made our way to join the end of the line.

She took stock of the people in line and squared her

shoulders. "We're allowed to take our daughter out for ice cream."

It wasn't a real answer and didn't do much to alleviate the sudden indecision I had about being out together.

It wasn't that I wanted to hide her away, it was that I wanted to hold her hand as we walked up. If I wanted to nuzzle her neck on a public sidewalk, I didn't want one of us to lose our job over it.

"Mac!"

I slowed and turned toward the familiar voice.

Great. Kylie, Jordan, and Leah were walking across the parking lot.

Kylie was a pistol-ball on the best of days. It was not a good thing for her to be here, because she was the one who originally found the TikTok video that started this whole life change I was going through. There was no telling what she might say.

But Kylie had her own story, and she and Thoren were part of the larger family, so I couldn't act like I hadn't heard her.

"Kylie," I greeted. "Jordan, Leah."

I also couldn't be rude, because as the fire chief, Olivia would eventually meet them at the station. So I sucked it up and made the introductions.

"Ladies, this is Chief Hawkins and ou—her daughter, Rosie." Fuck. That wasn't supposed to come out like that. I barreled forward, hoping they wouldn't catch my slip. "They're new in town, so I'm showing them all the best places." Why did I add that last part? It made it sound like a date.

"I love your hair, Chief," Jordan spoke first, her own blond curls fighting to be free from her ponytail.

They devolved into a discussion of curl care, and Rosie

had Leah in a discussion, which left Kylie the perfect opportunity. She turned her back to the others and looked at me with wide eyes. "Mac, is that…?" she muttered, jerking her head in Rosie's direction.

I couldn't dim the pride that swelled in my chest. Didn't want to. "It is."

"Holy shit, Captain." Kylie gripped my arm, her eyes wide, expression stunned. She had a way about her, not scared of anything, and definitely not scared of me like the others seemed to be. "That video was for real?"

I simply nodded and checked over her shoulder to make sure no one was listening. "She's my daughter."

"But you introduced her as yours and the chief's daughter—oh my God. That's, like, the biggest news of the year. How is it not all over town yet?"

"Because it's no one's business."

"And there's nothing going on with the mom? Just you meeting your new daughter?"

"Also no one's business." It felt wrong to deny Olivia, even though we were supposed to be keeping this a secret. Things had been quiet for her with administration. I didn't want to give them any reason to focus on her again.

But Kylie wouldn't shut up unless I was blunt. In fact, she'd probably appreciate what I otherwise shouldn't say.

"Olivia and I are friends. We are learning to navigate this new situation. I'd appreciate you helping us keep it on the down-low. Not trying to hide anything, just don't need any added outside interactions."

Her eyes bounced back and forth between mine, and I let her see how important this was to me.

In a fleeting moment of clarity, I knew Kylie understood my need for privacy.

"I hear you, Captain."

"Thank you, because if people make a big deal out of this, jobs will be on the line—mine and hers."

"But that's not fair. You guys should be able to co-parent."

"I agree. So we're going to prove that it can be done before anyone comes for us." I was making stuff up on the fly, but as I said the words, I felt them in my soul. I believed in us. We could do this. And hopefully by then, we would have a solution, and neither of us would lose a job.

A soft smile flitted across Kylie's face. "I'm really happy for you, Mac." With that, she turned to face the others. "Hey guys, let's skip the ice cream part of the night and go straight to the wine part."

"I'm in," said Jordan. They uttered their goodbyes and started walking away.

"Oh! Captain, did you hear about Francis?" Leah turned, calling back to me.

"I didn't. How is she?"

"She's at the rehab facility, terrorizing the nurses and pretty much creating havoc. They busted her for organizing a gambling ring." Leah chuckled, her eyes alight with adoration as she spoke of Francis.

"Who's that?" Olivia asked.

"Mrs. Francis O'Malley. Probably the biggest flirt you'll ever meet, and definitely the coolest woman I've ever met," Jordan supplied.

"What happened to her?"

"She fell and got a new bionic hip, as she calls it. She's threatening to lead hula hoop classes when they release her from PT." Leah shook her head as if she didn't know what to make of it.

Kylie grimaced. "I actually feel sorry for her therapist."

Jordan's eyebrows shot to her forehead. "Wow, that's saying a lot."

"So, she enjoys the facility?" Olivia asked. The sincerity in her tone suggested that she needed to hear confirmation.

"Oh, definitely," the three said.

"We've just had to place my father in a home. It makes me feel better knowing that others are enjoying their situation." The relief in her voice took me back a step. Other than right before her conference, I hadn't heard anything else about her father. One more thing she was keeping to herself, keeping from me.

But I guess in the grand scheme of things, though we'd met years ago, we didn't really know each other.

Rosie and I moved forward with the line, as Olivia and the others stepped aside to talk about caregivers. Was coming here, coming out in public with them, the smart thing to do? If it came down to having to choose between me or the job, which one would Olivia pick? And why hadn't she shared this bit about her father?

Clearly, now that I paid attention to her, I could see the tension in her in the way she held herself as she talked with the others, almost as if she'd held these women—hell, all people—at arm's length. It was only as she became more comfortable around the ladies did I see her shoulders drop, her smiles coming more readily, more earnestly. And seeing her talk about the secret worries she held, how she relaxed and let some of her burden go, gave me clarity. She needed these people around her. People who would befriend her, help her.

Would I ever be enough for her and Rosie?

I shook off the little twinge of doubt that reared its head. After all, I was supposed to be here with Rosie as much as with her mom.

Olivia joined us at the Adirondacks a bit later, all signs of discomfort gone. Apparently, having other women to chat with made her happy.

"I like them," she said, licking her cone and causing me to have an instant reaction.

I grunted. "They're good people."

"Uh, oh. He's grunting," Rosie quipped. "You know what that means."

Olivia looked at Rosie with a question in her eyes.

I lowered my cone and gave Rosie my best stern look. "What's it mean?"

"You aren't happy about something. You get all grunty when you don't like what you hear or what you have to say."

Olivia's eyebrows shot up. "He does, doesn't he."

"Okay, you two. It's not gang-up-on-Mac time."

"But it's so much fun."

I relaxed then, because my daughter's smiles were contagious, and she looked happy, and I was determined to enjoy it. Even if it meant becoming a sap over a stubborn, mouthy teenage female and her equally as stubborn, mouthy mother.

* * *

"You're coming tonight, right?" Thoren slung his bag into the back of his truck, parked next to mine in the empty back lot of the station. It was the end of shift, and everyone was heading out. Though the morning promised a beautiful day, the night before had been a long one, and I was more than ready to get home.

"I don't know..." For a while, we'd made it a regular thing to have cookouts. But since Olivia and Rosie had come into the picture, I'd avoided them. Too much to explain, too many questions I knew they'd ask.

"Capt, are you pissed at us?" Nate draped an arm on the bed of my truck. Thoren slammed his door and faced me. Between the two of them, I was boxed in.

"Got nothing to be pissed about."

"So, you'll be there?" Nate asked.

"Yeah, Nate's got a problem he needs manly help with," Thoren said. Nate's eyes flashed to Thoren, confusion written all over his face before it morphed, and he looked back to me.

"Yeah, what Thoren said. I need some help. I... have a thing."

I called bullshit. But then again, Nate'd been a dumbass once before with his girlfriend, and a not-so-gentle reminder from me had helped him, so maybe there was some underlying truth.

"Also, I've got this fence that I'm needing help repairing, and I need all the help I can get, so if you can, come earlier."

I didn't want to go to a freaking cookout. But I also didn't want to let Thoren down if he needed the help.

"Yeah, I can come help with the fence. But I'm not sure about the cookout."

"Sweet." He elbowed Nate in the chest. "You're still available, right? Don't be ditching me now."

Nate winced, rubbing his pecs. "I gotta make a stop, do some arranging of my schedule, but yeah, I'll be there soon."

I eyeballed the two again, sure they were up to something, but climbed in my truck, promising I'd be at Thoren's after a stop to grab my work clothes.

By the time I got to Thoren's, work was well under way.

I pulled into his long gravel drive, taking in the picturesque view of the rolling pasture and the old farmhouse that sat on top of the hill. I parked next to Nate and scanned the field beyond the house. Thoren, Nate, and Mike, from the looks of it, worked at the tree line in the distance. So this wasn't some bullshit, made-up thing, and we really were going to be working. Thank God. I needed a good, solid day of physical activity.

"Hey, Capt," Mike called as I reached them.

"Told you before, it's Mac when we aren't at the station. What's the plan, where do you need me?"

Thoren walked me through the project, and the four of us set to work, replacing fencing wire along the border of his property.

"What's happening with the arson case?" I asked Mike.

"Eh, not much. PD is still doing their investigation, and the officer who lost Watkins the first time finally got reprimanded. Other than that, we've just been chasing leads here and there. It'd be awesome if we could release a photo, but since T-Bird here is his identical twin, I hesitate to put it out there. After I released that news statement offering a reward for information and listed him as a suspect, I don't want to provoke him to escalate further. It was bad enough that he targeted the chief when that article went out. In my defense, I thought the reporter was going to be more discreet. But then again, the mayor had been in on that press conference, and he'd made sure to make it sound like Chief Hawkins was wasting time and resources on a dead end."

I stiffened at the mention of Olivia's name.

"The mayor is a jackass," Thoren grumbled. "So full of himself and his own political agenda. He's been salty ever since they fired his buddy and claps back at the council every chance he gets."

"He's salty because he's lost his kickbacks, and everyone knows it, but he just keeps getting reelected." Nate hammered the wire around the fence post with a little too much enthusiasm. "And he's taking too much joy in setting up Chief Hawkins."

What the fuck was he talking about? Olivia hadn't mentioned anything happening between her and the mayor.

Mo ambled up with a cooler mid-conversation, passing out fist bumps and taking a place opposite Mike.

"Speaking of Chief Hawkins," Thoren continued, unspooling the wire and handing a section to Mike, forcing me to step between the four of them to stay out of their way, "seems like you and the chief are making friends... Mac."

These fuckers. Got me all comfortable and then ambushed me into discussing my relationship with Olivia. I should've known when I saw their girlfriends at the ice cream shop.

"Leah said she's lovely," Mike offered. "And that's not Leah just being Leah. She really liked her."

"Jordan was bragging on her too," Nate added.

Thoren gave me a look. "You know Kylie gave me the deets, Cap—Mac. Said she saw you and the three of you looked cozy. Are you and the chief hanging out now?"

A little more than that, I wanted to say. I wanted to claim her. It felt wrong not to.

"From your silence," he continued, "which is scary as fuck most of the time, except for now, when you've got this 'Oh shit' look on your face, it looks like this situation is complicated."

"Yeah, Mac," Nate added, punctuating my name. "How's it feel to be around her, working for her every day? I mean, she's hot"—I frowned at him in warning—"and we know you have history. Is it weird working for your baby mama? Think you want to make it a second-chance comeback? Inquiring minds wanna know."

I wanted so badly to fess up. To shout to the world that Olivia and Rosie were mine. With anyone else, I'd have to deny it. And I was so tired of denying it.

I looked to the men who had worked alongside me for so many years. We'd been in life-and-death situations together. We had a bond forged in fire—literally. If I could trust anyone, it would be them.

"Things with Livvie are complicated." All four stopped and stared at me, and I realized my mistake. *Fuck.*

"You don't have a thing you need to talk about. Do you, Nate?"

"Nah. We were just covering all the bases to make sure you showed today."

They'd made some elaborate scheme and had me sweating for their damn gossip purposes. I sighed, knowing if the shoe were on the other foot, I'd hound the shit out of them 'til they talked about whatever was eating them. Might as well take a dose of my own medicine and be out with all of it.

So I told them. I told them about Rosie getting suspended and that leading to Liv coming to the lake house. I told them about how I forced them to come to my house when I realized they might be facing a threat. I told them how confused I was about all of it, except the part about knowing I wanted them close.

Mo passed out beers from his cooler. "What are you gonna do, Mac? You know how the city is against departmental relationships."

I scratched my head, because wasn't that the question of the year.

"You could go to PD," Mike offered.

"I'm no longer certified."

"Another city department?" Thoren asked.

"Nothing is open right now, but it could be an option."

"You're not thinking of leaving the city entirely, are you?" Nate hit me with a horrified look.

The truth was, I didn't know. Fighting fires was what I'd known most of my life. I didn't have any real skill set aside from renovations. But renovation work wouldn't pay for that balloon payment looming in the future.

"I'm not planning on going anywhere. I qualify for early retirement soon. I've been banking on using my leave payout, combined with what I've managed to save, and selling my Newman house to pay off a balloon payment on the lake house. I don't want to leave and lose that money. I've mapped it out, and it'll take all of my accruals, minus a few here and there for emergencies, but it is the only available option to keeping the lake house."

"Can you refinance it?"

"I don't know. I think the way it was structured meant that wasn't an option. I've been checking with my bank to see."

"What about selling?" Mo's deep voice cut in with the words that I dreaded.

"It was the place my parents wanted to retire to. Selling it, losing it, feels like a betrayal to their memory."

Nate reached for a second beer. "What's the lake house got to do with the chief?"

Mo looked at him like he was struggling for patience. "Because if the higher-ups get wind of the relationship, their jobs are at stake."

Thoren chimed in, "And that means losing his retirement payout."

"What about that training job offer you got a couple of months ago?" Nate asked.

"I wouldn't qualify for early retirement or my payout." The odds just continually seemed stacked against us.

Mike added, "And with the way the mayor is gunning for the chief, he'll try to make as big a deal as possible and fire them both. Make an example."

"And then where would that leave Olivia and Rosie?" I finished. "I can't take a chance on hurting them like that. Being fire chief was Olivia's dream. I don't wanna take a chance on losing the lake house, but I do want the opportunity to know my daughter, and maybe see where this leads with Livvie."

Silence fell between us. There was no easy answer. Someone had to lose in this situation.

"Well, we can at least help you keep the Livvie part a secret." Nate finally broke the silence.

"Thanks. For now, we're just trying to keep things normal, professional, and keep our distance from each other unless we are at home."

"Does HR know she's at your house?" Mo asked.

"No, she didn't change her address. No one knows except you." I thought of the conversation with Cal. "Well, maybe more. Cal mentioned it."

For an afternoon workday, this conversation had turned surprisingly deep. It felt good being able to confide in these guys. And maybe having more than just my ideas would help find an alternative solution.

"We'll help you any way we can, Mac."

"For now, just keep things quiet, and if you hear any grumblings or rumors, let me know."

"Speaking of rumors..." Mo started. "Did you guys hear that Cal is going to the county?"

"What? Why?" Mike, Nate, and Thoren all drew back.

"Just part-time right now, but I wouldn't blame him if he went full-time. Better benefits, more money," Mo replied.

"Yeah, because they work all that mandatory overtime." Thoren sneered. "It's a shit show over there, from what I hear."

It was time to put a stop to this before it became a full-on bash session. "Okay, guys. That's enough. We can't partner with them for mutual aid and then talk about them behind their backs. They've got some management issues. They'll get it sorted."

"Feels like Cal is betraying us."

Mo scoffed. "Not every station has a crew as cool as ours. Plus, I also heard he's been helping his sister and her kid. Probably needed the money and couldn't turn it down." Mo was a solid voice of reason for these younger guys. I clapped him on the shoulder in thanks for being the one to point out the obvious. My guys were good at their jobs. Smart, successful, competent firefighters. But sometimes they could just be stupid and self-centered about real life.

"Can't blame a man for taking care of his family." I spun and grabbed the next bail of wire. "Are we done gossiping? Can we get back to work now?"

* * *

Little did I know how big of a challenge keeping my distance and remaining professional around Olivia would be.

She sent out an email about physical testing, requiring all personnel to meet standards, pushing a ton of buttons and drawing criticism that it was fucking hard to remain silent about.

Then she called a mandatory meeting, where I had to pretend to be myself and not glare at an asshat from C-shift who continually stared at her legs.

"I just think it's ridiculous that 'everyone has to do it' was sent down," he said, putting quotation marks around the phrase, before sitting back with his arms across his chest. "We all know that 'everyone' won't be doing it."

I don't know how she maintained her calm, but her voice was ice cold when she replied, "Lieutenant. Are you implying that I will get a pass on this test?"

I was so fucking proud of her for not taking his shit.

"Just calling it like I see it."

"I see."

I loved it when she got all bossy and confident. I hoped she'd cream his ass. If anyone could, it was her.

The next week, she'd shown up at the training tower in full turnout gear, just like all the other guys, and proceeded to smoke his ass in the exercises, much to everyone's delight. No one liked that guy anyway.

But for her efforts, she won the open respect of my entire crew.

"Chief is a badass," more than one of them had muttered.

Only I knew what it'd cost her to go out and push herself to the limit. I'd made it up to her by running her an Epsom salt bath and giving her a very enjoyable full-body massage.

Still, on the job, she showed up in high heels the next

day and called a video conference, in which she congratulated the few who'd beat her times and let the others know she'd be ready for a rematch.

Issuing the challenge like that had been effective, and more than one person took her up on it.

When I asked her about it, she said, "They'll never respect me if I don't prove that I can and will do their job. I'll at least give it my all."

One week, then two, went by with no suitable solution. My guys had proven trustworthy, and even when Olivia was present at the station, they'd been true to their word to not say anything. Rosie went to homecoming with one of the little pricks she'd met after the art debacle. He'd withstood my glare fairly well. And Olivia and I had immensely enjoyed our alone time.

Olivia presented her budget with professional passion, and several fire staff had gone to the mat to show their support for her. The city manager, though he'd blustered a little, had capitulated and given her everything she'd asked for. But I imagine it would've been hard to say no when she was asking for equipment upgrades to meet safety standards, especially when the ones making the decisions had to look the guys they were putting at risk in the eye. Hard to say no when it became so personal.

Overall, things were going well.

Until one day they weren't.

Tones rang out for a structure fire, not our station, but we were running backup. Since the arsonist had been laying low, we'd not had many structure fires. With only one engine in each station, we usually had a second station moving for backup, either with zone coverage or pulling in to assist once the first unit arrived on scene.

As I jumped in the pickup to follow the engine, my cell

phone rang. It was odd that Olivia would be calling me, knowing I was responding to a call. So, though it wasn't the best time, I accepted.

"Mac." Olivia's voice was as panicked as I'd ever heard it.

I slipped the phone between my shoulder and chin, then flipped the lights with one hand and drove with the other. "Talk to me, babe."

"The address of the call, that's where Rosie is supposed to be."

The world stopped. Time stood still.

My heartbeat flooded my brain, and all I could do was focus on following the flashing red lights in front of me.

"I can't get her on the phone, and I can't find her location." Olivia's voice shook with emotion. She sounded as close to losing it as I'd ever heard her.

"Keep trying. I'll call you back. And Liv—" I paused and took a shaky breath. "I'll find her."

I slipped the phone into the cupholder and passed the engine, hauling ass. I was first on the scene, even beating the first unit. I jumped from the truck and headed around the back of the residence, reporting back to my crew. The adrenaline rush hit me, and though I tried, I couldn't keep the panic from my voice.

"No visible flames, no visible smoke."

No Rosie.

Hell, there was no one even at the house.

"What's up, Captain?" Thoren jogged up to me, Nate in tow, both wearing serious expressions.

"Rosie's supposed to be at this house." The words were hard to say out loud.

"Doesn't look like anyone is home." Nate eyed the house, whose alarm was blasting. "Could be a false alarm."

He was right, of course. Why didn't I think of that? "Contact 911 and see if they've made contact with the alarm company and homeowner."

"Ten-four."

A half hour later, we rolled back up to the station. False alarm due to faulty wiring on the system.

But no Rosie.

I paced the grounds outside the station, trying not to vomit, waiting to hear back from the half dozen officers I'd called in to look for her.

Technically, it was too soon for a BOLO. But I'd just asked that they keep an eye out while on patrol.

My phone rang, and I answered it before the first ring ended.

"She's home," Olivia stated flatly. I sank to the curb outside the station, so relieved I almost missed Olivia say, "You better tell her you love her before I kill her."

"Where was she?"

Big Mo, who'd been standing vigil, perked up at my words. He hurried to me and took a seat next to me.

"She was *who* she was supposed to be with. But she won't be allowed to have any unsupervised visits with *Ryan* for a very long time."

Ryan, the little shit from homecoming. Still, I couldn't get past the "she's home."

"I'm going to let you go so I can go grill your daughter about birth control now." Olivia's voice was ice cold and, frankly, a little terrifying. "I'll call you later."

She hung up before I could say anything else. My hand dropped uselessly to my lap.

Had we been a normal couple, I would've been able to be home with her. But under the current circumstances, I had to sit by and wait here at work, trying not to puke or break down in tears or make any sort of scene. Because fucking rules dictated that I couldn't let my feelings be known for Olivia. And it sucked.

Mo laid a hand to my shoulder. "Everything okay, Captain?"

I sat a little straighter. "Yeah. Yeah. She showed."

"She okay?"

I shrugged. "At least until her mother gets done with her."

His chuckle was a low rumble. "Moms and daughters can go for hours. Your best bet is to stay here, let them hash it out, and pick up the damage when they settle down a bit."

I nodded dumbly. I'd run the gamut of emotion throughout the day, cycling through everything from ice-cold fear, to heated anger, to blinding relief. And now I sagged from the weight of it all.

"How do you do it?"

"What's that?"

"You've got girls, a wife. How do you manage them?"

He chuckled again. "Dude. I don't. I just hold on for dear life most days." He clapped me on the shoulder, then pushed to his feet. "But man is it a sweet ride."

By the time I got home the next morning, Rosie and Olivia had made a truce. Olivia called in, and Rosie skipped school. So I took my girls out to the pond.

"Do I need to have a word with Ryan?" I asked, paddling out to the best fishing hole.

Rosie blushed but owned her mistakes. "No, Sir."

"We will be going to the doctor about birth control, though," Olivia added, and I nearly dropped the oar.

They both dissolved in laughter. Brought together by their pursuit to harass me, the sound so bright and such a relief, it didn't matter if they were laughing at my expense. I splashed them until they begged for mercy, making a mental note to definitely have a chat with Ryan.

But through it all, the thought that I should've been there was in the back of my mind. I should've been the one out searching. And I didn't know how I was going to survive parenting.

Chapter Twenty-One

Mac

It was amazing how fast time moved when you weren't paying attention. As I threw the ball with Buster one cool fall morning, I looked back over all that had changed in the few weeks since Olivia and Rosie had barged into my life.

For starters, tossing the ball with Buster was no longer my chore, and something that now belonged to Rosie. But she'd spent the night with her friend Shae, this only after Olivia and I had had a long talk with Shae's father about the day she'd scared the shit out of us by sneaking off with Ryan, so here I was in the yard while Buster played in the dew-covered grass.

I still didn't know if Rosie and Ryan had snuck off and had sex—didn't want to know because that would possibly mean jail time for me. What I did know was that not even a week later, he was out of the picture, and Rosie was hanging out with Shae more.

And this chilly morning, she was gone, and I had plans with my woman... just as soon as the damn dog was settled. Buster forgot the tennis ball and started making his necessary poop circles, spinning to the left and right in combinations of two to the left, three to the right, and we were in business.

I was trying to decide whether breakfast-in-bed seduction was necessary, or if I wanted to just go in and wake Olivia with my mouth between her legs, when the screen door banged behind me.

I looked over my shoulder to find her huddled in a big fluffy robe, cradling a coffee cup. The morning sun spotlighted her perfectly, giving her skin the softest glow. When she'd walked into that island bar, it had been the same. Just *bam*. The minute she showed up, my whole world turned on its head. As if the sun said, *This beautiful woman needs a spotlight, so here's a sunray of her very own.*

I turned to fully drink in the sight of her, aware that, once again, I was shifting on the inside. I'd never thought to find lasting love. Had given up on the idea of family.

And along came Rosie and Olivia, and now they made up my world. I couldn't imagine my life without them. There was still no real resolution to the job situation. I'd been checking to see if my retirement would transfer if I moved, but asking HR any pointed questions was risky. Couldn't tip them off. Who knew what they might share with the higher-ups, even though the conversations were supposedly confidential. I didn't trust them.

All I knew for certain was that I wanted this woman in my life.

She caught my eye and tilted her head. "What's that look for?"

I began a slow stalk toward her, letting all the heat and desire, and maybe even love, show in my gaze.

She turned to face me, her back to the porch rail as I crowded her, taking her mug in one hand to set it aside and untying the sash at her waist with the other. Her nipples peaked under the cold morning air. With the knuckle of my forefinger, I traced the edge of her low-cut silky gown, down the soft mound of one breast and back up to the opposite side, where I pushed the thin strap off her shoulder. The gown fell loose, exposing one tantalizing breast.

I shifted my stance and bent low to take her perfect tip into my mouth.

She exhaled softly, threading her fingers into my hair. I slipped the remaining strap off her shoulder, exposing her other nipple before circling it with my tongue. "I love these delicious tits," I said, palming her. The weight of her globes filling my hand, spilling over, the indent of my fingers in her soft flesh, the tips peaked in the cold morning air—all of it was a dream come true.

"I love this gown and how sensually it glides over your skin." I took one pert nipple in my mouth, sliding my hand down the soft front to cup the heat between her legs.

"No panties, Liv? Did you come out here bare so I could have easy access?"

Beneath my hands, she squirmed, her hips thrusting against my hand. I slid a leg between hers, pressing against her heat.

"Look at you riding my leg. Fucking gorgeous. You want me to slip the hem of this gown up? I could be inside of you in seconds. Is that why you came out here looking like a wet dream?"

"Mac," she whimpered, the longing and need in her voice matching the desire coursing through me.

I backed away from her with a groan of protest and took her dainty hand in mine, pulling her toward the door. "Problem is, gorgeous, I want to take my time with you."

Letting her see all the desire I held for her, I led her inside the house, the warmth of the kitchen hitting my skin. I pushed her against the door, swiping the robe and gown off in one move.

Her hands slid under the hem of my shirt, branding the skin of my stomach, my chest. I wanted her hands on me, needed to be inside this woman like I needed air to breathe. I craved the connection, wanted to consume all of her. Drink her in and let her passion give me life.

I cupped her hips and took her mouth, drinking from her, devouring her. It was a claiming kiss, a soul-destroying kiss, and I never wanted it to end.

She shifted, wrapping a leg around my hip as if she, too, couldn't get close enough.

I broke the kiss, lowered to a knee, and feasted on her until her cries grew loud, supporting her as she went limp around me.

I shoved my pants down as I stood, and then I buried myself inside her. Using the door to brace, I lifted her other leg around my hip and drove into her over and over again, giving her everything I had inside me.

Nothing mattered. Nothing except this beautiful woman and the way she commanded my body. Words rose from my soul with every thrust, "You're beautiful. You're everything. You're mine," until the pressure built and shimmered and, in a blinding flash, washed over me.

When I came down, I lowered her legs, slid my hands to cup her jaw, and kissed her, whispering her name against her lips like a love song.

She cupped my cheek and kissed me softly. "Mac."

I opened my eyes to find hers on me.

"I love you," I blurted into the tender moment.

She went still.

"I never thought I'd say the words to anyone again. I never thought my life would feel this full." I paused to kiss her again because I couldn't not. She cupped my cheek, her eyes glossing with a sheen of tears.

"I don't care what happens. I want you in my life. I'm tired of pretending. I want to claim you, let the whole world know that you are mine, but more importantly, that I am yours. All of me. Belongs to you."

Her thumb traced my lip, my cheek. Then she pushed me away and bent to retrieve her robe.

Not what I expected.

She slipped the robe on and slid away from me, gliding down the hall to the bathroom as if I hadn't just laid myself bare.

I stood frozen, staring blankly at the empty space by the door.

Had I misread her? All of the long nights we'd spent together, the depth of emotion in her eyes, the connection we had when we made love. The way she showed me in a thousand different ways that she cared. Had I made it all up in my head? Had I gotten it all wrong? If so, how big of a fool had I been?

One other time, a woman had walked away. I'd been so blindsided when Diedre stood me up, left me stranded and alone in front of a church full of guests like a fool. She'd taken a piece of me, my heart, and all my hopes and dreams for a loving wife and family. I'd waited over fifteen years to feel this depth of emotion again, to lose myself in a woman. Had promised myself I'd never be that vulnerable again.

For Rosie, I could live through the pain of Olivia not

loving me in the same way, but I didn't want to. I wanted all of Liv, the way she had all of me.

"Mac," she called softly from behind me. I spun like an eager child looking for a prize, to find her at the couch. She held out a hand to me, and like the fool I was, I staggered to her, stepping over the shattered pieces of my rejected heart.

I slipped my hand into hers, and she directed me to the couch like she was coaxing a wild animal. When she had me seated, she slipped into my lap, wrapping my arms around her.

Then, she smiled and kissed me.

"I had to go clean up," she said, running her fingers through my hair. She paused at my frozen reaction and leaned back to look into my eyes. "Oh, sweetheart. You look so stunned."

How could such an intelligent woman be so dense? "Liv, I told you that I love you."

Her lips tipped up softly. "I heard."

"You walked away." I choked on the words. It was all I could do to push them out.

"Is that what this look is for? Because I wanted to concentrate on the words you were saying, rather than the mess running down my leg?"

"Olivia." I said her name as a warning and made to shove her away. I couldn't be here for this flippant attitude. Couldn't sit by if she was going to make fun of me.

"Stop." Her voice held a command and required my attention. "Mac Collins. You need to learn something about me. When the man I love tells me he loves me for the first time, even though I've seen it in his gaze, felt it in his touch, and witnessed it in the way he takes care of me every single day... I don't want anything distracting me. Especially when he's scared to death and looks like he might bolt naked out the door."

Her words thawed my insides slightly, though the rejection still lingered.

"Let's get one thing clear," she continued, wrapping one arm around my shoulder and cupping my jaw. "I love you too. I wouldn't walk away from you, ever."

She kissed me softly, taking away a little more of the sting.

"Sweetheart, look at me," she whispered, cupping my jaw.

I did then, really looking deep into her eyes. What I found was compassion, kindness, acceptance, and love.

"I love you too." Her voice shook as the words left her mouth and became real. Diving deep into my heart, touching that soft wound that had never fully healed, that lonely place deep inside me that longed for someone to see me—to love me.

"Don't ever leave me." The pleading words came on a whisper, ripped from my heart and thrust into the space between us before I could stop them. "I don't deserve you, won't ever be good enough for you. But please don't ever leave me."

Her expression shifted, tears filling her eyes. "I won't. I'm so sorry, Mac. That was heartless of me to walk away a moment ago." She kissed me again, as if trying to soothe the hurt. "You've been so gentle with me, making me feel so secure. I just took for granted that you knew how I felt. I should've taken more care, been softer, especially because I know you have such a tender heart. Please forgive me."

I could and I would. But maybe I also needed to grow a pair and realize that just because she hadn't immediately responded the way I wanted her to, didn't mean her feelings weren't there.

"I shouldn't be so sensitive," I admitted, finally finding the strength to communicate.

"Mac, it's okay to be sensitive. It's one of my favorite things about you. I promise to honor your sensitive heart."

"You could make it up to me by marrying me." The words popped out before I could stop them. But once they were in the open, hanging between us, the future became real. I wanted her. Wanted her and Rosie in my life for always.

"How would that work? One of us would have to give up the job."

"I'd give up everything for you," I vowed. "I can find another job. I can sell the lake house. I can freeze my retirement. Hell, the way Rosie likes to spend money, I'll be working until I'm dead, anyway."

Liv studied me, her eyes flashing back and forth between mine. "I want to say yes."

"Then say it," I pleaded, "let's just do it. We'll sort the rest out later."

A beautiful smile spread across her face, and her eyes softened. "Mac, honey. It's not that easy."

"It is, Liv. It's just that easy." A little twinge of doubt sprouted low in my gut. "Unless you don't want me."

"I do, Mac. There's just so much at stake, and this feels really fast."

I scrambled for a backup plan. "How about we just make this a permanent move, then." I needed some commitment from her.

Silently, she watched me. Stroking a hand through my hair, studying my eyes, trying to read me.

"I'm serious, Liv. I want you here. With me. I don't care

what it takes. I'll turn in my notice at the station tomorrow if that's what it takes."

Her throat bobbed as she swallowed. "Mac, I'm scared they'll make me out like some kind of boss predator shacking up with a subordinate."

I shifted her on my lap, turning her to straddle me, and cupped her cheeks. Gazing into her eyes like I could will her to see how I felt about her, about us, and how the rest didn't matter. "We have a history. Long before the fire department. We have a daughter as proof." My heart thudded in my chest. Beating so hard, so fast. "Just be with me. Be all-in with me."

Her hand slipped over mine, lacing our fingers and pressing them to her heart. "I'd feel so guilty if you left the department you love because of us." Tears pooled in her eyes.

"Sweetheart, there's a reason you do this job when you're young." The corner of my mouth tugged up. "And I'm getting too old. I don't recover from all-night runs like I used to. I can't fall back asleep after tones drop, whether it's my station or another station. If I'm honest, I only stayed because I've been so close to retiring, and I thought if I could just hang on for another few years, I'd be okay."

I closed my eyes and admitted, "I love my guys, my crew. But I don't love the job anymore." The huge confession felt like a weight being lifted from my shoulders. "If I could've moved to a role that had more regular hours..."

"The role I took from you."

My eyes popped open. "Sweetheart, you didn't take the chief's position from me. You earned it. You do a hell of a good job, too."

That earned me a tentative smile. "So what now?"

"You and Rosie move in with me permanently, where

you belong. I'll turn in my notice and start looking for something else. We'll be a family."

We decided to wait for Rosie to get home to tell her our happy news and spent the day celebrating in bed. Later that afternoon, Olivia left to get her, and I schemed up a special meal for my ladies, complete with flowers on the table and steaks on the grill.

Rosie bounded up the stairs, Buster hot on her heels, and straight into my arms. "Hey, Mac," she cried like she hadn't seen me in a month.

"Hey, squirt. Oh, sorry, *Buttercup.* Did you have fun?" I set her back on her feet and watched as she folded onto the porch swing and patted the seat for Buster to join her, knowing damn good and well that the dog wouldn't jump. Except, to my surprise, he did.

"We had a blast. What'd you and Mom do?"

Olivia's shoulders rose to her ears as she looked at me with wide eyes, clearly asking if now was the time.

I checked the steaks and slipped the tongs onto the hook, then walked to Olivia and gave her a peck on the cheek.

Then I faced my daughter.

"We talked. And now I need to talk to you." I pulled a chair over to her and sank into it, dropping my elbows to my knees, not knowing how to go about this.

"Sweetheart, I think you know it was a huge surprise when I found out about you."

Her eyes shuttered as if she were afraid of what I might say. This kid. Stole my heart and put it back together without even trying. But now she looked scared to death. Of what, I wasn't sure. I extended my hand to offer her some comfort.

"Rosa Nell, will you look at me, please?"

She slipped her small hand into mine. Hands I'd give anything to go back in time and see when they were little. Still, hers were small and soft, and the sight of her trusting me made me a sentimental fool. I gave her fingers a reassuring squeeze. "I have a confession to make."

She swallowed, her eyes wide, face stark.

"I saw your TikTok a while back. When you showed up here that first day, I knew exactly who you were."

She paled and swallowed again. "Mac, I can explain."

"You didn't do anything wrong, sweetheart. Quite the contrary. Everything you did set us up to find each other, and I'm grateful that you did."

"I feel like there's a 'but' coming." She looked wide-eyed at Olivia. "Mom? Is there a 'but'?"

I didn't give Olivia a chance to respond. I needed to get this out in the open. "Rosie, it's not bad. I promise. And I'm sorry I'm messing this up. What I'm trying, badly, to say is that..." I squeezed her hand again, drawing strength from the contact. "I love you, sweetheart. I love your mother. And I want to make this permanent. For all of us. So I asked your mom to marry me."

Her wide eyes bounced from me to Olivia and back to me. "For real?" she squealed in delight.

I nodded, and then she launched herself toward me, abruptly bursting into tears. "Oh my God! We're getting married? We'll be a real family?"

Olivia bracketed our hug from Rosie's back and said, "Well, not exactly. I turned down the marriage proposal. But I take this to mean you're okay with it if I said yes?"

Rosie drew back, leaving my neck wet with her tears,

but her legs were still clasped around my waist, holding on like she never wanted to let go.

"Mom, don't be stupid. MacDaddy is a catch."

I flinched at the term before she added, "You'd better say yes."

Olivia didn't immediately respond, and the old doubt clamored forth, but this time, I knew I had my daughter on my side, and it was only a matter of time before her mom came around.

Chapter Twenty-Two

Mac

"Hey, Capt." Nate's voice came through the phone just as happy and chipper as ever early Sunday morning. Before I could even say a hello, he barged on. "Listen, I know it's short notice, but we're doing an impromptu cookout today. A little going away party for Cal since tomorrow is his last shift. My house around four."

Even though I'd rather hang with my girls at home on a Sunday afternoon, I couldn't really say no when we were paying respects to a brother.

"Oh, and make sure Chief Hawkins and Rosie know they're invited too."

I made a noise low in my throat, and once again, Nate continued, "Thanks, Capt. See you then."

"Who was that?" Rosie called from behind her phone.

"Nate. They're having a cookout this afternoon."

Rosie's eyes lit up. "Oh, cool! Can we go?"

My girl. Always ready to go and do.

I glanced over at Olivia lounging at the opposite end of the couch, book in hand. "Yeah, we need to."

Olivia glanced up. "Do we go in separate cars?"

As much as that sounded like it should be the smart thing to do, I was done with the games. "Nah. We go together."

"Oh my gosh, that dog is the cutest," Rosie exclaimed as we rounded the corner of Nate's house. The cookout was in full swing by the time we arrived—the grill smoking on the deck, and all of my guys milling around, no doubt talking shit. Their women were setting chairs up around a fire pit in the yard. Country music blared over hidden speakers.

"This feels a little like middle school," Olivia quipped. "Guys on one side and girls on the other."

I snorted. "It'll be like this until the sun goes down and the couples start their dancing. That's when I usually head out."

"You don't like dancing anymore? I seem to remember a time..." She winked at me.

"I do. I didn't like being the fifth wheel when everyone else had a partner."

"Hey, Mac! Hey, Chief!" Jordan bounded across the yard. "Hey, girlie, I like your shirt," she complimented Rosie, pointing out their matching Swiftie tees.

"Oh. Em. Gee! I love Taylor. I haven't seen her live in concert since we couldn't get tickets. But I really want to."

Olivia nodded toward the guys. "Should we go say hello?"

I grunted a response and followed her up the stairs.

"Hey, Chief. Want a beer?" Nate greeted, offering her a cold longneck.

"You guys know how to pull it together on short notice, don't you?"

"Eh, it's mostly Jordan. She's pretty much always down for a cookout and can pull it together in a flash. Some of the other guys are inside."

Conversation grew stilted and tense for a few minutes. My guys were never this quiet or awkward. It was like they couldn't relax around Olivia. She must've felt it, too, because she gave them a polite smile, not quite ice-princess level, but not her usual easy grin either. At the opposite corner of the deck, Cal sat gazing out over the backyard. A couple of guys from Station Three were chatting nearby.

"I'm just gonna..." She tipped her beer toward Cal and then grabbed a second beer from the cooler before making her way over.

"You guys still pissed he's going to the county?" I broke the silence.

"Maybe a little," Thoren said. "But I can respect why he needed to."

"Then don't you think it's kinda a dick move to leave him sitting alone at his own going away party?" Sometimes these guys could be so clueless. Regardless, they broke up and joined Olivia and Cal mid-conversation. I took a second to appreciate how my woman was giving her full attention to one of her soon-to-be former firefighters, giving him her ear and treating him like he still mattered.

"...that's understandable."

"I don't want to leave. Things have been much better since you've been on board, Chief. But their starting pay is nearly ten grand more than what I make now, plus the over-time... I can't turn it down."

"You don't owe me an explanation. I'd never hold you back from an opportunity. And if things don't work out, hopefully, we'll still have a place for you. It'll be hard to replace someone with your skill and experience. But if you don't mind, I'd like to use you as an example for some much-needed changes in our department."

"What are you thinking, Chief?" Nate piped up.

Olivia turned to face him. "We've got to make some changes before we lose more personnel. Better pay, updated equipment, and renovations to our other two stations. The list is endless."

Thoren snorted. "That's a helluva lot more than the last two chiefs did. You sure the council will go for it?"

Olivia smirked. "Probably not. But I've got to try."

The conversation expanded from there, and I stood back and watched while my woman essentially wooed the entire lot of them. I'd become burned out, dissatisfied in my role. It was painfully clear that the people in this conversation were invested in making a change for the better. I wanted to be a part of that. A part of something bigger. To leave something better than I found it.

Before Olivia, I'd been content to just do my job, bide my time. But what would it be like if I were in a role that could make a difference for the department?

"Are y'all done solving all the world's problems up there?" Kylie called from the yard. "We're ready to eat!"

Jordan gave out instructions for the food line, while Nate finished pulling burgers off the grill. Everyone ate and mingled for a short while, but most left soon after, including Cal, who cited needing to get home to help his sister with her baby as his reason for leaving early.

Eventually, it was just my crew left. Thoren set the fire in the pit ablaze. And Kylie changed the music, which immediately led to Mike and Leah slow dancing. I shot a knowing glance at Olivia, reminding her that I'd predicted this would happen.

"Awe, they're so sweet," Rosie cooed, bestowing her favorite compliment on the smitten couple.

"They're nauseating is what they are," Kylie supplied.

Thoren wrapped an arm around her shoulders and kissed her temple. "You know you're secretly jealous that I haven't swept you out for a spin. Although, I'd rather steal you away behind Pearl."

All the hairs on my neck rose, but Kylie stepped in just in time, muttering, "Watch it, T-bird. We've got little ears tonight."

"Who's Pearl?" Rosie asked, hopefully missing the innuendo.

Jordan joined the group. "Oh, Pearl's my camper van."

Rosie's face lit up. "Mom and I love to camp!"

Jordan's eyes darted between Rosie and Olivia excitedly. "We should totally take Pearl out for a girls' weekend."

"We could take Gracie and Buster somewhere they could swim!" Rosie, easily caught up in Jordan's excitement, began speaking in exclamation points. "We could take our bikes! That would be the best! Mom, please say yes!"

Olivia laughed. A full, real laugh. One that I was intimately familiar with, but my friends were finally seeing her the way I saw her.

"It does sound like fun."

"Awesome," Rosie cried, practically jumping into the arms of her new bestie Jordan. If I could do something so simple as take my daughter camping and make her this happy, I'd do it every weekend. As it was, I was immensely grateful that this friends group that had always included me in their parties now seemed to also be opening their arms to my daughter and my woman.

Nate stepped up beside me and gave me a shoulder bump. "She's a cute kid, Capt."

"Told you before to call me Mac."

"I know, sorry. But you'll always be Capt to me. Just like she'll always be Chief to me," he replied, nodding toward Olivia. "It's just a sign of respect. Not trying to make a big deal out of it."

I made a low noise in my throat. I could see his point.

"Anyway, I'm glad you guys came out. It's been fun. And heads up, Jordan will have that girls' trip planned before you know it. So if you aren't okay with it, now's the time to speak up."

I side-eyed him. "I think Olivia and Rosie can handle themselves."

"And if the girls go camping, maybe you'll see fit to invite all the guys to this lake house that you constantly talk about, but yet we've never seen."

"I've invited you."

"No, Capt. You've told us all about the renovations you've made, but you've never asked us to come help you, never called on us, even when we offered."

"What are y'all scheming over here." Thoren stepped to the other side of me.

"Eh, I was just telling Capt that if the girls go camping, the guys can head to the lake house."

Thoren's eyebrows shot up. "Hell yeah, I've been waiting on an invite for years."

For the first time in forever, I felt truly chastised. We were tight at work. Our jobs demanded trust and being able to work together. But I didn't realize that these men might actually consider me a friend outside of work, outside of being their boss. The realization was sobering.

Before I could respond, the women rejoined us,

including Kylie, and the conversation shifted yet again. So much in my life was changing, and so much would continue to change before it was over with. And suddenly, my eyes were open to all I would miss when I did leave the department.

Olivia slid in next to me, our arms barely brushing, and I envied the casual ease with which these men could drape an arm around their women—Nate with Jordan—or press a kiss to their hair—Thoren with Kylie. Her pinky brushed mine, and I latched on to it with mine like a lifeline.

Friends.

Found family.

Laughter and love and fun.

I could see the life I wanted laid out before me, but what would I have to sacrifice to get it?

Chapter Twenty-Three

Olivia

The court square was hopping with energy when Rosie and I went into town the next evening. The Main Street Planning Committee hosted events several times a year to draw visitors to the downtown area. Market vendors were set up on all four sides of the courthouse sidewalk, shop owners had their doors opened, with chalkboard signs offering deals to patrons, and restaurants and bars in town had different wines available for tasting. The sidewalks were a crush of people out milling around during the Sip-n-Shop event.

The historic old courthouse had opened its doors for visitors to tour the hundred-plus-year-old building. Children played in the small grassy areas behind vendors under the twinkle-lit trees, and on every corner, a different musician had set up, offering an array of different music styles.

It was noisy and quaint and everything small town.

"Oh, Mom, can we go to The Mercantile? They have a carving of a boat that I know Mac will love."

I followed her into the store, picking up a book that I thought he might also like.

"I can't wait until you guys make things official, and I can tell the world," Rosie said as we left the store and headed toward the coffee shop.

I grinned because I was as ready to brag as she was. Having to keep our relationship status secret was the only damper to the otherwise joyous weekend.

Across the courtyard, Thoren exited the courthouse, pulling a cap low on his forehead. Hoping that his girl-friend Kylie and her friends might be around, I called his name. I dragged Rosie with me and tried to catch up to him.

"Thoren," I called.

He slowed, looking over his shoulder.

"Is Kylie with you?"

He turned then, looking somewhere over my shoulder. "Nope." The muscle in his jaw ticked as his gaze lit briefly on me before shifting to Rosie.

"This your daughter?" His voice was off.

He tugged his cap lower on his forehead before shoving his hands in his coat pockets.

Beside me, Rosie laughed. "Of course, silly. Don't act like you don't know who I am because I kicked your butt at pool the last time I was at the station."

Thoren shuffled, watching his feet, the cap blocking my full view of his face. "You got me."

"Well, tell Kylie I said hello, please."

He nodded and turned to leave without a goodbye.

"Weird," Rosie complained.

Something didn't sit right with me over the exchange either. "Yeah." I watched him until he blended in with the rest of the evening crowd.

"Let's go down this block next." Rosie tugged me along behind her, Thoren already forgotten.

Minutes later, a loud boom sounded from the direction of the courthouse, and people began running out of the historic building.

I hauled Rosie to the corner and pushed her back to the brick side of the building, out of the way of the chaos.

I needed a radio, and I needed it now. Instead, I called 911 on their direct line.

"This is Chief Hawkins," I yelled into the phone. Fuck professional. Fuck calm. This chaos was real.

"I'm downtown, and there's been an explosion of some kind at the courthouse," I yelled over the screams as people ran by me. The building had been open for tours, and there was no telling how many people were injured.

"10-4, 1201. We've received multiple calls, units are en route." The wail of the engines started before I could even end the call.

Headquarters was only two blocks away. I could run Rosie down there for safekeeping, grab my radio, and make it back to the scene.

Smoke rose from under the copper dome and began pouring out of the building. People darted across the street, right out in front of cars. Someone was going to get killed if they hadn't already.

I glanced at my daughter, my heart thumping from the adrenaline coursing through me. There was no time to get Rosie to the station, even though it was only two blocks away. I couldn't leave this scene.

Engine One pulled up on West Court Square, blocking traffic.

"Rosie, come on," I yelled, grabbing her hand and darting through pedestrians, sprinting to the engine. I could put her by the truck, and she'd be safe, and I could keep an eye on her *and* do my job.

I made it to the crew as they were pulling hoses and ordered Rosie to stand at the back of the truck, out of the way of the crew, but in a safe zone.

Then I set to work. "Lieutenant. SITREP. I'm without comms."

He was busy working the pumps, looking at the hoses and back to the gauges. "Engines from Two, Three, and Four are en route."

In that moment, I felt like the most useless chief ever. I didn't have a radio. I couldn't take scene command. I didn't have bunker gear. All I could do was stand there and—

"Extra radio in the cab, Chief," he yelled over the noise of the pumper.

I went to grab the radio and established command. Mac would hear my voice and know Rosie was on scene with me.

Water flowed into the hoses as the first two interior crews approached the structure. Despite the personnel packed up and ready to go, and the ones waiting to go in next, we'd need more backup if we were going to save the historic building. We needed all hands on deck, plus mutual aid. I made a quick call to the county chief and requested help to cover zones and provide an additional aerial truck.

Moments later, a rescue squad truck and a second engine from the outlying stations pulled in.

The police department established a perimeter. A relief ambulance stationed behind the trucks.

With a glance to ensure that Rosie was still safely tucked where I'd left her, I walked toward the opposite end of the courthouse to get a visual of the crew entering.

I saw Mac pointing, leading his crew. His bunker gear

hung on his hips, jacket on but unbuttoned. Well-used helmet on his head.

Seeing him was a relief I hadn't known I'd needed. Just one moment of clarity and stability. Mac was that touchstone.

I clicked my mic to tell him that mutual aid had been requested. Nothing. My radio was dead.

Jogging across the square to him, I called his name as I got closer. He scanned me quickly, and his expression lightened almost imperceptibly.

"Do you have an extra radio in your truck?" I asked. "Mine died, and we've got flames showing on the first floor. South side. I need you to relay that."

Around us, the square was packed with firefighters in bunker gear. Plump hoses filled with water crisscrossed the lawn. Smoke rose in the early evening sky. Red lights flashed from the tops of the engines, reflecting off the glass of nearby businesses. The whole scene was chaotic, and yet, it had a beautiful rhythm to it.

"No radio." He scowled, yelling over the drone of the diesel engine. "The damn spare won't hold a charge."

Inadequate equipment on a life-and-death scene—the idea made me nauseous.

Things had to change. I'd started the process, but there was still more to accomplish.

I pitched the useless equipment into the truck. "I need you to establish command, because I have no comms." I knew full well this was not my best option. As chief, I should be in charge of the scene. But without the ability to communicate, my hands were tied.

"Okay." Ever confident, capable. That was my Mac. "Where's Rosie?" The worry in his voice mirrored my own and nearly set me over the edge.

"She's at the back of Engine One. I'm going to check on her now. I've called in mutual aid. County should be here with their aerial soon."

Relief flooded his features, I imagined both at the news that Rosie was fine and that help was on the way. "Good."

"If this thing gets any hotter, we'll have to go to defensive stand."

His jaw went taut. "Give us a chance, Chief. We can't give up. Trust us. Let's see what we can do."

Of all the people on this scene, I trusted Mac the most. He was the only one I would've relinquished command to. He stood before me, tall and proud and strong and one hundred percent ready to give his all.

With a nod and a long look that I hoped said so many things I couldn't voice, I turned over command, taking his radio and announcing, "911, NFD 1201 turning command to NFD 1222."

"10-4, NFD 1201. Establishing NFD 1222 as Incident Command."

I stepped back and watched as Mac shifted into leader mode.

In that moment, I'd never felt like more of a failure. My crew needed me. The citizens depended on me, and I was left without a radio. No way to dictate decisions, to support my crews. They could get my decisions through Mac, but it wouldn't be *my* voice directing them. Letting them know I was in charge, that they could trust that I would take care of them.

I prayed that the mayor wasn't on scene and watching me hand over command.

My probationary period was nearing the end, but he'd been looking for a way to terminate me since day one. This might be his opportunity.

My dad would be so ashamed of me.

I swallowed my pride and squared my shoulders. I wouldn't go down without a fight. And what better way to fight than to let the best do their job.

I caught Mac's attention and motioned toward Rosie.

He nodded my way, attention already shifted to the job at hand, issuing orders. The first attack teams—three crews, six personnel—were already inside, relaying scene details. Knocking down the raging fire.

Two-man teams from each of the four trucks paired off, their backups waiting for the call for relief. Mac made the call to send in secondary support, and two teams from the eastern block of the court square raced across the lawn.

And I stood helplessly and watched.

Chapter Twenty-Four

Mac

Pacing the perimeter of the building to the opposite corner, I called for a headcount check and status update from my teams inside. Flames lit the interior of the second story. This side needed more attention.

The radio crackled. "1253 to command," Nate's voice called over the radio, a hollow, static-filled crackle. "Staircase is fully engulfed."

"10-4, staircase is out of commission. Command to Aerial Two, see if you can get inside that second-story window."

The fire shifted and rolled, licking out of windows, growing hotter and hotter. We were losing it. Looked like Cal would be leading a crew on his last shift. "B-team, take the south entrance."

A loud crack sounded from across the court square, and radio traffic went nuts.

Cal, the lead firefighter, jerked and fell to the ground.

"What the fuck?" I barked.

Crack. Crack.

The other crew dropped low to the ground as screams rose above the cacophony of the scene and the chilling retort of rifle fire.

"Active shooter, take cover!"

I wrapped my arms around Olivia and slammed her against the engine, covering her body with my own, before glancing over my shoulder in the direction of where she'd left our daughter. Too much distance separated us from her, the length of a city block.

Policemen barreled in behind us, providing cover. Guns drawn, radios squawking.

"It had to come from the roof of the Alamo!"

"I've got visual on a subject."

More shots rang out, pinging the side of the engine. We ducked behind the safety of the firetruck as the bullets struck true.

"He took out the pump panel," I yelled.

"Jesus Christ, he's cut off water supply to the crew inside the building." Her words were barely audible in the din around us.

Out on the lawn, one of the firemen dragged Cal's prone body to safety. Olivia gripped my hand, squeezed her eyes shut, and prayed, "Please let him be okay, and please let Rosie be hiding."

"She's smart. She'll be okay," I growled in her ear.

A staticky voice came across the radio of the officer next to me. "Lost visual."

Olivia shuddered, hand gripping mine. "I left her by the engine on the other side of the court square." Fear laced her words—fear that sliced into me and went straight to my bones. "I've got to get over there, Mac." Wide, terror-filled eyes met mine.

"No fucking way. You can't run across that yard. You know how to control the panic, Liv. Breathe and think. Where was she?"

"At the back of the engine."

"Okay, can you see her?"

Olivia peered around the end of the engine, and her shoulders relaxed. "She's talking to someone. I can't tell who it is, but it's one of our guys."

"Okay, let's get our head back in the game. We've got to get these crews out of the building."

From behind us, someone called out, "Chief."

Olivia looked over her shoulder and cursed. "The mayor is waving me over."

I looked over to find the mayor, halfway hidden behind a glass door, motioning at Olivia. "Go. I got this. Stay low and get inside the building."

I clicked my mic to call for a report and got nothing. "Dammit. Fucking cheap-ass battery."

I pitched the useless radio and sprinted behind the barricade of an emergency vehicle to the pump engineer manning Aerial One. Over the truck radio, I could hear the interior crews calling for direction. "Four personnel are inside, hunkered down without water," I barked at the engineer. "I want all the water you can get dousing this bitch." Taking a chance that there might be a spare radio, I ducked into the cab, and *score*, one last fully charged unit.

No further shots had been fired, so with any luck, the shooter had run off. That, or he was waiting for us to get complacent and would then start taking us out again.

I scanned the scene.

PD was on high alert, trying to keep people from sneaking out of hiding. The aerials were dousing water on the structure.

Halfway down the sidewalk, out in the open, not under any cover at all, Olivia was arguing with Mayor Smith. His round face, mottled with anger, shook as he yelled right into her face.

That motherfucker.

I strode across the street, ready to hand him his ass. I knew damn good and well she could take care of herself. But no one was going to yell at my woman while I stood by and let her take it.

"Chief! Chief Hawkins!" I raised my voice until it boomed over the chaotic din.

She turned, looking pissed as all hell.

"You're needed."

I couldn't go up and accost the man, even if the thought of planting my fist in his face was a heady thing. Instead, I gave her an out.

She spun, leaving him with some parting shot over her shoulder, and stalked toward me.

"Thanks. I was two shakes away from getting myself fired."

"No problem." We made it back to the original command point and stood taking in the scene. Olivia scanned the area with an experienced eye. "You know I trust you, Mac. But they've got maybe five minutes before we need to pull them out. That shooter is long gone, and this thing is getting out of control. I don't give a damn how old this building is, it's not important enough to lose one of our men or women over it. Pull them out."

"10-4, Chief. Understood."

"I'm going to see if I can find Rosie, and I'll report from the other side of the square," she said, taking off before I could get a word in edgewise.

I keyed up my mic. "NFD 1222, all personnel."

Another loud flash and boom sounded from inside the structure. It was then that the guys in the building started calling out in panic. The second story was caving in.

Another crackle of urgent radio traffic.

I sprinted to the west side of the building in time to see Thoren and Nate hauling Mo out of the building, backlit by a wall of fire. Thoren and Nate had been partners. Where in the hell was Mo's partner? My heart rate kicked into overdrive, and my vision tunneled to what was happening before me.

"NFD 1222, all personnel. Retreat and report," I commanded, yelling into the mic to be heard.

I ran forward to help Nate and Thoren get Mo to the ambulance. Dread pooled in my belly, but I had to know. "Where's Burgess?"

"He's with Three's crew."

Relief flooded hot and fierce through my system.

The remaining crews from the other stations all reported in. Burgess was being brought over by the two who had helped him out of the building.

They were all banged up but alive.

I looked behind the two men supporting Burgess, expecting to see Olivia and Rosie somewhere in the distance. But now that we'd moved to exterior defensive, there was no way to see beyond the massive amounts of water being dumped on the building.

The hair on the back of my neck stood. Something was off. I didn't buy that the shooter had been taken out or run off.

But I knew what Olivia would want me to do. She'd want me to stay put and help her injured people. So I fought the urge to go search for her, for them.

Chapter Twenty-Five

Olivia

My panic was in overdrive. I'd been so sure I'd seen Rosie at the back of the fire engine with Thoren—until Thoren tumbled out of the burning building. When he'd ripped that BA mask off his face, my heart stopped. If Thoren had been inside fighting the fire, who had Rosie been with?

I sprinted down the sidewalk, shooter be damned. "Excuse me, have you seen a teenage girl with curly blond hair?" I asked a man standing inside his business door. He barely paid attention to me, giving me the briefest head shake.

Hyperaware that the street had been cleared, I noticed every crack in the sidewalk as I jogged to the next cluster of onlookers and asked them the same question.

I stopped every stranger I saw. I was two blocks away from the court square and swallowing bile when a little old woman poked her head out of a used bookstore.

"My dear, you look affright. Can I help you?"

"Yes, please." My voice broke on a sob I couldn't quite contain. Rosie was fine. This was all a big mistake.

"Take a breath, dear. What can I help you with."

"My daughter. I can't find her. She's fourteen, wearing a denim jacket. And light jeans. She's about this tall and has blond hair." I tried to calm my nerves and make sense of the situation, but every moment that ticked by without finding her let more panic sneak in.

The old woman appeared to be thinking hard, her gaze distant. She glanced down the street, away from the fire, and then back at me. "Does she have curly hair?"

"Yes!" I grabbed her hands, clutching to her words like a life preserver.

"I saw a young girl a bit ago. I figured it was just a dad dragging his kid away from trouble. You know how kids—"

"Which way did they go?" I had no time to waste on her theories of troubled teenagers.

For a split second, she acted as if I'd offended her by interrupting, and then her face fell. "I'm sorry, dear, I only know they went that way." She pointed away from the fire. Just beyond her shop was a four-way stop.

Straight ahead, the road led to a residential neighborhood. To the right led to a large church that took up the whole block. And the left led back into the business district.

"I couldn't see much beyond this door, and I was paying more attention to the courthouse."

I swallowed hard. "Thank you."

I stumbled forward to the stop sign at the corner. I needed to think.

He wouldn't have taken her back toward the businesses. Too many people that way. Same for the neighborhood. Too many onlookers checking out the fire.

I spun on a heel and called, "Ma'am, what's behind the church?"

Her brow knit with concern. "It's an empty lot. It used to be a playground. But they let it grow over. Kinda spooky back there with the empty shed buildings."

And suddenly I knew where that shithead had taken her.

I sprinted through the church courtyard as fast as I could, jumping over planters that lined the walks to the building, trampling the neatly groomed grass. I turned the corner of the building and found the empty lot.

The old woman had been right. The entire lot was overgrown with vines. In stark contrast to the neatly groomed church grounds stood two neglected buildings, one on either end of the lot, their dilapidated wood frames listing to the side. A dim orange streetlamp barely lit the area.

Hiding in the shadows, I forced myself to be still. Forced my breathing to slow. Tried with every ounce of control I had to keep my movements minute because every slight noise seemed magnified.

In the stillness, two things registered. One, I needed backup. Two, I was going to kill this son of a bitch if he hurt my Rosie.

I pulled my phone out of my pocket, careful to keep the face to me while I lowered the screen brightness. Then I dialed 911. They could get PD here the fastest.

I was two blocks away from at least half the shift.

The operator answered, sounding harassed. They'd surely had almost as dramatic a night as we'd had.

"This is Chief Hawkins," I whispered.

"Ma'am, can you please speak up? I can barely hear you."

"No, I can't. A man has abducted my daughter, and I

have reason to believe that he's holding her hostage in one of the abandoned buildings behind the old First Baptist Church."

"Do you have a visual on your daughter."

"No."

A huge sigh crossed the line. "Ma'am. What makes you think your daughter has been abducted."

"Because I can't find her. She's not where she's supposed to be. I think I saw her with a man."

"How old is she?"

"Fourteen."

"Ma'am, I'm sorry. Is it possible she's just run away?"

I combusted. "You listen to me. My daughter did not run away. Stop wasting my time. You need to get on the radio and send one of those fifty personnel you have lining the sidewalks. You tell them Fire Chief Olivia Hawkins has a missing child. I need some backup, and I need it now."

I reiterated the location and hung up.

Probably, I was on my own with this. And definitely, flaunting my position would likely get me a reprimand. And that operator was just doing her job, but my daughter's life was in danger.

I slipped my phone in my pocket.

The smart thing to do was wait. But it was excruciating.

Still, I remained in my hiding spot for a heartbeat, praying that she'd be okay. That I would hear something that would give them away.

Two blocks away was chaos. The distant drone of the engines and the shouts of fire crews working were like another world away. Like a movie scene playing in another room. Distant, but there.

Here, it was deadly silent.

I focused on breathing deeply, though every sound,

even my breath, seemed magnified in the stillness of the area.

Across the bleak lot, just beyond the misshapen chain-link fence, from the direction of the least sturdy of the two buildings, came a high shriek that abruptly cut off.

But I'd heard that shriek a million times over her life-time. *Hold on, baby. Momma's coming.*

The door to the shed burst open, and a mass of blond curls tumbled out, followed by long lanky limbs I'd recognize anywhere. Her jacket gone.

She landed hard on her knees and scrambled back to her feet.

"Rosie," I screamed.

She whipped her head in my direction. "Mom!"

I bolted as fast as I had ever run. To her. My baby girl.

A man stumbled out of the building behind her, wiping his mouth with the back of his hand. Rosie changed direction, leading him further out of the building.

"You little bitch," he growled, running and reaching, nearly catching her by the shirt.

He heard my footfalls just as I leaped into the air, shoving my feet toward him in the most epic side kick I'd ever done.

We landed, and I screamed for Rosie to run.

Beside me, the man rolled from his back to his side, then rose on hands and knees.

"Thoren," I gasped, heaving myself upright, trying to catch the breath I'd knocked out of myself when I hit the ground.

He pushed to stand. "Wrong brother, bitch. But I like how you think."

Thoren was a twin. The realization stunned me. His first punch was unexpected. He got in that one good shot, and then I turned my righteous fury loose on him. I pummeled him, throwing everything I had into smashing the bastard who had hurt my daughter—hurt my people.

With a roundhouse kick that caught him across the jaw, we both went sprawling in a duet of grunts.

I recovered first, scooted over, and landed on him, hard. I planted my knee in his back, wrenched his arm behind him with one hand, and clenched a fistful of hair with the other. "You son of a bitch," I screamed, yanking up and back until he cried out in pain.

"Get off me, bitch," he growled.

I wanted nothing more than to smash his face into the ground.

"Easy, Chief." Around me, voices started filtering in, lowering the red haze my vision had become.

"On your left."

Mike Harrison. *One of mine.*

I relaxed my pose slightly and realized I was snarling.

"I got it from here, Chief." Mike placed his hand over mine, allowing me to release my grip.

I looked up into his warm brown eyes.

It was over. We'd stopped him.

Other hands slipped under my elbow, helping me stand. I stared back at the man who'd done so much damage to our town, to my family. Mike snapped handcuffs on Loren Watkins— arson suspect, murder suspect, and attempted kidnapper.

"Liv." Mac's choked voice cut through my stunned daze. I found him standing off to the side with our shaken daughter wrapped around his torso, his thick, strong arms holding her safe.

And on legs that felt like jelly, I stumbled to them.

Chapter Twenty-Six

Mac

I'd been standing with Thoren and Nate, waiting to give direction to the medics on which hospital to take Cal, Burgess, and Mo to, surrounded by a mix of concerned PD and FD crews, when a radio call-out sounded from the PD radios.

"911, NPD. Respond to the area behind First Baptist Church. Possible abduction in progress. Fourteen-year-old female, unknown male. Caller states she thinks she saw them in the area."

Every hair on my body raised, and I locked eyes with Mike Harrison.

"Olivia," I mouthed, unable to form words through the dread coursing through my system.

I stumbled back, spun, and ran.

Down the long blocks, dodging people, dodging hoses still pumping water on the fire. My heavy boots thumped on the concrete. Past the stores locked up for the night, toward the darkness that lay beyond the immediate downtown area.

My heart pumped. I couldn't draw enough air. My God, Rosie had been taken. And Olivia was out there on her own, chasing down our daughter.

Somewhere in the back of my mind, it registered that I needed to relinquish command, but I couldn't stop. I had to get to them.

At the corner of East Washington and Main, I stumbled for a heartbeat, barely registering the scene before me.

Two people fighting in the shadows of the poorly lit park. Someone running toward me.

"Dad!"

I braced as Rosie slammed into me. Mike sprinted past.

My arms closed around her automatically, lifting her as I kept moving to Olivia. I had to get to her, but I couldn't seem to let go of Rosie. My arms locked in a tight grip around her slender body.

In the park ahead, Olivia spun an impressive round-house kick, taking her attacker to the ground, detaining him. She was powerful, all beauty and grace. And mad as hell.

Mike ran up and took control of the situation.

Two other officers showed, one helping Olivia to stand.

And there she stood, my magnificent woman. I was so damn proud. So fucking scared. So livid that she'd taken even the first hit.

"Liv," I choked out. Unable to move or really speak, barely able to breathe.

She saw me then. Our eyes locked across the distance. She took one stumbling step toward us. Then another. Slowly at first, then faster, until she was nearly running.

In slow motion, I watched her run to my open arms as she joined us, hugging our shaking daughter between us.

I closed my eyes, holding on to these women for dear life. Because they were my life.

I'd been alone and happily solitary when they found me. But now I couldn't imagine my life without them.

"Why aren't you at the fire command?" Olivia finally found her voice.

I opened my eyes to find Mike and the other officers had Loren Watkins on his feet, shuffling him forward, hands cuffed behind his back.

Rosie had quieted, but Olivia looked ready to go to war.

"Come on." I ignored her question and turned us into the light, needing to get them to safety, unable to let either of them out of arm's reach. "Let's get out of here."

At the corner, an elderly woman stood wringing her hands. As we drew closer, I recognized her as the leader of the Public Safety Foundation.

"Oh, thank goodness," she exclaimed as we drew into the light, coming back into the block off the court square. "You found her."

Olivia said, "Yes ma'am. Thank you." She let go of us, and it was all I could do to not voice my objection until she said, "Can I give you a hug?"

She embraced the older woman tightly. "Thank you for paying attention. You helped me find her."

The words were soft-spoken and heartfelt, and the elderly woman pulled away and patted her cheek with tears in her eyes. Olivia took a step back, her own eyes sparkling with unshed tears. I slipped my arm back around her, needing to touch her, to feel that she was alive and well. I never wanted to see her cry or hurt again.

From the other end of the block, the mayor's voice boomed. I looked up to find him laughing with one of the business owners, the sound so jarring and out of place, it took me a second to register what I was hearing.

Who could laugh at a time like this? I glared in his direction, willing him to feel my anger.

A woman and her child were attacked.

My woman and *my* child were hurt.

A very bad man was taken off the streets.

Our historic courthouse had burned to almost a total loss, and we'd had a man shot and two injured in the line of duty.

The need to walk right up and deck the mayor burned as hot and bright as anything I'd ever felt in my life.

As if the man himself had been the one to hurt them.

But in a way, part of tonight's shit show had been a direct result of his actions.

"Mac. Head back to the scene." Olivia gave me a low warning.

"Fuck that. It's his fault that scene was such a shit show."

"The mayor's? How?" the elderly woman asked.

"He's one of the ones who cut the funding for our equipment, forcing us to go with cheaper options. Options that failed when we needed them most," I ground out.

"Mac, go back to the scene," Olivia demanded. "Take care of the guys. Do your job."

I looked her right in the eye. "I mean this as respectfully as possible. Shut up, Chief. I'm not going anywhere." There was no way I could act all business as usual when the two most precious people in my life had nearly been lost.

"Mac," she warned again. "We can't be seen like this."

I ignored her, slipping my arm around her because she was too far away.

"Hush up. Y'all can fight about it later," Rosie finally spoke, still tucked into my chest. If a voice could hold an eye roll, hers did. "The whole world can see how in love you are. You aren't fooling anyone."

"Exactly, even the ones who can ruin everything," Olivia ground out.

I kissed her temple.

"Let them look. I don't care who sees. I don't care if I have to leave the department. I can find another job."

Olivia turned to me. "But..."

I quieted her with a kiss. "We'll figure it out, baby. But go easy on me right now. My two favorite people in the whole world were just in a fight for their lives. I need to hold you. I need you close. Let me have that. None of the rest of it matters."

Chapter Twenty-Seven

Mac

Two days after the courthouse fire, I got a call—a demand, really—to attend to one Francis O'Malley at the Brightside Rehab Center.

It had been two full days of making statements to investigators with the Georgia Bureau of Investigation and the state arson investigator. Loren Watkins had been arrested on scene, and this time, he was placed under maximum security. The evidence gathered from Harrison's detective work, combined with the eye-witness accounts of the shooting at the courthouse fire meant Watkins had multiple pending charges, including homicide and attempted murder.

So, with all the legal stuff being wrapped up, and after visiting Cal at the hospital—Burgess and Mo had been treated and released the night of the fire—I walked into the rehab facility as summoned.

The nurse behind the counter flirted while I signed the guestbook, until an uproar rose down the hall. She tilted her head in the direction. "That's probably where you'll find her."

Mrs. Francis was known to be a meddler, so the assumption fit.

Olivia and I had gone through scenarios and what-ifs, both of us bracing for the council hearing. But when Mrs. Francis called, it was usually important, so I made the time to swing by.

I stalked down the hall, halfway nervous but curious as to why she'd demanded to see me.

The community room in the rehab center was set up with gaming tables. Little old people all sat in circles, cards in hand, and stacks of chips in the center of each table.

"Well, would you looky here." Mrs. O'Malley's voice rang out loud. "See, Eunice? I told you he'd show. Y'all, this is Captain Mac Collins, firefighter extraordinaire, rescuer of little old ladies with broken hips. And Mr. December in the annual calendar."

I managed to hide my cringe at the mention of that damn calendar and made my way to her, taking the wrinkled hand she offered.

"Sit," she ordered me. "Deal him in, Gerald," she ordered the elderly black man next to her.

"I can't stay, Mrs. O'Malley—"

"I told you, it's Francis. And yes you can." She gave my hand a tug. Resigned, I took the seat next to her, willing to play along if only to make her happy for a moment.

"I really can't," I said. "We have the council hearing today."

Francis slapped a hand over the cards Gerald dealt and directed her gaze across the table. I glanced over to see the elderly woman from the night of the fire eyeballing Francis. A whole conversation happened in their stare down.

Francis broke first and pulled her cards to her, picking them up, fanning them out, and rearranging them. "That's why you're here, Macmillan Collins."

She shifted a card from one side of the hand to the other. "You see, Eunice here says that lily-livered bastard is trying to make your woman a... what was it you said?" she asked her friend.

Across the table, Eunice, the woman who helped Olivia, scowled. "That sorry excuse for a mayor is trying to make your woman a scapegoat."

I perked up at this. Suddenly finding all the time in the world available.

Eunice continued, "I heard what she said the other night. And I'm downright mad. We have funding available to buy equipment for the department. But when I've inquired about donating, he's shut me down. But it was obvious the other night that it's time he's removed from office."

Francis nodded beside me.

"What's the hearing for?" one of the card players asked.

I didn't want to answer because the truth was. It was my actions that caused the hearing. And for the past two days, Olivia had been under an incredible amount of stress because I had refused to return to the fire.

I'd relinquished command of the scene and stayed with my girls. It should've been grounds for termination.

I knew she was conflicted over it, needing us to be together, while at the same time, I'd outed our relationship and put both our jobs in jeopardy. And likely it would be hers.

But I had a plan.

"It's a personnel hearing," I admitted reluctantly.

"What time is it?" Eunice asked.

"Three o'clock today."

She looked at me across her glasses. "Isn't that their regular council meeting time?"

I nodded. "Yes, ma'am." Because this asshat was making a big deal about taking down the fire chief.

"In a called public meeting?" Mrs. Francis frowned at me, then at her friend.

This was doing me no good, sitting here witness to an old-folks' poker game and surreptitious glances. I had a plan to carry out, action that needed to be taken. Plus, I wanted to be there for Olivia before, during, and after the hearing. I didn't know what the mayor had on his agenda, but I could guess. And none of the scenarios were good.

"Mrs. O'Malley, I need to get going. Was there something you needed me for?" I didn't want to be rude to my elders, but I itched to leave, already headed to my next stop in my head.

"No, dear. You have enough on your plate." She patted my hand.

I rose and, on a whim, kissed her forehead. "Glad you're feeling better."

"You too... Santa Daddy."

I walked out of the room right as my phone rang in my pocket. I answered and slid it to my ear to hide my burning cheeks.

"Mac. It's Childers."

"Hey, man," I greeted my old friend. "Thanks for returning my call. How's it going?"

"It's good. Things are good." The hesitation in his voice told me otherwise.

We'd met years ago in the service and then reconnected in the fire academy. He'd since gone on to run the academy, and we met for drinks every time I went back. We didn't talk often, but once a part of the brotherhood, those ties ran deep.

"You don't sound okay. What's going on, Hal?"

"I'm at my wit's end. One of my instructors is leaving to head out west and join a search-and-rescue team. None of the applicants are qualified, and I feel like I'm spinning my wheels, again."

I could feel his frustration through the phone.

"Who's leaving?" A tiny seed of hope sparked. The reason I'd called him in the first place was to feel out the situation at the training academy. I was grasping for solutions.

"Bohannon. Did you ever meet him?"

I reached my truck and climbed in, noting that I still had time to make it to Olivia's hearing. Regardless of what the mayor was calling it, this council meeting was going to be a hearing about Olivia.

I focused on Childers. "Bohannon? Tall guy? Had a thing for jumping out of planes?" I recalled taking a CPR recert class from him.

"Yeah, he's going out west to fly search-and-rescue missions. I think it's so he can just get his kicks for jumping out of perfectly good aircraft. But what do I know. He's also had some trouble at home lately. Anyway. It's been hard as hell to find a good replacement for him."

"I hear you, brother. What can I do for you?"

"I don't suppose you know of anyone who's certified that might be interested in teaching?"

It was hard enough trying to find people to work in the fire service. The long hours, lack of pay... not many people wanted to work a career where you were away from home every third night. Not to mention all the bullshit that came with dealing with some crappy people from time to time. I couldn't imagine what the pay as an instructor would be, but I was sure it wasn't much.

I glanced at the clock, time to head out. "Maybe. I'll think on it and let you know."

"Sure. You aren't interested, are you?"

I swallowed thickly. "You know, I would be... but I'd have to give up my retirement plan. I'm so close... and the training center would mean a pretty hellacious commute." I voiced my concerns, even though I'd originally called to see if he did indeed have a place for me.

"I get it. It'd be hard to leave knowing I only had a few more years." He heaved a beleaguered sigh.

"But I'll give it some thought," I said as I rang off.

I drove to city hall, forcing the conversation out of my head. Right now, Olivia was my focus, and I wanted to be there to make sure the mayor didn't come down hard on her.

Chapter Twenty-Eight

Olivia

Cathy knocked lightly on my office door. "It's two o'clock." The solemness in her voice did nothing to alleviate my trepidation.

I spun the ring on my finger and drew a breath, searching for the confidence I knew I'd need to face a room full of men who had it in for me. That was unfair. There was only one or two who might be gunning for me. But in such a small town, who knew which pockets might be lined.

On that chipper thought, I faked a smile. "Don't be so glum, Cathy." Truth was, I needed her support.

Mayor Smith had announced a called city council meeting. My actions, or inaction, the night of the courthouse fire were being called into question.

Or maybe it was that Mac hadn't let go of me after taking down the arsonist-slash-kidnapper and had needed to have me within arm's reach. Or the fact that he'd stood there in front of everyone with his arm around my shoulders, kissing my temple, lingering there as if he needed to breathe me in to remind him that we were all right.

Basically, Mac and I had both broken the rules, and the mayor thought he'd finally found a reason to fire me.

"Did you hear from the attorney?" I stood, gathering my paperwork.

"Not yet."

Upon returning to work the day after the fire, after working with Human Resources to ensure that the injured men were sorted with the support that they'd need, I'd contacted an attorney of my own. I'd suspected that the mayor might take this opportunity to pull a stunt. So I'd dug up as much dirt on him and the city manager as I could and passed it along to her.

I went to the ladies' room to check my appearance. I'd tried to cover the bruising from the few licks that Loren had managed to land but couldn't do much about the still-swollen eye. It was my first look in the mirror that had softened my anger toward Mac. Half of my face was swollen, and a cut over my eye had bled profusely. I couldn't blame him for being overly touchy once the fight had ended.

And if I were being honest with myself, I'd needed the comfort of his arms and had drawn strength from him.

But the fact remained that one—or both—of us would lose our jobs after this meeting. Even though the local news, both paper and citizen word of mouth, labeled us as heroes, one of us would have to pay the price.

The woman in the mirror before me didn't look like much of a hero with her slumped posture and defeated expression.

Failure was a suffocating blanket on my shoulders.

I'd wanted to be a fire chief for as long as I could remember, following in my dad's footsteps. Had I thrown it all away? Lost my dream job? Lost my chance to honor my roots and make my family proud?

I'd busted my ass for this place. This career. Had my weakness of needing to be with Mac in the heat of the moment cost me that dream?

There was some measure of peace in knowing that I'd made a difference in the world. I'd negotiated for better equipment for my crews. Hell, I'd saved my daughter and stopped a killer.

But that knowledge and those deeds wouldn't get me a paycheck or benefits for Rosie. Who would hire me once it got out that I'd broken the rules.

Anyone would.

The words in my head sounded like my voice but held Mac's strong attitude.

Where had the badass woman who'd been hired for this role gone? She wouldn't stand and stare morosely in the mirror, cataloging all the ways she was wrong. Hell no. She'd catalog all the ways she was right and the system was wrong. She wouldn't be defeated. She'd tell that cocksucker mayor where he could stuff his rules and blaze her own trail.

I squared my shoulders. I'd played by other's rules for too long.

I reached up and grabbed the hair clip, releasing the severe bun I normally wore. Why was I minimizing myself? I loved my curls and didn't like my hair up, but I'd taken to the style when I realized that I got more respect as a peer when I hid my feminine aspects.

And that was total bullshit. I deserved respect because I was a hell of an administrator in the fire service. I shook out my curls and fluffed them.

This mayor could kiss my ass.

This was my firehouse. They needed me. I'd done more

for them in the few months I'd been here than anyone had in the last five years.

And whether these people liked it or not, they were mine, and I was going to continue to fight for them.

I turned on a heel and stalked out of the bathroom, wearing my cape of righteous indignation. Let these assholes come for me. I was ready to take on them and the rest of the world.

* * *

Municipal meetings were boring and uneventful unless there was an inflammatory topic on the agenda. I walked in with Cathy by my side and went directly to the front row, right where the council members and the mayor had to see me.

I made eye contact with each member as I got comfortable in my seat.

The meeting agenda included a mix of contract approvals, a financial presentation, and declarations.

Nothing about me or the fire dept.

Still, I didn't trust that something wasn't about to go down.

Beside me, Cathy leaned close to murmur in my ear. "I'm just making it look like we have a secret to discuss."

I pressed my lips together to keep from smiling. "Will Trina be here?"

"I'm not sure, I couldn't get her on the phone. Hopefully."

The meeting was called to order and moved forward with agonizing slowness.

The back door opened, and the click of heels could be

heard coming down the aisle. A woman stepped in front of me and sat to my left.

"Sorry I'm late," Trina murmured.

I smiled darkly at my kickass attorney.

Another agenda item was ticked off the list before the back doors opened again, and this time, the sound of a group entering interrupted the speaker. He stumbled over his speech as he looked to the back of the room.

I turned to see what the commotion was and had to fight against the tears that burned my eyes. All of the fire department staff filed in. Every last one of them, on duty and off. Taking up rows of seats, starting with the row behind me, until they filled them and lined the wall. They'd come together as a unit to make a show of entering as a team.

I wondered who was covering their zones and then realized it'd be okay. If they got a call, they were in the city limits and could respond quickly. And make a show of it while they were at it.

So what if they were late to the meeting. They'd made it known they were standing together and standing with me. I didn't really care if they made a distraction. They'd shown up to support me, and that realization solidified my desire to fight for them.

I nodded to the few who braved eye contact with me. I wanted to search for a particular man, the one who'd held me close in the morning hours as I worried over the meeting. I wanted him to come sit beside me, stand with me as my partner.

But I also wanted to keep my job, so I turned my glacial attitude on and faced the council of men who held my employment in their control.

The atmosphere in the auditorium grew tense. A low

murmur of voices lifted until the chairman banged his gavel, demanding order. The crowd grew quiet as the council moved through the agenda and finally called for any non-agenda items.

The mayor sat up to his microphone.

"I'd like to add an item pertaining to the events of October 3, the night of the courthouse fire."

A ripple of activity rolled through the audience.

The clerk motioned for the mayor to continue. He cleared his throat and picked up his paper. I swept a hand down my uniform jacket to wipe my sweaty palms. Inhaling deeply, I squared my shoulders, prepared for whatever he was about to throw my way. Next to me, Trina practically vibrated.

"Now, we all know that the courthouse fire was devastating," he began, his tone and demeanor reminding me of the few times I'd gone to church revival and been subjected to theatrical judgment. "The fine folks of this community have looked to the courthouse for nearly a century. The history that we lost that evening is incomprehensible."

It was all I could do not to huff, because this man was such a showman with his downcast expression and melodramatic sorrow.

He looked solemnly at his audience, making a grave point. "But I'd like to also bring to light other events of that evening."

"Here we go," Trina muttered.

"On that awful night, the entirety of our fire department was battling the blaze that destroyed our fine courthouse. Except there was an obvious absence of leadership on the scene. Now, most people would assume that with something as tragic as this event, the chief would be on the scene and in command. But it has come to light that the newly appointed fire chief was not on scene. In fact, she left the scene, leaving a lower-ranking officer in charge."

He peered up at the council, making sure he had their undivided attention, his expression horrified as if I'd committed the worst sin imaginable. No mention of the active shooter. Or the arsonist who set the fire.

"In addition to that, I have confirmation that the fire chief has broken city Human Resources rules and has instigated a relationship with said lower-ranking officer. Now, I can imagine how that officer might have felt, suffering the advances of his higher-ranking female chief."

He made a show of moving some papers around on the podium before him, frowning with grave intensity before continuing his monologue. "I'd like to gently remind you fine folks, sexual harassment goes both ways. And our fire chief walks around taunting her subordinates with her... tight skirts and her high heels. It's a grave injustice to expect the lower-ranking staff to remain steadfast to their committed duties when she's flaunting her assets like a common whore."

The silence following his speech was deafening.

The mayor preened. Oblivious to the undercurrent of hostility, he slipped his fingers into his coat pocket and puffed his chest out.

"Now, I realize this position falls under the jurisdiction and authority of the city council. But I'd like to make a recommendation to remove this temptation from the fine men of the fire department. I make a recommendation to remove the fire chief from office."

A roll of murmurs through the crowd forced the council chairman to bang his gavel to regain control.

"Thank you, Mr. Mayor."

I sat as still as I could, afraid to draw attention to myself.

Afraid to look my people in the eye. I should be jumping up and down at the insane accusations and blatant ignorance the man spewed.

"Well, if that's not the most ridiculous thing I've ever heard," a lone elderly female voice piped up loudly from the back of the room.

"Mrs. Eunice, please take your seat."

"I'll do no such thing, Herbert," she told the council chair. "I don't care about your meeting rules, so just pipe down. Paul here is the one who is making private matters public. So I'm going to say my piece, and you're going to listen."

She passed my row, leaning heavily on her cane, until she limped up to the mayor and thumped him on the chest. "Sit down, Paul."

"Who is she?" Trina asked from the corner of her mouth.

"That's Eunice Whitaker," Cathy said under her breath. "Founder of the Public Safety Foundation. Probably the scariest woman on the planet."

"Now, let me tell you the truth about that evening," Eunice began, thumping her cane against the podium to gain attention. "That night, a sorry sack of human set fire to our beloved courthouse. Then he popped caps, injuring some of the very men sent to battle that fire. That's all on the bad guy who's currently behind bars. But the real travesty. The real issue that Paul here isn't mentioning is that the batteries in the radios that the personnel used failed. Why? Because the mayor cut the fire department's budget. The former chief doled out contracts and bid awards to his buddies, and they purchased inadequate equipment. Now, normally, the Public Safety Foundation would happily provide grant support for these supplies, but the former chief declined any assistance because, and I quote, 'the mayor was going to take care of them' end quote from emails between myself and the former chief. To be clear, our Chief Hawkins was on scene, but due to Mayor Smith's failure, she couldn't do her job."

The councilmen looked between themselves.

"Further," she continued, "Chief Hawkins left the scene because her daughter was kidnapped. I'm sure I'm supposed to say allegedly here, but since I was a witness, there's no alleging to it. I saw him with my own two eyes." She banged the cane against the podium again.

"How dare you threaten to fire a woman for saving her child. Especially when that woman was also responsible for capturing the jackass who set that fire and the others. And as for her relationship and all that bluster... get over it. They have a child together." She shook her head, brandishing her cane again. "We all know what happened before, Paul. If you don't want your own dirty laundry aired, you need to pipe down and apologize to Chief Hawkins. If anyone is a whore around here, it's you."

Shocked silence rang through the room.

"Now, one of you fine young men help me back to my seat." She motioned for the man nearest her to come assist, turning back to the microphone as they began to lead her away. "And Mr. Chairman, remember, your momma is my neighbor at the nursing home."

As chaos reigned through the conference room, the meeting was ended abruptly, with no resolution, though I wasn't so sure we'd heard the last of the mayor.

Outside city hall, Trina turned to me. "What just happened? I've never seen anything like that in my life. That whole meeting needs to be thrown out. It was totally illegal."

"Welcome to small-town politics," Cathy said with a grin.

Trina's eyes lit with glee. "I may have to come here more often."

We said our goodbyes, and I watched as they walked away.

No matter what kind of disruption had happened, it was a matter of time before the council decided to act. I just knew the mayor wouldn't let this go.

My crew didn't deserve to be put through this. They'd had enough turmoil. My job was to be their support, not create problems for them.

A familiar pickup truck pulled up to the curb, the passenger window rolled down, and Mac stared back at me.

I didn't want to give him up and separate him and Rosie. But we couldn't continue like we had.

With a heavy heart, I walked to his truck and got in.

Chapter Twenty-Nine

Mac

Olivia and I skipped out for the rest of the day. I took her home and made love to her, using our bodies to show her how much I treasured her. Cherished her.

She looked defeated and so damn sad.

I left her curled on the couch, with a cup of caramel-bourbon-laced hot chocolate while Buster and I went to pick up Rosie from school.

"Is Mom okay?" Rosie's brow furrowed in concern. "How did it go today? Did they fire her?"

"No, Buttercup. It wasn't pretty, but nothing has happened yet." And I was determined to do whatever it took to get us both what we wanted.

"Thank God. She's worked so hard and finally made chief. It would be terrible if she lost this job."

I hated that my baby girl was concerned over this. She should be worried about regular kid stuff, and this whole situation was worrisome even for adults. It didn't sit well with me.

For so long, I'd only had to consider myself. And I thought I'd been okay with that. But the moment they came back into my life, I realized how wrong I'd been. I was so in love with them and couldn't imagine even a day without them.

Guilt and this sense of failure roiled around in my chest.

If it weren't for my stupid need to hit that retirement goal, none of this would've been an issue. The Watkins attack and the courthouse fire would've still happened, but this fallout wouldn't be an issue.

"Plus," Rosie continued, absently loving on Buster, who sat behind her with his head propped on her seat. "I really like it here. What if mom loses this job? We'd have to leave and move somewhere else. Moving sucks. I've just now made friends."

I glanced to see her cheeks a bright pink.

"That's selfish, I know. But it's the truth. Plus, Mom's happier than she's ever been. And then there's you. I wouldn't want to leave you."

The more Rosie talked, the more she drove home that it was up to me to fix this situation. Olivia would only leave if she had to. And if she left, she'd be taking Rosie. And that was not going to happen. I didn't care what decisions had to be made. I'd find a damn way to keep my family together.

When we got to the house, Rosie flew through the door. Olivia was at the kitchen table scrolling on her laptop. I dropped my keys in the basket they'd bought to collect my things and leaned down to drop a kiss on her head.

On the laptop screen was a web page for job postings.

"What the hell is that?" I didn't even pretend like I hadn't snooped over her shoulder.

Olivia squared her shoulders, the ice queen preparing to go to battle.

"Nope, don't even go there." I stopped her before she could start. "Don't tell me you're thinking of leaving NFD. That's not going to happen."

"Mac, we have to be reasonable about this. Smith isn't done with his tirade. I've already hurt the department enough."

"How?"

"By casting us in such a negative light."

Her words felt like a slap across the face. That's what we were? That's how she felt? That we were negative.

I clenched my teeth, biting back the hurt and anger.

And then reality sank in. She was planning to leave.

Her goals and dreams meant so much to her that she was willing to leave. Sure, she could try and find something close. But we both knew fire chief positions didn't come easily. And it was likely that it would mean relocation.

I stood stock-still, the truth of it staring me in the face.

I wanted to pitch a fit. Yell. Ask her what about me? What about us? What about Rosie?

But the truth was... she didn't love me enough to stay and make it work.

I turned on wooden legs and stumbled out the door, walking aimlessly toward the shop, then past it, Buster hot on my heels.

One thought going through my head.

She didn't really love me, and she was leaving. And my whole world would crumble when they left.

I dropped to the grass on the bank of the pond, the emptiness in my chest a void greater than I'd ever known.

I'd been through this before. I'd faced a quiet house for so long because it hurt so damn bad to know I wasn't worth fighting for.

I sat there until the sun began to set, an orange glow across the water that usually brought me peace. I couldn't look at the house that would be empty. I couldn't think of anything beyond how quiet it would be without them. How lonely I would be. All the nights I'd been here, alone, had never mattered until they came and filled up the space. My life.

My whole fucking body hurt at the thought of losing them.

A shuffle behind me brought me back to the present. A blanket landed on the grass next to me, and then Olivia sat. I couldn't look at her beautiful face anymore, so I stared out over the water.

"Hey. You okay?"

I couldn't believe she was asking me that. "No, I'm fucking not okay." The words came out gruff, laced with hurt and anger.

"Mac. Talk to me."

Good God, would I ever get over hearing her voice? I swallowed thickly, still searching the water, unable to conjure a response.

"Mac, hey." She dragged my hand off my knee, gripping it with both of hers. I stared at the place we were connected, not understanding how we could fit so well together and still seem so far apart.

"Mac."

I watched as her hand squeezed mine. Strong, capable hands, with fingers that knew when and how to be delicate. Fingers that were now shaking. Fingers with busted knuckles because she'd fought like a champ. I imagined those knuckles healed, and those fingers decorated with my ring.

Then she pulled my arm aside and slipped over my legs, straddling me. Releasing my hand and cupping my jaw, her thumbs tracing over my cheeks. I closed my eyes because she was just too beautiful to look at when my heart was so raw.

"My sweet man," she whispered, dropping a soft kiss to my lips. "I love you so much. You have the biggest heart of anyone I've ever known."

I swallowed thickly, realizing she was wiping tears from my face, feeling like the biggest fool in the world.

Her arms slipped around my neck as she pulled me close.

Finally, my body responded, my arms wrapping around her. I buried my face in her neck, breathing her in like she alone could sustain me.

"Liv," I choked out. I didn't know what I wanted to say —so many things, but none of the right words to say them.

I squeezed her tighter, unable to stop myself from clinging to her. Her head fell to mine, her gentle breath providing the calm that eventually seeped into me.

She shifted, her lips trailing my ear. "Sweetheart," she whispered. "Tell me what it is. What's wrong?"

"You can't—" My voice broke on a sob. Fuck, I couldn't even say the word.

She squeezed me tighter. Her body shaking against mine. Was this unbearable pain something we shared?

Her breasts rose on an inhale. "You think—" She paused before continuing, "Of course it is. You thought it meant that I wanted to leave." Her palm skimmed my face, and she pressed a kiss to my forehead like the fucking child I was. "Mac, I'm so sorry. It's killing me to see you so upset."

I pulled back, the need to see her eyes urgent. "You're not going anywhere," I declared. "We'll figure it out."

Something slipped through her eyes as she leaned in to kiss me. "Come on back to the house. Rosie is worried."

I let her pull me to my feet and walked arm in arm with her back to the house. Rosie had set the table and prepared supper and was oddly quiet. Buster lay at her feet.

Under her watchful eye, I forced myself to eat her meal, having to chew each bite twice to get it to go down. But I couldn't get the image of the three of them driving away out of my head. Because I knew that if they did leave, I'd send Buster with Rosie.

We watched a little TV and spent a quiet night with the three of us snuggled on the couch, one under each arm, stretched out with our feet kicked out in a line on the ottoman. I couldn't quite make it past the two smaller sock-clad feet flanking mine to pay attention to whatever show they'd picked.

My mind spun the whole time.

When we went to bed, Olivia made love to me gently, sweetly. My heart decided it was another goodbye.

We dressed, me in my sleep pants that she loved so much, her in her silky nightgown. When she curled up next to me, pressing her back to my front, I held her tightly in my arms and lay there listening to the sounds of her deep breathing, sifting my fingers across the soft fabric of her nightgown as she drifted off to sleep.

The glow of the moon lit the bedroom enough for me to tell when the door opened quietly. Rosie peeked around the doorway. I lifted my head to let her know I was awake.

She padded closer, fidgeting.

Without a word, I rolled to my back and lifted an arm

out to her. She curled up, head on my shoulder, her body giving a soft shudder every once in a while.

The vise grip on my heart tightened even more. My girl had been crying, and I hated knowing it.

Buster jumped up and, after his three requisite spins, curled at Rosie's feet. Only then did she fall asleep.

I lay there for I don't know how long, just listening to the sounds of the ones I loved most in the world sleeping. Comforted by their nearness.

I didn't know how I'd manage it. Maybe it would mean giving up the seniority I'd built and starting over. I would sell the lake house and the boat, or maybe even go work for another fifteen or twenty years somewhere else. Maybe we'd eat ramen and not take vacations.

One thing was certain, I'd give up everything I owned, but I wouldn't give them up.

And if Olivia keeping her position was the thing that would make her happy and keep them with me, then I would make it happen. I'd do anything to keep us together.

I swallowed thickly. On the one hand, I wasn't ready. Wasn't ready to say goodbye to the career that had defined me. The family I'd made with my crew.

On the other, it was time.

The all-night calls, the twenty-four-hour marathons.

The adrenaline highs and lows.

Leaving my shift would be hard. But being with Olivia and Rosie would be worth it. This was what it meant to be loved. Sharing dreams, sacrifice. Sticking around in the hard times.

Love wasn't just kept in memories and old houses. Love was in the foundation of the family that lived in the house.

And these two loved me.

Despite my grumpy nature. And my solitary habits.

These two made my world brighter. So bright, there would only be darkness if they weren't in it. So it was up to me to keep that brightness. To prove myself worthy of their love.

My mind made up, I drifted to sleep as the night sky faded and the sun began to rise.

Around mid-morning—after too few hours of sleep, even if I was surrounded by the loves of my life—I made a phone call to Trina, Olivia's HR attorney. Her excitement at going against the city was palpable even through the phone, and I found her waiting outside city hall by the time I got there.

Together, we stalked down the long hallway to the Human Resources office, where I was informed that the director was in a meeting with the mayor and city manager.

"You can't go in there!" Her words bounced off my back as I pushed through the door.

"I don't care what the handbook says..." The mayor, red-faced, with spittle gathered from the corner of his mouth, loomed over the desk.

"Tsk tsk, Mr. Mayor. Now, I know you don't want to violate your adopted Human Resources handbook and open yourself and the city up to litigation." Trina sounded almost gleeful at the idea. The woman was a shark. "Generally speaking, of course."

"What in the hell are you doing here? You can't be in here. I'm calling the police and will have you escorted out of here," he blustered, jowls wobbling as he aimed his furious words at us. Mr. Bloom audibly groaned, and the HR director looked defeated.

I had a feeling I knew why the man would be willing to risk breaking their own handbook. Was it legal and enforceable? I had no idea, and that's why I'd called in Trina. And I hoped that by the time I walked out, we'd have some resolution.

"I have a proposition for you, Mr. Mayor."

An hour later, I walked out feeling lighter than I had in years. After leaving Trina at her car, I stood on the sidewalk, looking out at the park in the distance. The artwork that had been destroyed in the tornado was starting to be replaced, slowly and surely, with new pieces. I strolled down the block to get a better look. Someone had created a chalk drawing on the concrete at the entrance to the park, the image of a beautiful sunrise over the city.

I didn't know what direction my life was about to head in, what career I might find. I just knew that Olivia and Rosie would be with me.

Chapter Thirty

Olivia

In the days following the council meeting, I made it a point to visit every station and thank every single person individually for coming to support me.

I vowed that I would fight not only for my job but for my people, because they needed a leader who would put their best interests first.

And every word out of my mouth was a lie because I'd still been looking and still had no resolution to this fraternization problem. On the morning after Mac's breakdown, he rose quietly, later than normal, took Buster for a run, and then came back and made us breakfast. I was surprised to find that Rosie had joined us, but she'd climbed into bed with me as a little girl whenever she was troubled.

Her sneaking in in the middle of the night made me realize that our little family implosion was worrisome to her.

Add to it Mac's quiet, reflective mood, and it felt like we were all walking around waiting for the other shoe to drop.

It felt like he'd withdrawn, and I worried about what might be going through his mind.

"You're staring out that window, looking like you've got something on your mind," he said, catching me off guard at the end of the second day.

He'd gotten a phone call in the middle of dinner and had gone out the door as he answered. The move was unusual for him and just added to the trepidation I felt.

"Maybe I do. Maybe I'm just looking for a way to make things all right. If it weren't for my job, we could get married."

He crossed the room and slipped his arms around my waist, pulling me into his chest and brushing a kiss to my temple. A deep, satisfied sigh left my lips because no matter what, this was where I belonged. Nothing else mattered except being with him.

"Sweetheart, I need to tell you something." His words felt weighty. Meaningful.

The seriousness in his voice sent a direct shot of anxiety to my system. He drew in a deep breath and said softly, "I quit."

Every muscle in my body froze. He quit? Quit what? Me? Us? My thoughts were racing as he continued, "You don't have to worry anymore. I took care of the problem." He spun me to face him, placing a gentle kiss on the tip of my nose. "I promise you, if it's in my power, I'll always take care of your problems."

I leaned back to gaze into his eyes. "What?"

"That call I got was from Trina. The city accepted the terms of my resignation. So, Chief Hawkins, this is my official notice that I quit."

I stared at him, unable to comprehend the words.

"What about your retirement? The lake house? What about the station? The guys?"

With the tip of a finger, he pushed the curls from my forehead, his gaze tracing the movement. Those eyes swept my face, and when they met mine, they were full of so much love.

"I froze it. So I'll still get my pension, I just won't be retiring like I'd planned." His fingers trailed down my arms to link with mine. His deep, soulful eyes, warm and so full of love, made my heart hurt. "I'm selling the lake house."

Horror rose up in me. "Mac, no!" He couldn't do that. That house held so many dreams for him. He'd been planning his future in that house since before his father died.

"Sweetheart, I choose you. Always. You and Rosie are what makes life worth living. You're my anchor; you hold me steady. I was a fool for letting you go the first time." He kissed me on the nose again, tightening his arms around me. "I'd give up the world, but I'll never give you up again."

Chapter Thirty-One

Mac

My last shift was solid evidence that it was the right time for me to leave. We'd run all day, endless ridiculous calls. The kicker came in around seven p.m. when we were dispatched to save a cat from a tree.

A collective groan rose. We'd just sat down to have the first meal of the day.

We pulled up to a familiar address, and I glanced across the street, wondering when Francis had gotten out of rehab, and why she hadn't just called Mike to come over and rescue her damn cat.

The guys all piled out, and we made our way to the door.

As I hit the top step of her porch the front door swung open. "Thank God you're here. Come on, follow me."

"Hey, Mrs. Francis," I greeted. "Good to see you back in action."

She waved me forward, and I followed, assuming we

were going to the backyard. I passed through the front doorway into her front sitting room, and the light clicked on unexpectedly.

"Surprise!"

My whole shift waited in that room, ridiculous party hats, blowers, everyone yelling and cheering. My guys from my station sidled in behind me, slipping on more stupid-looking party hats.

Further in the house, firefighters from other shifts, police officers, medics who ran calls with us, and even some of the county guys were there. An entire houseful of men and women I'd worked with over the years.

Olivia emerged from the back of the pack, smiling from ear to ear, with tears in her eyes.

In stunned silence, I watched as she put her radio to her mouth and said, "NFD 1201 to 911. Please be advised, NFD 1222 has received his final call."

It was fucking hard to breathe as I realized what was happening. I'd taken part of plenty of last calls—some from retirement, some from death. This last call was my mine. Marking the end of my identity as NFD 1222. My eyes burned as tears filled them.

The room grew silent, all the men and women who had become family gathered to honor me, as the familiar voice of a 911 operator gave my last call over the countywide radio system.

"It is with great honor that we announce the last call for NFD 1222, now-retired Captain Mac Collins. With over two decades of service, in which he has received numerous commendations for his leadership and bravery. The entire 911, EMS, Fire, and Police Service wish to thank you for your endless dedication to the service and safety of our citizens. Congratulations, NFD 1222. It's been a pleasure serving with you, Captain."

The operator signed off, and Olivia held her hand out to me. "Your radio, sir."

I was frozen. I couldn't move. A massive weight sat on my chest, and I couldn't look anywhere but at my beautiful woman through a watery gaze.

Like she knew I was having trouble even functioning, she stepped forward, making a show of unclipping my radio and clicking the mic. I just had to say the words.

Drawing strength from the love shining in her eyes, I cleared my throat and croaked, "NFD 1222 is out of service."

Olivia rose on tiptoe and wiped a thumb across my cheek, catching a tear. With a gorgeous smile on her face, she wrapped her arms around me and kissed the life out of me while my crew whistled and cheered around us.

Nate and Jordan, Thoren and Kylie, Mike and Leah. Mo and Teresa. My found family. All here with me, cheering for me, for us.

Olivia stepped back as Rosie barreled into me. I hugged them close and lost the battle against my tears.

One by one, through back claps and watery smiles, my friends congratulated me. They meant congratulations for my retirement, but my real win was Olivia and Rosie. The two ladies who stood at my side, the two I'd do anything for.

After the initial rush, the crowd thinned as on-duty staff went back to their stations with full bellies and leftovers, courtesy of Francis, Leah, Jordan, and Kylie.

Nate stepped up, offering his hand. "Congrats, Capt. Happy for you. We're gonna head back to the station now."

"Yeah, I guess it's time to get back to our zone. Somebody's gotta work around here," Thoren said with a smirk.

Mo chimed in, "We'll see you when you come clean out your locker later."

I walked them to the front porch with a heavy heart. I'd miss these guys.

I watched their easy banter as they fought over who was driving the command truck back to the station, when Nate spun on his heel, walking backward. "Oh, hey, Mac... cookout at Thoren's next weekend."

And just like that, it hit me. My friendships didn't have to be over. "Make it my place and you're on," I called back.

Three sets of thumbs-up.

A sense of peace washed over me. I still needed to find another job, another source of income. But things would be okay. I caught a glimpse of Rosie tossing a ball with Buster.

Yeah, we'd be okay.

"Mac." County Fire Chief Roman Slater stepped up beside me and handed me his business card. "Give me a call." And with a handshake, he left.

I flipped the card over, noting his cell phone scrawled across the back. Arms slid across my waist as Olivia stepped into my side. "What was that?"

"No idea," I said, slipping the card into my back pocket and then draping my arm around Olivia. "Thanks for today, babe. Not sure if you'll ever know how much you mean to me."

She rose up and placed a gentle kiss at my jaw. "I love you, Mac."

I kissed her forehead, watching our daughter play in the yard with our dog. This was my life now. *They* were my life now. "I love you too."

Epilogue

The following summer

I slid a rag over the bottom of the canoe one more time, brushing away nonexistent dust, feeling like a sentimental fool.

"This looks so great," Rosie said from the doorway of the garage. "Are you excited? I'm excited."

I was, and for more reasons than I wanted to admit. "Yep."

Behind Rosie, her best friend Shae tossed a ball with Buster, who promptly ran down the bank and splashed into the lake.

Rosie bopped to the open garage door as the crunch of tires on gravel sounded, followed by the sounds of car doors opening.

"Yay! You guys made it." Rosie's delighted squeal was an echo of my own excitement.

I dropped the rag and went to greet our guests. Mike and Leah, Nate and Jordan, and Thoren and Kylie all piled out. We exchanged handshakes and backslaps and hugs.

"Thanks for having us, Capt," Nate said.

"Nate." I made a noise low in my throat.

"Sorry... Mac."

We got them settled in the house and the one next door that I'd rented from my neighbor for the weekend. The plan was for the guys to head back when they had to report on duty, but the women would stay and hang for an extra day at the lake.

"Okay, Mac. We're ready. What can we do?" Thoren asked.

"Nothing, just relax."

"You didn't invite us out to relax." He glanced around like he was looking for something. "Did you?"

"Of course we did," Olivia chimed in. I think she knew how badly I'd been missing my guys. It had been her idea to have everyone come out after we opened the lake house for the summer.

But I knew she'd done it for me. I wasn't handling unemployment well. There were only so many side jobs I could find. In a nutshell, I needed more to do.

"You guys hear from Cal lately?" I shifted uncomfortably, the weight of the county chief's business card heavy in my wallet. Heavy on my mind.

"Yeah, actually," Nate replied, "Ran into him in town the other day. He's all healed up, back on duty."

"Things good for him at the county?"

Nate shrugged. "They've got their share of problems, but he looked good. Tired. Working his ass off. Said he missed us, but the money was good."

"It's about time. Now we just need to make sure we leave him with the tab sometime." Thoren grinned. Cal's dipping out on buying a round at the bar had become a running joke.

"Well, Mac..." Thoren ran his hands down his thighs. "Gotta say, I half expected you to run for mayor. Please tell me you're making your bid now that you don't work for the city anymore."

I chuckled and shook my head. "No politics for me."

Nate chimed in with "Well, I'm glad you guys decided to keep this place, knowing how much you've loved it. Don't you have some kind of project we can help with? I mean, we're all here."

I took in all that encompassed the lake house. The garage I'd spent countless hours in, the freshly pressure-washed exterior and deck. The boat house that gleamed with new ropes and updated bumpers. And the woman who'd made it all happen when she signed her name next to mine on the refinanced mortgage stood proud and strong chatting with the other ladies.

"We didn't invite you guys to work."

"But Dad," Rosie piped in, and God, I'd never get tired of hearing her call me that. "We could use their help to take the canoe out. She deserves a good send-off on her maiden voyage."

The wooden canoe that she'd taken such pride in helping me complete wasn't so large that we couldn't handle it alone, but one glance at my girl, at the light dancing in her eyes, and I clamped a hand around the back of her neck, pulling her under my arm. "Yeah, sweetheart."

"Wow, that is beautiful," Kylie exclaimed as Mike and Nate carried the boat out of the garage and down the embankment.

"Thanks," Rosie said as we followed the guys. "Me and Dad finished her. I can't wait to ger her on the water."

My girl, acting like the boat was already her second best friend. Maybe someday we'd tackle building a sailboat together. I had plans to take her to the ocean over the summer, rent a sailboat and see how she liked it.

"Wait," Jordan cried as the guys neared the water. She raced toward us, Buster and Gracie hot on her heels, a bottle of beer in hand. "Don't boats need a proper send-off?"

Rosie giggled as Jordan handed me the bottle.

I grabbed my daughter's hand and tugged her to the bow of the boat. "Here you go, sweetheart. You do the honors and christen your very first boat."

Rosie's eyes went wide, filled with tears. I pushed through the tightness in my throat. "It's not a car, but you'll probably enjoy it more than a car anyway."

Rosie crashed the bottle over the hull, Olivia quickly following to gather the shards of glass, tutting about dogs and vet bills. And then my girl climbed into her newly refurbished canoe and set out across the slough, wobbling the canoe and squealing the whole time.

"She'll never catch a damn thing squealing like that," Olivia muttered, slipping her arm around my waist. She had a point. I made a mental note to make sure we were outside when I handed over the Taylor Swift concert tickets I'd scored.

A chorus of laughter rose as my friends witnessed my daughter promptly flip her brand-new boat. Buster dove in to rescue his girl, Thoren right behind him.

I felt a now-familiar tug at my heartstrings. This was how it was supposed to be. What this house, this place, had been meant for. Not a solitary life post-retirement. It was meant for family and friends. Squealing, happy teenage daughters, and dogs who barked incessantly.

And I couldn't wait for more.

"If I haven't told you lately, I love you, Mac Collins," Olivia said with a smile in her voice.

I looked down at the woman in my arms and kissed her forehead. Happy and content. "I love you too."

* * *

Want more? Click below for a special bonus !

https://dl.bookfunnel.com/44vo3u2jeu

Author's Note

Ending a series is hard. I'm ready to move on to new ideas, new places. And yet that final book needs to feel perfect, needs to do the series and characters justice and tie up all the loose ends.

When I finished the first draft of Mac and sent him off to dev edits, I cried like a baby. It was the first time that sending a book out was more about letting go of a character than feeling scared of the editing process.

Mac appeared as I was drafting Nate, fully formed, standing patiently off to the side, shoulder propped against the wall as if he were watching me build every scene. A warm, steady presence through every book, every revision.

Going in, I felt like I knew him. This warm yet gruff hero. Tender and stalwart. The rock-solid foundation that kept it all together. The voice of wisdom to his younger team, and to me. Until it was his turn... and he went silent on me.

Mac had been through the storms of life, had felt all the heartache. I knew that he loved deeply and hurt deeply. And try as I may to make him be a total grump—to showcase that gruff exterior I'd grown to love... when his heroine entered his life, he just rolled over and presented his tender side. Just threw the towel all in for her. And I loved him even more.

I couldn't conceive an end for this book until the third round of professional edits. Editor Jess was patient with me, allowing me space to percolate the perfect ending. I finally realized that I just couldn't let Mac go. I didn't want to say goodbye. Somewhere around my fourth or fifth revision, I finally found the answer to how to do Mac's HEA justice. But even then, I couldn't say *The End* on him. So he's coming with us to the next series, and I hope you'll join me as Cal earns his happy ever after.

Stay in the know about Cal's book by joining my newsletter here:

https://raefields.com/news/

Also by Rae Fields

Mike and Leah
Ignition Point

Nate and Jordan
Burn Point

Thoren and Kylie
Flash Point

Acknowledgments

Much like it takes a village to raise a child, it's also taken a village to raise this baby author.

To my family and friends I say thank you for understanding when I've had to bow out and huddle up in the writing cave. Thank you for supporting this crazy dream of mine.

To Editor Jess, thank you for believing in me and my stories, for challenging me to make every book better, and also for listening to me whine. Someday I'll get you that yacht.

To Editor Brooklyn, I'm so happy that someone knows how to use commas, and that it isn't me. And thank you for loving Mac as much as I do.

To Mia, Mary-lou, Julie, and Karla, thank you for your endless support, your willingness to brainstorm and beta-read, and most of all thank you for your friendship.

To my 6 a.m. Squad and my HEA crew, thank you for showing up every damn day, for picking me up when I'm down, and for being the best cheerleaders ever. Rising tides my friends, rising tides.

About the Author

Rae Fields is beginning her publishing adventure and hopes you'll come along for this journey. She feels weird talking about herself in third person and hopes you'll join her newsletter and socials where she can just talk to *you*, and not feel weird about it.

Find all my links and join my newsletter at

www.raefields.com

Want to stay in the know on all things Rae? Join my newsletter here!

https://raefields.com/news/

www.ingramcontent.com/pod-product-compliance
Lightning Source LLC
Chambersburg PA
CBHW031209310726
48969CB00001B/279